Shadow Hunter

Iris Kain

Also by Iris Kain

Eternal Spring

Sour

Blood Tribe (Book #1 in the Blood Tribe trilogy)

Blood Trials (Book #2 in the Blood Tribe trilogy)

Blood Treason (Book #3 in the Blood Tribe trilogy)

Shadow Hunter

To my mother, Norma, who always told me to pursue
my dreams, and who had faith that I'd achieve them.

CHAPTER 1

August 2005

When Delroy Ducharme started his lifework, avenging his parents' deaths, those who lived near his childhood home had been safest. But now, as the body count grew high and the mission reached its nerve center, he knew he needed to be more careful.

Tonight, as dusk fell, the heat of the Alabama night was intense. Now, in the shadowy hours past midnight, the temperature made his skin as clammy as the summer that never left the forefront of his mind.

A slight breeze smelled of the waist-high grass around him and his perspiration. He smiled, the motion tight and unfamiliar on the corners of his mouth. His newest prey stomped through the dusty gravel erratically, weaving slightly from side to side as she rummaged in her voluminous purse mumbling something about calling for a car. Luxurious chestnut hair fell before her eyes, and she brushed it back with a wobbly hand sparkling with diamonds.

Delroy watched with amusement as she pulled a tin of mints from the bag and opened the box. Cylinders of minty freshness tumbled to the ground at her feet. Her slender ankles, topped by pale blue sandal straps, quavered as she watched them fall. By chance, she managed to save one in her delicate palm. She smirked at her clumsiness and popped the candy into her mouth, ignoring those that had fallen in the dirt.

She removed a keychain from her pocket, zipped the bag shut, and brushed off her stylish, baby blue dress, brushing off both the dust and the memory of her gracelessness. She moved as if she was headed to a boardroom on a ship at sea, weaving and riding waves only she felt. Her oval face ended in a jaw set on reaching her destination. Her brow appeared as though trying to furrow but was frozen in place with ample doses of Botox.

The keychain held a small container of pepper spray, he noted. A bit of concern rose, but quickly faded. Had she sensed them? No. Impossible. His prey never sensed them. Not even when they stood close enough to breathe on the back of their necks.

A canvas bag dangled in his left arm. The ghostly silhouette of the spirit within, signified by an emblem surrounding his right triceps muscle, seemed to glow in the starlight. He consulted the spirit about what weapon they would use tonight. The knife? The wire?

No, they decided, it had been too long since he'd touched a dying victim, felt the last breath on his face, and saw the soul leave the body. This time, he'd use his hands. At least at first. But after they'd killed her…

He advanced, his feet impossibly soundless on the gravel and leaving no trail in his wake. He weaved as she weaved, always directly behind her so as not to alert her with a shadow from the street light.

When he grabbed her, her eyes opened wide in surprise. Her perfect mouth opened in a beautiful expression of astonishment as they struck her, knocking her unconscious. Her feet etched dual dirt trails as they dragged her into the tall grass on the hill beside the road, trails that vanished as if brushed aside by ghostly hands as soon as they came into sight.

He waited until she regained her senses before he allowed the furor to consume him. Her blood covered him in seconds. He smiled as they quickly—but not too quickly, she must suffer—took her life. His heart did not race; it sang with joy as he exacted punishment and offered her in sacrifice.

After Delroy tore her leg from her torso, her spirit abandoned the body. With no life, there was no pain. Though his thrill was nearly gone, he didn't stop. There were a few details left before moving on.

Her spirit hung nearby, at times hovering over his shoulder, watching as he finished his macabre work. Her ghostly face wore an expression of unrepressed horror, and he reveled in knowing that she watched as he took the knife and cut her delicate neck from ear to ear, as he positioned her eye so she winked, knowing in death what those in life would never know.

He stood. The hillside was red, covered with her life fluid. It was shining, viscous, magnificent.

"What are you?" she asked. "Why me?" Her ghostly voice was exquisite, and he realized he hadn't heard her utter a sound as he took her life. He wondered why. Most of them screamed loudly and often. Tonight, there had been no music but the sound of her body against the ground and his inhumanly strong hands.

"Because you were there," Delroy replied. "Because you were there."

CHAPTER 2

Detective Noah Halabrin turned from the cold corpse and sighed. The vic had been a young one, a woman no older than his sister. But where Brittney was tall, blond, and trim—a slightly older, female version of himself—this woman had been short, pale, dark-haired, and gaunt. From her ill-kempt appearance and bruised arms, he surmised she was a drug user.

"What do you think happened, Detective?" Captain Blanch asked. "I know you didn't drop in on this crime scene for nothing. You had a whole weekend ahead of you. For once." She turned from the corpse and gave him an inquiring stare. Her hazel eyes, small and deeply set into an oval face framed with short, strawberry-blond hair, told him nothing of her suspicions—either of the case or his drop-in. "Been listening to the scanner again?"

"You know me," he murmured.

Blanch's eyes shrugged. She did know him. Maribeth Blanch, although curious, never voiced concern over Noah's attraction to the murders in Gryphon—the few the town had. Noah understood his captain well enough to recognize that while she had confidence in her conjectures, she was curious to hear his. He always had theories about the deadly ones. And often, they were uncannily reliable theories.

A handkerchief waited in his back pocket, and he withdrew it, mopping the sweat from his brow and wishing he had a similar tool for removing the smell of death that hung in the humid air that stank of metal and burned plastic. It was nights like this that he questioned the wisdom of living in an industrial northern Alabama town that was stifling in the summer and too far away from Birmingham or Huntsville for any culture. Gryphon's sole advantage as a town was its large manufacturing base, which meant jobs for the many undereducated lower-middle-class families there. One of the town's two known homeless people discovered the body in one of the factory warehouses—an abandoned one off of Rhodes Street.

Halabrin turned his back on the crime scene for a moment, and his hands moved, twitching and swooping a little before his torso. The captain cocked her head and tried to watch what the detective was doing, but his body blocked most of her view. She knew this strange ritual was a custom near the beginning of his investigations—especially the murders. It was a topic of many a squad room chat. Most of his coworkers thought it a nervous twitch, but Captain Blanch wasn't too certain. A twitch, maybe, but nervous? Not Halabrin. Never Halabrin. The man was the proverbial rock.

Detective Halabrin nodded, but not in anyone's direction. He turned back.

"Murder."

"Murder? You're sure?" Halabrin's success rate on his cases was the highest in the department. His captain often wondered what made him so sure, but she rarely doubted him.

Halabrin nodded again. "Get the lab guys in here. Do a scan for toxins. I think they'll find her levels are through the roof."

His captain scoffed. "No shit. She's a junkie. I have no doubt she's been banging meth for years from the look of her. An overdose isn't unusual."

"Of battery acid?"

Blanch's eyebrows shot up. She gave the corpse another glance, looking for the clue that had led Halabrin to his conclusion.

"You can't know that from looking at her," she said, incredulous. *How on earth did he come up with that?*

"Look at the size of that bruise on her foot. It's massive—much too large for a drug to have caused it. It's injected between the toes, which isn't so odd with a junkie, but a bruise that size says something wasn't right. She must have injected something corrosive. Whatever she injected—or was injected with—it tore up all kinds of shit in there. Check it out. I have a feeling I'm right."

Blanch's eyebrows remained hidden under the straight bangs that covered her broad forehead. She turned to the crime scene analysts and the detectives who'd made it to the scene earliest. "You heard him. Full tox scan, and check for anything unusual in her bloodwork."

"Yes, Ma'am," Detective Chartier replied. His green eyes shot daggers at Halabrin, who pretended not to notice.

Halabrin mopped his head again before returning the sweaty handkerchief to its pocket, then turned to the door and walked out past the shadow that he alone saw—a ghostly young woman with translucent tears sliding down her gaunt face.

CHAPTER 3

Delroy was losing a two-day fight against exhaustion. He fought off his drowsiness as long as he could, dreading the nightmares that always accompanied sleep, and now—thanks to his new spirit friend—he often stayed awake nearly three days at a time. But the sleep always won out, pulling him into an undertow of black, nightmare-filled slumber. Although he rarely remembered the disturbing phantoms that haunted his dreams, he often woke with a hammering heart and a body drenched in reeking sweat, sometimes with one of his tools in hand, at the ready.

His pleasure at settling another score was dying off, and he knew it was perhaps an hour before sleep overtook him. Murder was the ultimate high, one that peaked near ecstasy and it abated what felt like minutes later, leaving him drained. It was time to retreat for a while.

His victim's car was black and well-maintained. As he slid into the driver's seat and caressed the steering wheel, a smile crept across his bloodstained face. He'd never driven anything so opulent: leather seats with sheepskin covers, and a dash with more buttons and gadgets than he had time to explore.

His family had never wanted for money, when he'd had a family, and Delroy thought he recalled them driving a Mercedes as well, but he was too young to drive back then, and cars hadn't mattered as much. That had been a long time ago. Too long. So long ago, at times, he hardly remembered.

Other times, it was as if he lived there still, with the hateful spirits of his dead parents still berating him, correcting him, controlling him.

The car started with a growl, then a purr. A female operetta voice swelled from the speakers and, irritated at the noise, he jabbed the Stop button with a finger, leaving a red smear on the button that faded and vanished. He saw a cell phone on the passenger's seat and tossed it from the window before pointing the nose toward his hideaway. He tapped a button, and the window slid soundlessly into its sheath. Warm, humid night air flowed through the car, wrapped around him like the comforting embrace of a familiar blanket.

Too comfortable. Soon, he grew drowsy. He wanted to turn on the stereo or crank up the air conditioning, something that might ensure his wakefulness, but he didn't risk it. Attempting to manipulate controls he wasn't familiar with was risky; he might get distracted trying to find a decent radio station, drive off the road and wreck the car, or weave and draw the attention of the police. Not a good idea.

Maybe putting a stop to Miss Annoying Opera hadn't been such a good idea. At least she'd grated his nerves enough to keep him awake.

He drove on, warm, in silence. To help him stay up, he hummed a tune from a children's movie about chimney sweeps.

Steering out of town, he chose roads without streetlamps, roads that were protected from the brilliant sun during the day by an awning of ancient trees. These roads frequently curved, sometimes sharply, and he fought his exhaustion to maintain control of the car around the dangerous bends.

There were no billboards to distract himself with. The

homes on the street had been built far from the road, and those with the lights on were mere shooting stars passing by his windows. At this distance from town, all that filled his senses were trees, moonlight, the green smell of the night air, and the continually swerving motion of his headlights as he steered around the curves.

The first time he caught his eyes drifting shut, he risked taking his eyes off the road long enough to switch on the air conditioning. Gusts of arctic air turned his clammy skin icy. Goosebumps rose, and his focus grew long enough for him to reach his destination.

He parked the car at the curb outside a wrought-iron fence only yards from his shelter, a risk he normally wouldn't have taken, but exhaustion was pulling him under again, and quickly. His eyes fought to stay open, and the muscles in his arms and calves cramped with fatigue. The spirit would not be denied his chance to feed. Delroy couldn't run the risk of parking it elsewhere and backtracking; he might not make the journey if he tried. He'd hate to be discovered unconscious in the ditch on the side of the road—or worse, run over by an unsuspecting motorist.

He locked the Mercedes and threw the key he'd found hidden under a wheel well into a bush. It wasn't his key, it wasn't his car, and tempting as it was to keep it for a while, he wouldn't use it again. Although the police would undoubtedly find both the vehicle and the key, Delroy wasn't concerned.

As he turned away, the blood from his recent kill evaporated from the seat, the steering wheel, and the floorboards. The hair he'd left on the headrest faded to nothingness. The few remaining fingerprints vanished.

He opened the padlock on the gate and let himself inside, locking the gate behind him. His vision grew dimmer; dancing stars obstructed his vision. Exhaustion threatened to swallow him with every step. He could barely make out dull lumps of gray and black on the ground before him in time to step around them. The grass was a sea of green.

He had to get inside. Soon.

When Delroy found the door to his sanctuary, almost blind with fatigue, he opened the heavy portal with what felt like Herculean effort and carefully closed the door behind him.

No police officer would find him. They'd never know. The gray man within made sure of that.

He crumpled to the floor and slept.

CHAPTER 4

Friday nights: most people live for them. To Noah, a Friday night was, more often than not, the same as any other night. It often meant long hours and lots of legwork, many times with nothing more to show for it than more questions than when he started and a fraction less tread on the bottom of his shoes.

Tonight, however, was different. Tonight, the tox team did their work up on the dead junkie on a case that wasn't his, and until the official results of her scan came back with the results Noah had foreseen, he had a couple of days off. Until then, they would treat her case as another OD. After that, he had no doubt Maribeth Blanch would call him in on the case to assist, hinting heavily that she was dying to know how he'd managed to narrow down the cause of death so precisely.

He'd assist the follow-up on the young woman's case, wandering streets in the stifling heat to ask friends if she'd been feeling suicidal, was it uncommon for her to take lethal amounts of crystal methamphetamine intravenously, and he'd do all the perfunctory police workups. Hopefully, when he had a chance to make his way back to the crime scene alone, he'd have a chat with the girl.

She already told him she wasn't going anywhere.

He supposed he could've gone back and talked to her tonight, but it would mean going against Captain Blanch's orders. Officially, it was Chartier's case, not his. Blanch had informed him that he needed to go home and have a beer in a tone that brooked no dispute. Direct orders. He recalled how her thin lips had flattened into a straight, harsh line as she leaned toward him, giving her words emphasis with one hand planted on a sturdy hip and the other waving at him with a pointed finger.

"Halabrin, you work too hard. If you don't take tonight off, you'll be pulling another eighty-hour week. I need you rested. The lab won't finish up until Monday, if then. For God's sake, go home."

He shut the refrigerator door and raised an amber bottle in the air, tossing the cap in the general direction of the wastebasket.

"Here's to you, Maribeth," Noah said, raising his bottle of Hefeweizen to the slowly oscillating ceiling fan. "Captain's orders." He took a long swallow and sat back on the bare futon, reveling in the air-conditioning. His TV sat dead, glared at him from across the room. A coat of dust rested on top, and dust kitties were starting to gather near where the bottom rested on the wooden floor. He'd never bothered to buy an entertainment stand.

"What?" he asked it. It stared back, one enormous, glassy cyclops eye to his two bright green ones. A distorted and inaccurate reflection of his curly blond hair and oval face was almost recognizable in the dark, mirror-like surface.

The phone rang.

"I didn't ask you," he barked. He swallowed another sip of beer on the way to pick it up. He had a feeling he knew who it was, and his heart picked up its pace a little.

"Halabrin?"

He wasn't disappointed. It was the sweet, female voice he longed, yet hated to hear—especially when he was about to begin a night off. Valerie Acquistapace. From the tone of her voice, he could already envision her stern face, her thick lips set in a frown, her espresso brown hair tight in a bun, highlighting her strong jaw and flawless brown skin. He cleared his throat.

"Sorry. Nobody named Halabrin here. You've just reached Dial-A-Prayer."

"Cut it out, Noah. This shit's big."

"Not big enough to get me out tonight, Val. I've started drinking. Can't drive. Sorry."

On her end, Valerie picked at a paperclip and prayed he'd only just cracked his first bottle. "This is a case you can't stay home for," she said, her voice too close to begging for her taste. "Blanch told me we're on this one together whether you like it or not. She apologizes for interrupting your night off. Hope you haven't had more than a sip."

Noah took another pull on the bottle and opened the refrigerator. A half-eaten meatball sub and five unopened bottles still coated in condensation stood among various condiments that held most of their contents.

"What's so pressing I've got to miss my hot date with a six-pack?"

Valerie, his sometimes partner—when the Leland County police department judged a case large enough to assign partners—paused. Noah's stomach clenched like a fist. He inferred from Valerie's reticence that her news wasn't good. Most of the time, she was the first to dive into a big case with zeal.

She bit her thumb. *Don't get his hopes up, Valerie. He won't be unbiased at the crime scene if you give him false hopes.*

"It's big. Another murder, second in Leland County in the same night—which, as you know, is unheard of. So naturally, Blanch wants you, Mr. High Solve Rate. But I think it's more than that. There's something at this scene... I've told Edwards to go ahead and process, but not to move the body or anything until you've seen... I don't know,

Noah. I think it's a connection, but I'd hate to be wrong about this." She paused, and Noah wished he could see her expression, which always gave her dead away.

What she said next nearly knocked the wind from his lungs. "Weren't your folks at Lightning Fork?"

Noah's beer slipped from his grip and landed on the wooden floor with a dull plunk. Pale beer foamed over the planks and tickled his toes.

"I'll be ready. How soon can you get here?"

"Ten minutes."

"I'll be ready in five."

CHAPTER 5

August 1987

Noah didn't want to die. And although he had a suspicion his death was coming, he sat in the backseat, agitated and dumb with fear, stuck between his two older, taller, and blonder twin sisters, Ashley and Brittney. They blatantly ignored him. He'd been acting weird all day.

His parent's Blazer handled the country roads leading to the campground like a luxury car, but Noah's stomach tightened as if he was sick nonetheless.

He didn't want to know. He didn't want to, but he did, and the knowledge made him as helpless as a baby, unable to change what he knew was unavoidable. He had seen his parent's death coming, and he'd never been wrong in his dreams. Ever.

Jenny and Robert Halabrin, Noah's parents, and his two siblings were unaware of his trouble. He supposed they thought he was having one of his quiet days. Perhaps if they'd known why he'd chosen that day to impersonate a mime, they'd have drawn him out, pulled his fears from him like a banished demon.

They didn't know about the nightmares.

It hadn't mattered so much before—his precognition. He knew that was what it was called; he'd looked it up in his encyclopedia. None of his dreams had affected anyone he'd known well before last night, and none had been so clear in its picture of the disaster about to happen. He supposed that it might have to do with how close he was to the victims.

He hated thinking of his family with those words. The victims.

The first time he'd had a precognitive dream, it had involved Mr. Freeman, the good-natured man who delivered their mail with a smile every day. On Saturdays, Noah always waited on the steps for him. From time to time, he was rewarded with a postcard from his grandmother or a letter from his cousin studying abroad at a college in Rome. Sometimes, Mr. Freeman gave him a treat, like a stick of gum, for waiting. Mr. Freeman looked a lot like Morgan Freeman, the actor, and Noah had asked him one day if they were related.

"No, son," Mr. Freeman had replied. "Not that I know of. I'm just handsome, I guess."

Noah dreamed that Mr. Freeman had gotten into an accident during his rounds. An ambulance had hit him as he was crossing Delta Street, and as it swerved, it crashed into the huge elm tree up the block. Both Mr. Freeman and the other man being rushed to the hospital in the ambulance that had hit him died.

A frightening dream, not to mention depressing. After he had woken up, he'd dismissed it as nothing more than a nightmare. Still, the eerie sound of the ambulance siren haunted Noah. He wondered how he could remember that the sound had changed into a sick-sounding warble on impact.

It had seemed so real.

It didn't help matters that the next day Mr. Freeman's rounds were taken over by a tall, meaty blonde woman named Miss Geiger. When Noah offered his hand to take the mail, the woman shook her head brusquely.

"Are you the Halabrin boy?"

"Yes. I can take it."

"No. I need your mother's signature for a package."

Noah waited for her to ask him to get her, but the woman hefted her leg onto his step and said no more. He rose, annoyed that she took for granted that he'd oblige her, and called for his mother.

As she signed for her package, Jennifer Halabrin asked about Mr. Freeman.

"Hit by an ambulance yesterday," the chunky woman said. "I thought for sure you'd know. Happened right up the road, here." She raised a thick arm and pointed toward Church and Delta, the intersection Noah had dreamed about. There were huge gouges torn from the bark of the elm. "Right shame. He was a good man. One of the few."

That night, Noah's mother related the story to his dad, and Noah learned the meaning of the words "irony" and "lesbian."

A few months later, Noah awoke in a sweat, a scream fading on his lips. The dream about Mr. Freeman had been horrible, but this one was worse. It had been terrible to watch Mr. Freeman die in his last dream, but in his second dream, *he* was the victim. He'd been a dying woman lying in a pool of her own blood as her boyfriend hovered in the shadows, waiting for her last breath. His—her—blood flowed from massive wounds in her chest and stomach that burned, ached, brought tears to his eyes. When he clenched his fist, he felt the scratchy carpet fibers on his finger pads.

When he woke, he lay immobile in the dark, his throat dry and his heart beating so hard his ears rang. He ached to crawl out of bed and see if his parents were still up. At eleven o'clock, it was early enough that they might be up watching the late shows. But what would he tell them? Would they believe him? His mother would most likely worry and wonder how he'd dreamed up such terrible ideas. At ten years old, he wasn't allowed to watch horror movies.

As the moonlight cast shadows on his bedroom walls, he waited. It felt like hours before his heart slowed down, but he finally made himself creep out of bed for a drink of water to soothe his aching throat. The cool drink tasted coppery as it went down. He stood in the well-lit bathroom, basking in the warmth and security that went with knowing there was no one else in the room waiting to kill him. After over twenty minutes of talking quietly to himself, of reassuring himself that the bleeding woman was only a dream, Noah crawled back in bed and prayed for a dreamless sleep.

Two days later, he came down to breakfast, the nightmare all but forgotten. It was Mom's turn to cook, he noticed with relief, and his father sat at the table with the Gryphon Tribune and his usual mug of coffee. Noah grabbed a plate and silverware from the stack beside the stove and sat, patiently waiting.

Noah wasn't normally interested in the Tribune, but it was hard to miss the headline. It screamed at him in bold letters, the lettering much taller than usual:

"Gryphon Woman Dies at Knifepoint."

Noah's stomach turned as his nightmare came flooding back. The pain, the tears, the way he felt the burning injuries, the feel of the carpet under his fingers. *Knifepoint.* It made sense. In his slumber, he had somehow shared a body with the woman who'd died—had felt her pain.

When Noah's mother saw him studying the bold print, she chastised his father and made him fold the newspaper, tucking the headlines underneath.

Noah thought the headline was untrue. *More like* Knife Points.

His clairvoyant dreams continued over the next two

years. On occasion, they were pleasant—like the time he knew their neighbor—the retired widower, Mr. Whittaker—was about to receive an inheritance from a rich relative he hadn't spoken to in years. But most often, they involved violence, death, or both. *And what is an inheritance,* he thought later, *but a gift someone gets because of someone's death?*

Then, one day, he noticed the people. Or, more specifically, the shadowlike people. Real people weren't transparent, didn't look like a misty black-and-white movie, and they didn't vanish at whim. Still, the ghostly people didn't often interact with living people, so that was how he thought of them. Shadows.

It started as wisps of motion from the corner of his eyes—a fleeting movement that he attributed to a swift animal, maybe, or an overactive imagination (that he was often accused of having). Slowly, though, the motions grew less fleet, the shadows less vague, until he was able to make out limbs, heads, and finally faces and details of their see-through clothes.

It should have frightened him, he knew, but they never seemed scary. Most of the time, these shadow-people hung around doing not much of anything, just watching the actions of normal people.

One day, as he was walking through the woods behind his house, he came upon a shadow sitting on a stump. His gray hands rested on his legs, and his face held a peaceful, lost-in-thought expression. His eyes and mouth looked used to smiling but held no smile right then.

Noah looked around, made sure he was alone, and approached it.

The shadow appeared a little older than his parents, with a fringe of hair around a bald head with glasses perched on the bridge of a wide nose. He blinked his eyes and ruffled the back of his head with the same air of surprise as Noah's mother when someone at the door disrupted her. Then the old man smiled and met his eye, and Noah knew he understood that Noah saw him.

Noah clung to the long stick he'd been using as he walked as if it was a potential weapon, which he knew was silly since he knew the man was probably not only see-through but feel-through. Still, he clutched it until his palm hurt.

"Are you a ghost?" he asked. The ghost's face registered surprise but also pleasure at the unexpected conversation. The man smiled again and bobbed his head.

"What's your name?"

The man opened his mouth and moved his lips, but no words came out—or, if they did, they were soundless.

"I can't hear you," Noah replied, disappointed. He finally had the chance to talk to a shadow person, and he couldn't hear them!

The man paused, nodded heavily, and shrugged, palms facing the sky.

"Can you hear me?" he asked. The ghost indicated he did.

"Why can you hear me, and I can't hear you?"

The man removed his misty glasses, rubbed them on a transparent handkerchief pulled from a gray trouser pocket, and thought. An idea occurred to him, and he put the glasses back on and shoved the handkerchief back in place. He motioned with his hands, signaling that he would like to speak with them.

"Sure, that works," Noah said, hoping he'd understand.

The old man pointed at Noah, then at the woods around him, and used his hands to show that Noah was one hand, the woods the other. Then he moved his hands around in flat circles, always keeping them level. Noah nodded, showing that he followed him. Noah and the woods were together, on the same level. Then the ghost pointed at himself with the right hand, the hand he'd used to symbolize Noah. He moved the hand level with the "woods" hand and then moved it up and down.

"I'm stuck in one place, and you can move between more than one?" The ghost paused, considered the answer, and shrugged in reluctant agreement, moving his palm in a see-saw motion to show Noah was on the right track but not quite there.

"Wow," Noah breathed. He'd never spoken to anyone quite like this before. It was scary but cool. "Can you answer some questions for me? I'll keep them to yes or no answers."

The old-timer nodded and scooted over on the broad stump to make room for Noah.

That afternoon, Noah had returned to his house and asked his parents for lessons in sign language. His mother, who'd never known Noah to have a deaf friend, asked why.

"I think it looks neat, that's all."

Jenny, who'd always supported her children in their pursuit of knowledge, agreed. After a few phone calls, she found out that the local community center taught classes to young men and women, and she signed Noah up for six weeks of classes. Noah knew that she supposed after learning the alphabet, the names of a few animals, and how to count to a hundred, he would lose interest and would look for pursuits that were more normal for a ten-year-old.

She was wrong.

Noah absorbed the language, far outpacing the other children his age. After the six weeks were over, he begged his mother for more advanced lessons. This turned out to be much more difficult to find, and she placated him in his thirst for knowledge by renting books that taught sign from the local library. Then she lifted her limit on television usage and allowed Noah to watch as much of a public broadcasting show that taught sign as he wanted. Soon, Noah's knowledge of signs envied his spoken vocabulary. He knew that his thirst for knowledge baffled her, but he didn't care.

The shadows signed back.

He gathered from them that the reason they knew how, even if they hadn't known how to in life, was because knowledge was more readily accessible on their plane, or dimension, or whatever. He didn't understand the particulars, and he didn't care. He knew they understood him, and he knew that they knew how to talk back through whatever means. While his mother thought he was practicing his lessons, he was having an active conversation with beings she never saw. It helped him uphold his sanity.

The shadows knew he saw them. From the way some of them caught his gaze in kind or discouraging ways, it was obvious. He stared at them as they hovered over the shoulders of friends, family, and strangers, watching without a word, an easygoing expression on most of their see-through faces as if they had all the time in the world—which, he supposed, they had. Sometimes they gave him a friendly tip of the head or smiled. Noah smiled back if they looked pleasant enough. Most of the time, though, they ignored him, which suited him fine.

On the Halabrin family vacation to visit his uncle Trevor in Hawaii, he saw the strangest ghost of all. A man paced up and down in the hallway to their hotel night and day. When Noah tried to talk to it, the man ignored him, shaking his head and muttering to himself words beyond the hearing range of Noah's ears. Funny, he thought, when most of the ghosts at the USS Arizona had been so nice.

He didn't want to admit to anyone that he saw the

shadows. He might have been young, but he wasn't stupid. He knew no one else saw the shadow people, or that the few that did kept it to themselves. More importantly, he knew what happened to people who claimed they saw things that no one else knew were there.

More than once, he wondered if he was crazy, if the shadow people weren't there. But deep down, he believed. He knew his dreams were real, and the headlines had confirmed it too many times.

And if they were real, the shadows were, too.

At ten years old, he was the only person he knew with his gifts, if one could call them gifts. Noah hadn't known what to call them, except when referring to it in his mind. Then, it was his problem. As in, *It's okay to lie to Mom and Dad and say that everything's all right. They don't know about my problem.*

Then came the night he'd dreamed of his parents' deaths.

Now, it was more than a problem. Now, it was a curse.

AUGUST 2005

"What makes you so sure it's got to do with the thing at Lightning Fork, Val?" Noah asked as she sped through Gryphon's unoccupied night streets, hazard lights flashing, siren off.

The sun's descent hadn't cooled the town much. If anything, a low cloud cover made the heat more oppressive than it had been when Valerie had left the stationhouse at sunset. The heat penetrated her clothes like a sentient fog, working against all the paraphernalia she used to uphold the mistaken belief that she didn't sweat—she glistened. She strove to smell like she had showered only moments before; today she'd wager she smelled more like a Super-bowl locker room at halftime.

Valerie was one of the few officers referred to by her first name, but it was nothing sexist. Most other officers were unable to wrap their tongues around the name Acquistapace without rendering it painful for her to hear, so she preferred that they used her first name. Not that she usually had to ask.

"Don't get your hopes up," she warned as she swerved around a slow-moving Corolla, missing it by inches. Noah sucked in a nervous breath as he leaned away from the pas-senger-side door. Valerie's driving always made him jumpy.

She veered off toward the low-income part of town where zoning was questionable, and factories shared blocks with houses. "There's only one death involved, and it's a completely different location. I guess it might be nothing. But—"

"'It,'" Noah said, shaking his head with frustration. "The way you keep saying 'it' makes me think you've found some sort of evidence. What is 'it'?"

Valerie winced as if he'd used biting words instead of his usual deep, soothing voice—a voice that had helped many victims feel ready to describe the pain of a crime they'd endured mere moments ago. A voice she'd be will-ing to hear read one of her dad's old boring-ass history books from start to finish if he expressed an inkling.

Turning her head, she saw Noah leaning forward to meet her eyes, an expectant expression on his handsome face.

She hated the idea of raising Noah's hopes; she knew how long he'd wrestled with the pain of his family's death. She'd seen his need for closure in his relentless pursuit of the few murderers Leland County had seen in the ten years he'd been on the force—five now as a detective. His need to put his cases away in a tidy, completed fashion had helped him achieve his rank quickly in a small county station not inclined to hand out promotions.

After his sister Ashley's suicide five years ago, Brittney was all he had left. From what she gathered in the brief moments when he'd opened his clam-like shell, Brittney had fallen apart without her twin in her life. The bond they shared, and their happy life before her death, made her sister's absence a blow that Brittney was incapable of coping with.

Many times, while out on patrol, they'd had to take Brittney home drunk in the back of the squad car. After dropping her off at her apartment one night, Noah had mentioned—surprisingly without the faintest traces of bitterness or maliciousness—that alcohol was the mildest of her vices. If anything, he'd sounded frustrated, as if he wished he could take away his sister's need to self-medicate.

She sympathized with Noah's family's loss but knew that her point of view was a glimpse at the surface of a bottomless pool. She knew what it was like to lose someone close—someone who shared both your blood and your life. Salvador, her older brother and a sergeant in the Army, had been taken out by a car bomb during Operation Iraqi Freedom at the age of twenty-three.

Still, Noah's loss seemed much more tragic. First, Noah and his sisters lost their parents at the hands of a psychopath, and then Ashley took her own life. For Brittney to lose her twin... Valerie couldn't imagine what that blow must have been like. Valerie's family was as close as any tight-knit Italian clan, but she knew the bond between twins must surpass even the Acquistapace norm.

She turned a corner and slowed down, to Noah's relief, nosing the car down a gravel road that traveled beneath an underpass. Behind them, an aging row of industrial units shared bent and rusting chain-link fences. Ahead, a sloping hillside covered with weakening saw grass dipped toward the muddy, drought-starved river.

Two cruisers waited at the crime scene marked off by yellow tape. Four officers stood outside the border, their backs turned toward the scene. Ron Wallace, the criminalist, scoured the area by the inch, searching for evidence. Merl Edwards, Wallace's lean, freckled trainee, stood at Wallace's side, ready to photograph all the evidence Wallace uncovered.

Outside the yellow tape, one of the men in blue had a cigarette dangling from his lips; Valerie saw the orange glow through the murky light provided by the street lamps. From a distance, the hair looked crew-cut and blonde, the body Cro-Magnon. *Looks like Telleman's not too eager to help out.*

"I told Wallace not to move the body until we got here," she reminded Noah. "The small stuff he's processing, but... I want to see if you notice the same thing I did. And, of course, what you make of it if you do."

Unknown to Valerie, Noah was already noticing things; a ghost in designer clothes, now gray with death, stood in the center of the crime scene. She wrung her hands and watched the criminalists with a furrowed temple as they studied the place of her murder.

He tore his gaze from her. *Later. I'll talk to her in a minute. Now, I need to act like Joe Detective and see if I notice what Valerie did.* He wished he didn't know that he was looking for something Valerie had found significant. The knowledge might throw off his perception of what otherwise might have been incidental.

His ability to see what had caught Valerie's eye was her test of what she believed to be either a mind-blowing coincidence or a key piece of evidence. He hoped it was the latter. He also hoped the specter didn't wander off before he had a chance to talk to her.

Valerie put the unmarked car—a plain, black Dodge Durango—into Park, and they exited together. She came around the car and stood beside him, her head scarcely reaching his shoulder.

The muggy air seemed thicker here, the air cloying. Despite the drought that Leland County had experienced that summer, the air here had no lack of moisture. Valerie fingered the clasp on her holster as if preparing to draw her weapon. Whatever had happened here, it had unsettled her in a way he'd rarely seen before.

"Oh, I should warn you," Valerie said with more than her usual share of I'm Not Bullshitting in her voice. "This one's a real stomach-turner."

That would explain why no one but Edwards and Wallace are studying it, Noah thought. *The blues are saving the unpleasant job for those of us who'll be doing the heavy work.*

Wallace let out a heavy sigh and stood with effort as Valerie and Noah approached. Average height but heavily built with an abundant stomach, Wallace looked like nothing if not a young, beardless Santa Claus. And, like Father Christmas, he was impossible to dispirit. Years of studying criminal cases hadn't removed the devilish sparkle from his eye or the bellow from his voice.

"Real gross one, man," he said in greeting, catching his breath from the effort he'd exerted standing. "I'm glad I don't have to hunt the person responsible for this down. Damn sicko."

Another time, Noah would've expressed surprise at Wallace's choice of words, but from ten feet away, Noah saw that Wallace was right. Inside the ring of police tape was a crime site worse than a murder from splatter screen late-night horror flicks—the type that reveled in the ability to shock the viewers with as much blood as possible.

The body lay to the left of the overpass, within a field of yellowed, dried weeds and trash blown in from the highway overhead. Noah approached, keeping watch for the clue Valerie had spoken of, but seeing the entire crime scene with practiced skill with a detective's eyes.

Within the tape, the field had been painted with a massive coat of thick, red fluid. An arm lay nearest the left perimeter of the crime scene, fingernails still unchipped despite the ordeal the body had endured. The sparkle to her rings looked yellowish under the sodium vapor lamp. A leg, torn at the knee, rested to the right. The Louis Vuitton shoe had escaped a bath of blood, but barely. A matching bag lay near her detached right arm. The trunk of the body lay at the foot of one of the concrete overpass supports. The killer had cut the victim's throat so severely that her head reclined in an extreme tilt. Her suit, an expensive designer number she must have bought several hundred miles away, had been opened, and her stomach sliced until there was nothing left but a meaty pulp. It looked as if the stomach had exploded from within.

Even from this distance, Noah saw that her eyes had been played with; either one had been closed after death, or the other had been opened. She was frozen in an everlasting wink.

He noticed a candy wrapper flapping against one of the stakes thrust upright into the ground to give an officer an object to wrap the yellow tape around.

Valerie waited to see what he had to say, studied the way his strong jaw jutted out the way it usually did when he was first evaluating a scene. Two minutes of silence passed, and her patience gave in.

"What do you think?" she asked.

"Robbery wasn't a motive," he noted. "Her rings are most likely real, and he didn't touch 'em, and her bag is closed. Most robbers don't bother closing the bag once they've stolen what they want. Don't figure it was rape—her skirt doesn't look as if it's been pulled up, underwear is still pretty much in place, just stained with dirt and grass and blood. If I had to guess now, I'd say it was a psychopath, probably someone with a vendetta against her. Who found her?"

"Patrol car, Robles and Telleman. There were no witnesses."

Noah frowned. "Classy woman like that in this neighborhood? Any other time, I'd think her body was moved, but all that blood... There's no way this crime happened anywhere but here. I'd be surprised if the cause of death is anything but exsanguination. When was she found?"

"Less than ten minutes before I called you. Robles and Telleman called it in at one twenty-seven."

Robles turned his head at the sound of his name spoken from a distance. Tall, dark, and muscular, he was the poster boy for machismo. Tonight, he lit one cigarette from the butt of the previous, gave Noah a respectful tip of the head before turning his back to the crime scene once more. It suited Noah fine that the beat cops kept their distance this time. Locard's principle of exchange worked both ways; the fewer officers behind the tape, the lower the chance of crime scene contamination. Not that they weren't great guys who'd do their best, but sometimes it was better to leave the detective work to the DTs.

Noah raised the tape and approached the body with great caution under Wallace's unblinking scrutiny. From this angle, he saw a small set of keys in her hand, the finger poised on the panic button. There was a cylinder of pepper spray attached as well. He wondered if she'd gotten any on her attacker. *Probably not, but who knows? There's no telling in this mess if there was a struggle.*

"Where's her car?" he asked. No answer. He moved his gaze to the apparition, waited until she noticed he was studying her, and said firmly, "Anyone know where her car is? She's got her keys in her hand. She should have a car. The keyring looks like Mercedes."

The ghost, thankfully, caught his unwavering gaze. He held it, to make sure she knew it wasn't a coincidence.

The lips on the ghost moved as she tried to explain, and Noah shook his head almost imperceptibly, his eyes never leaving hers. Her expression of surprise was almost comical, her mouth formed a perfect "O." Noah was about to move his hands before his body and begin his usual questioning of the victim when he saw something from the corner of his eye.

He knew the instant he saw it that this was the evidence that Valerie had spoken of. If his gaze hadn't flickered to the side to see if anyone was watching, he wouldn't have caught it.

Above the victim's all but severed head was what Noah had first believed to be graffiti; the concrete was full of various clichés and promises of undying, yet initialed love. This, however, was smaller than most of the others. Spray paint had not been the media. It looked to Noah to be paint; it was too red to be blood.

A dark cloud, and stemming from it, a fork of lightning, its jagged edge pointing straight to the victim's head.

CHAPTER 6

Delroy dreamed.

As the raised flesh of his scar, his constant reminder of the night that changed him, pressed into the unyielding floor beneath his cheek, he dreamed of black books with yellowed parchment pages and bloodstained print that smelled of copper, decay, and mildew. His heart galloped, and adrenaline raced through his system in panic and frustration as he dreamed of places where voices of young men were dismissed, belittled, and laughed at. He dreamed of pain and suffering—his, and theirs. He dreamed of fury. He dreamed of justice.

He dreamed of drums and ceremony, of scorching fires, of promises given and promises denied. He had visions of small sneakered feet dragged along a red carpet, of headdresses and golden suns, of black obsidian knives, gray feet, red blood, stinging silver needles, and questions, always questions.

In his mind, pleading voices rang as blood dripped down from his hands to his elbows, dripping to the floor and painting it red.

Next came books, books, books, so many books to read, so much to learn. Prayers to the sun, prayers to gods, any god, every god that might listen and make him what he knew he was supposed to be. That would give him the power to make things right.

He dreamed of standing on a grassy hillside and watching in terror as his parents collapsed with their hands drenched in each other's blood.

He dreamed of a thick man with a walrus mustache and a shiny badge who told him a story about a young couple with a lust for power and an unhealthy interest in the occult.

Fury rose inside, along with the urge to lash out, to hit, but he was suppressed with powerful, unseen hands. The man with the badge was wrong! That wasn't it! His parents knew about life, about death, they knew how to use them, they'd never be a victim to something like that!

Delroy told the mustachioed man that he'd seen the stranger who attacked, who killed his parents without provocation, and who vanished without a trace, but the man turned away. Delroy tried another adult. Then another. No one listened. No one believed. No one looked for the assassin who'd disappeared into the woods because no one but an eight-year-old boy—no one but him—had seen him. No one knew the real killer existed, but not in the world they understood.

Eventually, Delroy stopped speaking of it at all. Instead, he made a promise to himself and his parents.

In his slumber, Delroy recaptured the moment when they shuffled him off to a box truck filled with other, miserable children. Next, he was pushed into a windowless building, a hovel surrounded by death and rot, where visions of his parent's spirits caused sweats and hallucinations.

He couldn't think. He couldn't think. He wasn't alone. His parents pleaded with him from the grave for vengeance, for blood. He couldn't think.

What to do? How was he to get rid of the voices? How was he supposed to feel free of the constant harassment, the nights and days of memories reminding him of the debt he owed to all those who had promised him a better life after this one in exchange for his one meager miserable existence?

He searched. He searched in yet more books—this time, he found volumes of darkness and other things he understood, things he'd learn to survive, to be perfect. He worked the musty-smelling ground, dug holes for the dead, and learned more about life and what came after. Mostly about life through death. He was uncovering the greatest secrets of eternity.

He found a young woman, a black book, and an answer to his myriad questions. A real answer, an answer that would ensure he kept his promise both to himself, his parents, and to a dead gray man who longed for life again.

He died.

He dreamed of gifts of weapons humankind had never seen and didn't understand, weapons not possible to trace, impossible to duplicate.

He dreamed of the man with the walrus mustache, now garroted with a thin wire, incapable of telling any more of his heinous lies. The young man—not so young anymore, and certainly not as weak as he once was—smiled and retracted his weapon. He put it into a satchel, along with his book of power and a promise of eternity.

He awoke and was surrounded by death.

August 1987

The night before their camping trip, Noah had gone to sleep with a smile, his heart light and filled with anticipation of the camping trip to come. His bags waited at the foot of his bed, packed full of bug spray, his Chicago Bears hat, and his favorite shorts and shirts. He was ready to spend a week in the mountains of Leland County with his family. It was a trip he looked forward to every year.

Ashley and Brittney, his fifteen-year-old sisters, were also eager to go, their enthusiasm brought on by thoughts of boys, suntan lotion, and showing off their new swimsuits at the lake.

The morning of their departure, he woke up in a puddle of sweat, his teeth clenched, his heart pounding, unable to move. Fear paralyzed him as it never had before. But never before were his dreams about his own life.

His mother opened his door in the morning with her usual, "Time to get up, Noah." She'd moved on at once, not pausing long enough to see the look of horror the nightmare had pasted on his face.

He forced himself into his robe and down the creaky wooden stairs to their sunlit eat-in kitchen, where everyone else was already having breakfast. The smell of eggs, sausage, and pancakes normally made his stomach growl. This morning, it made him ill.

His mother had made a huge spread for the occasion—a pre-camping tradition. She always said, "We aren't gonna eat well for another week. Might as well eat healthy this morning." Which was silly. Lightning Fork Campground —with its showers, ample plumbing, and modern snack and dining facilities—was hardly roughing it, but she liked to joke. It wasn't as if eating was important to her. At forty-five, Jenny Halabrin had a figure similar to that of her two teenage daughters. But it was a running joke in their family and had been for the ten summers, or so they'd spent a week at Lightning Fork.

All of Noah's life. Or—more accurately, he supposed— what was left of it.

Noah forced himself to swallow a few bites of pancakes and washed them down with orange juice. His stomach churned, and he stared at the glistening syrup on his plate and grimaced.

He had to tell them. He had to.

"I don't think we should go," he said, trying to make it sound forceful but reaching only a mutter.

Jenny paused, and the spatula she held tipped until she came close to dropping the sausages on the floor instead of Brittney's plate.

"Not go?" Robert Halabrin said. His large, brown eyes reflected little concern. "Noah, you love camping." His father, although not as slender as Noah's mother, had a young face. He was younger than Jenny by five years, but they looked the same age to Noah.

"I have a bad feeling this time," he said. And that was all. His mind froze, and any argument he'd dreamed up vanished.

They'll think I'm crazy. They'll have me locked up. And what if I'm wrong?

His sisters eyed him curiously, and his mother dismissed him with another helping of sausage, though he hadn't touched the first.

"Everything will be fine, honey," she said. "You'll see. You'll get there, and you'll remember everything you love about camping."

It's not that I don't like camping! I don't want to get there. I don't want any of us to get there. HE's there.

He shivered at the memory of his dream, which lingered in his mind as clear as a photograph. He wanted to throw up. He opened his mouth, but the words wouldn't come out. He stared at the pancakes, drowning in syrup. It reminded him of the bodies from his dream, dripping blood from dismembered torsos.

He leaped from the table and ran to the bathroom to vomit. No one questioned why. No one guessed it was any more than pre-vacation jitters. New, but normal for a boy bordering on adolescence.

Later, sandwiched between Ashley and Brittney, he sat with his eyes closed more than open, wishing to god that their mindless banter would unseat the thoughts that obsessed him. The more he tried to suppress the images of blood and mangled bodies, the sicker he became. Even his sisters' taunting couldn't chase away the demons that haunted him.

They passed a sign that showed that Lightning Fork campground was twenty-two miles away. Noah's mind ticked through the math.

At sixty miles an hour, that's less than half an hour. I'll need at least that long to convince them I'm not joking, maybe longer to convince them I'm not crazy.

The twins were in a heated debate over the pros and cons of a popular actor, and the banality of the conversation with the lives ahead of them so short drove Noah to the breaking point.

"I have something to say," he announced, a little louder than he'd intended.

Perhaps it was because he hadn't uttered a word the entire trip, or maybe it was because of his earlier comment about not wanting to go, but his family turned to face him and pay closer attention. Robert pivoted in the passenger's seat and gave him his serious, ready-to-listen face. His mother glanced back in the rearview as often as the drive allowed.

"I have something important to tell you," he continued, trying to sound as adult as possible. "And you're going to think I'm crazy, but it's true."

"We don't think you're crazy, Noah," his mother assured him. Her foot eased off the gas for a second as her eyes caught his in the mirror.

"You haven't heard what I have to say yet," he replied, trying to sound lighthearted and failing. He paused. Every argument he'd thought of now sounded laughable, unlikely, and impossible to prove.

"Go on," Robert coaxed.

"There's a... danger at the campground this year." His hands, ready to gesture the severity of his words, dropped, unused, to his lap.

Robert's brow furrowed, revealing worry marks. His mouth turned down at the corners. He let a moment pass, obviously wondering how he should respond. He blinked. "I can't help but wonder how you can know that, son?"

"I have dreams."

"Do you mean nightmares?" Robert smiled, the worry lines disappearing. "Everyone has nightmares, Noah. It's perfectly normal."

Noah winced. "Not when they come true."

His father suppressed his grin. "I can assure you that it won't—"

"But they *do*, Dad. They have before. And this one will, too. It's been happening for a long time."

He half expected them to laugh at a ten-year-old who used the words "a long time." Maybe it was the earnest way he pleaded, but his family listened.

Noah couldn't believe it. They were listening! He had to keep going, had to keep their faith in him strong.

"I knew Mr. Freeman was going to die. I dreamed it the night before. And that woman that got stabbed last year—I dreamed that too. I knew when it happened. He stabbed her nineteen times, one for every girl who dumped him."

"You can't know that!" Jenny exclaimed, her brow furrowed by the graphic depiction of death her son had described. From the disdain on their faces, Brittney and Ashley clearly wished another seat was available—one far away from their crazy brother.

Noah shrugged, his green eyes having a hard time

staying off the floor. "But I do. And Dad?"

Robert's eyebrows vanished into his longish hair. Worry lines near his mouth accompanied those on his brow. Noah knew he didn't want to ask, but as a father, he knew he must.

"Yes?"

"Granny Halabrin told me a long time ago to tell you she's sorry Uncle Trevor turned out the way he did. She blames herself for spoiling him because he was the baby. And—and she knew you wouldn't believe me, so she told me to say, 'Tell him he'd better believe you, or I'll tell you his nickname.' But she told me anyway because she knew you wouldn't believe me. It's Bubbie. Short for Robert, or Bobby, or whatever."

Noah's mother was so staggered she hit the brakes, and the Blazer tires squealed as it escaped skidding off the road by a narrow margin.

Noah cringed. He hadn't wanted to worry his family, but better worried than dead.

Robert was confused for a moment as he searched for a logical explanation as to how his son knew a nickname he hadn't been called in over thirty years given to him by a mother who had passed before Noah was born. Even Jenny only knew because his mother had still joked about it when they started dating—jokes that finally came to a stop once Robert had his children.

"Hold on, son," he said as a thought struck him. "Which is it? Do you see ghosts, or have premonitions in your dreams? Because it sounds like you're saying—"

"I have both," Noah finished. "I know it sounds incredible, but you *have* to believe me!"

Aw, crap. I went too far. But I had to tell them about Granny's ghost, or he'd never believe me about the premonitions! And without knowing about the premonition, they'd have no reason not to go camping. Oh, heck. God, I hope they believe me. Dear God, please let them believe me!

His parents exchanged a glance, and Noah sighed. He knew that look. It was the same look that he saw when his sisters told his parents that it was all right for people with driving permits to drive without a licensed adult in the car, the same look he saw when he'd told them that having a dog was good for a boy's grades. The look said that only that morning, a little boy had said he thought they shouldn't go camping because he "had a bad feeling," and now he's claiming to see ghosts and have premonitions in his dreams. It was a look that said they had their doubts.

"Tell me about this omen, son." Robert coaxed.

Noah paused. He had to be sure they believed him. If they doubted any word he was about to say, then they'd most likely dismiss the whole episode as a childish cry for attention.

It wasn't fair! He'd never been an attention-seeking child. As the youngest of three and the solitary boy, he'd never starved for attention, never craved any limelight. If anything, he'd done the opposite, hiding in the shadows of the twins' center-stage family performances: cheerleading, drama, ballet, and jazz dance recitals. All Noah had were his action figures and his sign language, and his ghosts, which nobody had heard about until now. And compared with the ghosts, the action figures and signing were, to say the least, a letdown. That his parents took this moment to behave as though he was in the habit of telling stories... well, it just wasn't right.

"A killer will be there," he said. *That's good. Get their attention, but stay with the facts. Don't sound like you're trying to do anything other than be honest with them. So far, so good.*

Jenny frowned, her attention divided between the road and watching Noah in the rearview mirror.

"And who will he kill, Noah?" she asked.

Oh, heck. Why'd she have to ask that? It doesn't sound believable. I saw it, and I'm having a hard time believing it.

Noah studied his hands. Now, more than at any other point in his life, he hated his problem. He hated knowing what no one knew and being helpless to prevent it from happening. The burden of his knowledge was too much for a man so young; even he knew it. For some reason, fate had cursed him to witness people's deaths, and he hadn't a clue how to stop it from happening.

He swallowed, wishing he could lie. He couldn't.

"Everyone," Noah murmured. "Everyone dies."

"Everyone?" Robert said. "That's a lot of people, Noah. And you mean to say no one will get out alive? And one man kills them all?"

"Well, I *think* it was everyone," he said. "I... it's hard to tell. I only know what I saw, and everyone I *saw* was dead. I guess that doesn't necessarily mean he killed everyone. Just everyone I saw in my dream."

He hoped his logic would show them how sincere he was, maybe even a little wise. He raised his gaze from his hands to face his father. Robert indicated that he was listening with a tip of his head, but he didn't disagree with him or tell him to *Stop his foolishness right now, young man. We're going camping whether you like it or not.* Noah's heart lifted a little.

"And what else did you see, Noah? Do you know who did it?"

"A man with a scar on his cheek," Noah continued. "He's got this weapon... something new, or a ghost weapon or... I don't know... it's hard to explain. Something that no one else has. It can reach long distances and cut people in two. And I saw that I'll see your ghost. And Mom's. You're going to... you'll die if we don't turn around."

"He has a scar?" his dad said. "And some high-tech or possibly supernatural weapon?" Noah agreed and didn't realize until the tone of his father's voice sank in that Robert didn't believe a word he'd said. A man with a scar. A weapon no one had seen before. It sounded like a bad story from a cheesy horror movie, but it was true! And if his father didn't believe him, chances were good his mother didn't either.

"Noah, I'll tell you what I'll do," Robert said. "I'll change our reservations if it's not too late. Instead of you kids having a cabin to yourselves, you can stay in one of the big cabins with your mother and me," Ashley and Brittney's cringes and groans of disappointment made Noah slump in his seat, "and we'll stay together all week. When did you, uh, foresee this attack happening?"

They didn't believe him. None of them believed him.

The twins shot him a warning look that said he'd taken his little scheme for attention about as far as they were willing to allow, but he didn't care. Maybe if they were together, he'd stand a chance of getting them out of there before the killer struck. Or, if he was lucky, perhaps by opening his mouth this time, he'd changed the course of fate, and they would be spared.

Do I believe that?

He didn't have a choice. He'd have to cross his fingers and hope. He didn't have the strength to move his mother out of the driver's seat, take over the van, and force them to drive home. And if he couldn't convince them, the best he could do was try to protect them.

"I don't know when it's supposed to happen, Dad. But I know it will."

Robert sighed, gave Jenny a look, and she nodded. His parents were like that. They didn't have to talk sometimes to know what the other was thinking.

"I'll see about getting a big cabin for all of us. We'll stick together, okay? No one can get us if we stick together, right?"

Noah studied his hands and hoped his father was right.

"Way to go, Twerp," Ashley growled. Brittney slugged him in the arm, hard.

He'd failed to convince anyone. Now all he could do was pray.

CHAPTER 7

The human half of them that slept woke sometime around four a.m. feeling disturbed but stronger. He had no clock, but he didn't need one to know the time; thanks to the spirit with whom he shared his body, his mind had attuned itself to a vast source of knowledge that only the gray folk could access. He did not doubt that the spirit could tell him the earth's exact location in the universe if he was inclined to ask.

His muscles ached, so he stretched them, feeling with each extension the amount that they had grown as he slumbered. Every hour he slept, he grew stronger than when he last lay down—sometimes a lot stronger, but most often, just a minute amount. A normal human wouldn't have perceived the tiny increments of strength his body achieved, but he wasn't entirely human anymore.

He rose, shook off his clothing, and made his way outside. Quiet reigned, save for the songs of a few cicadas and night birds. He sighed, and with his breath, he savored the mélange of fragrances floating in the thick night air, the cloying smell of night flowers, the lingering fragrance of cut grass and earth, and the underlying stench of death. It was beautiful.

The gray man within stirred as a new bit of knowledge made its way to them.

We are being hunted.

Delroy shook his head. *Impossible.*

Someone knows. Someone has made the connections—the fork of lightning points to you.

Well, yes. That made sense. It was vital that, in the end, someone understood why his victims had died. Now that the list was shorter than ever, it was time to let the world know why he had chosen them. It was time to show the world their guilt.

It is more than that. They know of you. A survivor has seen our last work.

A survivor. *Damn the survivors.*

Unbelievable. No one knew they existed. He left no traces at crime scenes, and any documentation of their life on earth should have been obliterated. Still, he knew through the infinite intelligence of the gray man within that someone was seeking him out, someone who wanted to harm him—or worse, to stop him from completing his task. Someone who knew what he was. What *they* were.

It didn't seem fair. His entire mortal life, someone or another had sought to do him in. His parents had loved him until he was of no use to them. After they died, his educators took their place, always telling him he never worked hard enough, trying to keep him from advancing, from achieving his full potential, from learning all there was to know about life and death, and the secrets the latter held. And women? They sought power they knew he'd someday hold.

He recognized the odds were slim he'd ever be found. It was impossible to track a person who left behind no physical evidence. Still, the thought that someone knew he existed was a little unsettling. Did this person know about the gray man, too?

He sighed, inhaled more deep night air, redolent with jasmine, blood, and decomposition. He forced himself to relax. Turning from his shelter, he strolled in the grass he tended more or less with care, and observed the waning moon above hidden behind wispy, gray clouds and tree branches. His quiet, isolated environment usually brought him peace when he felt stressed.

Not that he feared his hunter. Not at all. He'd made a deal with forces beyond the control of humankind—forces who ensured neither he, nor the gray man inside, had to fear the grave.

Anyone who wanted to harm him was hunting for his or her death.

CHAPTER 8

August 1987

Day two at Lightning Fork Campground dawned sunny and humid, and Noah's parents decided it was a perfect day to pick berries.

No one had shown much interest in camping since yesterday's arrival at the cabin, a blue-gray, two-story A-frame, and built, Noah thought, a lot like a modified church. The bottom was a vast, rustic living area with a stone fireplace across from the front door. Upstairs, in what might have been a choir loft, three queen-size beds with worn flannel sheets and quilts rested against the wall.

The family had spent the previous afternoon unpacking their clothes into the sturdy chests of drawers and shadowy closets before spending the evening resting. That night, they'd set up the campfire grill and cooked bratwurst and hot dogs for dinner. Brittney and Ashley had avoided Noah like last year's fashions. No had one talked much.

That morning, the senior Halabrins were determined to turn their camping experience into a positive one. Berry picking for all. Noah nearly vomited at the suggestion of gathering food. He couldn't shake the feeling that his stomach insides resembled thick oatmeal—or maybe paste. Not that he'd eaten much in the last twenty-four hours. Every time he tried to take a bite, images of bodies hacked into pieces entered his thoughts and made it impossible for him to eat.

The twins hadn't spoken much to him since his

outburst, with the minor exception of a few barbed insults given when his parents were out of earshot, some of which were pretty creative—like booger muncher and ass hair. He'd tried to make up to them by telling them each they looked pretty in their new camping clothes. Flattery had always worked well in the past, but he guessed his delivery must have been off. Neither one had as much as smiled when they flounced by him with an air of disgust.

After a late, leisurely breakfast, the Halabrin clan followed the trails in the woods behind their cabin to the berry patch. They only took two wrong turns—a personal best for Noah's folks—before finding the tangle of wild blackberries growing with abandon in a circle of tall white pines at the west end of the campground. The shrubs, which the campground gardener neglected, relished the lack of attention. Some of the fruits were as large as the tip of Noah's thumb.

Nothing was able to distract him. Not the brambles on the vines that pricked his fingers and thumbs. Not his sisters joking with one another about boys or clothes or favorite TV shows. Not the bees buzzing nearby, or the hot sun, or the feel of cool water from the thermos on his tongue.

Now, as the afternoon of day two drifted into evening, he wondered if his premonition had been nothing more than a nightmare. None of his visions had involved his family before. None had ever been so gruesome, involved so many people, or made so little sense. He hadn't considered how incredible it sounded until he'd tried to explain it to his parents. One man—even if he was partly shadow person—killing everyone in his path? With some crazy ghostly weapon? It was weird. Perhaps he'd mistaken it for an omen because it felt so real.

The more time he devoted to reflecting about it—and

he'd allowed himself more time to think about this one than any other—the more he doubted it was a premonition at all. Could the powers who had given him this horrible gift be that cruel?

A gallon milk jug with the top cut off was slung over his shoulder and chest by a large canvas belt. It was already three-quarters full of berries. He couldn't imagine eating that many if he had all week. Which, if his premonition was correct, he might not.

He'd spent more time keeping track of where everyone was than gathering fruit, and his lack of attention caused him to prick his fingers again. The little spots of blood were lost in blackberry stains.

Stop daydreaming and pay attention, Noah. Don't let anyone get too far. You can't risk letting them out of your sight.

He lifted his head and made sure no one had wandered too far, though it was only a few seconds past his last search. Robert caught his eye, and they shared a weak smile. Robert's eyes held a lot of parental concern.

Noah wondered how long it would be before his parents sat him down for a long talk about telling stories. So far, apart from swapping to a huge single cabin instead of two smaller neighboring ones, his parents hadn't acknowledged Noah's strange outburst. It was as if they wanted to ignore the whole episode.

Every second that ticked by, his nerves grew more and more frayed. Whenever he saw a happy group walking past on the nearby trails, he tried to remember if they'd been in his dream, and he wondered if they would survive the week. He wanted to scream a warning to them all, to tell them all to leave, go now, run away, and don't come back until after *he* leaves, the strange gray man with the scar carrying evil weapons from God knew where. But he didn't.

After all, what if he was wrong this time? What if his

"problem" was developing into a genuine problem—the inability to distinguish dream from reality?

He didn't want to be locked up in a hospital. Ghosts lived in hospitals, and although he was sure a mental hospital would be different from a sick-person hospital, he didn't want to spend the rest of his life surrounded by gray people. What if someone caught him talking to them with his hands? They'd never let him out.

A thought jarred Noah from his musing. *How long has it been since I've seen anyone other than my family? It must be almost an hour since we've run across anyone else.*

Did it matter? His relatives were okay. They walked, and talked, and laughed, all of them barely out of arms reach from him. Mom and Dad were a little farther down the same stretch of brambles, Ashley and Brittney on the other side of the shrubs, clearly within shouting distance if the scarred man emerged from the woods. They were all doing fine, for now. What did it matter what the other families were doing?

Maybe I changed it all by speaking up this time. Maybe it will be okay.

That was when the mountain lion leaped down from an overhead branch.

Brittney screamed and grabbed her sister's hand. The cat paid them no mind, its yellow eyes set on closer prey. Having landed between Noah and his parents, the predator did what centuries of instinct had bred it for and directed its attention to the weakest and smallest of the pack: Noah.

Robert and Jenny tried their best to distract the cat, but it was as if they weren't there.

"Get a stick!" Robert yelled, his arms sheltering his wife, his body ready to leap at the animal if the need called for it. Jenny obligingly rushed under the canopy of pine boughs and searched, but everything at her feet was too small to make a decent weapon. Desperate, she grabbed a handful of prickly cones and hurled them at the slinking mountain lion. Robert found a rock, threw it, and cuffed it on its ear. The cat growled, shook off the blow, and advanced toward Noah.

"Go!" Robert said to Jennifer, "Get help. I'll—I'll try to lead it off."

A sickening sense of familiarity washed over him, and he stifled the urge to scream in terror and despair as the opening sequence of his dream came back in a rush. He knew this was when it happened. This was exactly where his dream had begun.

He didn't want to follow the course of action he knew now to be preordained, but if he stayed, he'd be easy prey for the mountain lion. If he died, he'd be powerless to help anyone.

He ran.

Déjà vu washed over him as he pumped his legs, one after another. He tried to shake the feeling that he was reenacting a script, but it was almost as if he had no choice but to follow the path he'd known was before him. He reached the trees and swiftly climbed the nearest one with low-hanging branches, hoping that the mountain cat had changed its mind.

It hadn't.

Its sharp claws found easy purchase in the soft bark and meat of the pine, and it scaled it with little effort. Noah turned back and saw the predatory gleam in the animal's eyes.

That's right. He came after me. He came after me, but he didn't get me because—

Just as Noah predicted, a gray shape emerged above the cat; a ghost, dressed in bib overalls, who hollered in his ghostly tongue and made shooing motions at it. The cat growled, let out an angry snarl, and retreated with a resentful swish of its tail.

The ghost turned to Noah, a proud gleam in his eye.

"Thank you," Noah motioned. The ghost, who had spoken to Noah on his campground visit the year before, answered Noah's greeting and perched on a limb beside him.

"But whatever you do," the ghost signed, "don't go down. Stay here. Safe."

Noah's breath caught in his throat. "Why?" he asked. The ghost gave him a reproving gaze.

"You know why," he motioned vehemently. "You can't fight him. Don't go down, or you'll die, too. There's nothing you can do."

Evidently, the ghost knew that Noah understood what was happening. For a second, Noah wished he was dead as well, if only to tap into that fountain of knowledge he knew was available to those in the afterlife. Then, he might have a clue about how to stop the man from killing his parents.

"I'm not afraid to die," Noah told the specter. "I know I don't die for good. The worst that happens is I stay here, a gray person like you." He took a breath and screwed up his courage. "I have to try to help."

The farmer shook his head. "I took care of the cat," he motioned. "But the man... I can't take care of him."

Noah had already begun his descent. He had to fight. He had to take action. Sitting up in a tree while his family was killed was stupid. It wasn't like him. He had to try.

He paused, leaned over the limb, and supported his body with a branch under his armpits to free his hands. He motioned, "Thank you." The ghost shook his head.

"You can't fight him, you know," the ghost signed. "He's one of us."

Noah's fingers slipped, but he caught himself in time. His heart hammered louder than he knew possible.

One of them? He's a ghost? That doesn't make any sense!
"Then how can he—"

"That's what I mean. You can't fight him. Nobody can. We can't, and neither can you. He uses both worlds. He's different."

Noah wanted to understand what he meant, but he knew time was running out. "I have to try," he repeated, and he hopped to the ground. He didn't bother to look for the cat. He knew what was coming.

The ghost shook his head. "Good luck," he signed. "See you soon."

Noah had no doubt what the farmer meant by that.

CHAPTER 9

August 2005

"Amazing what a couple of psychopaths will do with their free time."

Wallace's voice arrived over Noah's left shoulder, disturbing his thoughts and nearly sending him through his skin. He paused for a second before responding to give his balls time to descend to their former position. Meanwhile, he cleared his throat and turned to face Wallace.

"You think there was more than one?" he asked.

"Had to be," Wallace said with confidence. "A loner could've pulled an arm from the body, given enough strength and enough time and a tool or two. But that knee was yanked from its joint. No way could a single person do that. It would take more than two people, pulling in opposite directions to achieve the leverage needed for a stunt like that, at least." He shuddered, an action he seldom used after decades of examining human remains with detached candor. A repulsed expression crossed his ruddy features. "I wonder if she was alive throughout any of this."

"You can't tell?"

Wallace shook his head. "Normally, a good indication at this point would be the amount of blood lost, but..."

Noah flinched and stared at the bloodstained hillside. In his mind, images of the carnage at Lightning Fork rose. The likenesses were impossible to ignore, even if the death count was much smaller. However, he didn't want to make connections where none existed. Assumptions lead to shoddy detective work, and he'd learned to not jump to conclusions when he saw evidence that, at times, seemed obvious to a fault. Many times, clues that turned up with little or no effort could be likened to the adage: if it seemed too good to be true, it probably was. He'd followed more than his share of planted clues to believe in coincidence. Criminals tended to be more desperate than smart.

"What do you make of that?" he asked, jabbing a finger at the symbol. Wallace leaned forward, squinting.

"Looks like a cloud with some lightning coming off it."

"Think it's recent?"

Wallace raised his eyebrows. "One way to find out."

He strode with his unique waddle-strut to his kit and returned with a swab and a collection bag. He knelt at the corpse's head, mindful not to disturb anything that he might need as evidence later. With the tip of the swab, he daubed at the cloud portion of the symbol. He studied the tip.

"Still a tiny bit tacky," he remarked with a shake of his head. They'd been close to catching this one. He added a drop of clear liquid he pulled from a kit at his side. There was no reaction. "'S'not blood," he said as he placed the swab into the container for later examination. "We'll run a test, see what the chemical makeup is. I'll let you know."

Noah didn't doubt that he would; Wallace was nothing if not reliable. As the older man returned to his work, collecting anything that might turn out to be a valuable clue, Valerie joined him in scouring the gently sloping crime scene.

Noah turned his back to them but motioned to the ghost discreetly with his head to follow him so she was in a position to see his hands at work. He then began what the department was quick to dismiss as a personal quirk: he fingerspelled words.

It never took more than a try or two before the ghosts understood what he was about. This time, it took three. He supposed it might have caught her off guard when he signed "How many?" The other option involved throwing up his hands, palms up, fingers splayed—a motion that might be mistaken for something other than an attempt at communication.

Once she understood, she held up a single, polished digit.

"One killer?" he motioned.

Now that she understood that his hands were talking to her, he moved on to using full signs when he needed them, using subtle movements if it meant using his hands near his face or past his sides.

"You see him?"

She shook her head.

"Not until after," she signaled, moving her right hand away from the left with a graceful forward motion. It was then that Noah realized she was beautiful.

"You know the man?" he asked, using English in the way that sign sometimes required. He had no "him" to point to, and, therefore, his grammar was more correct.

This time a shake of the head answered him. Noah sighed.

"Can you describe the man?"

Her hands flew in front of her face, and for a moment, Noah thought she was protecting herself from an attacker not visible in his realm—an otherworldly assailant. Then he realized she had used the sign for "dark." She paused for a moment and then motioned with her hands at about what she believed her attacker's height to be.

"Dark skin?" he asked. *If it's not a white man, it's not the same being that killed my parents,* he thought, surprised at the relief that flooded him with the thought. To his disappointment, she shook her head.

"Dark how?" He signed.

She thought about it for a moment, then put her thumbs to her temples. Her ring and pinkie fingers curled, and she extended the others and coiled them up twice, adding a facial scowl for emphasis.

The sign for demon.

Noah's brow furrowed in the middle. The ghost he'd seen eighteen years ago had said that the Lightning Fork killer was both man and ghost. This woman said her attacker was a demon. Might a ghost and a demon appear the same to someone who'd never seen the shadow people?

"Noah?" Valerie's voice called, straining to not sound irritated, "We could use your help searching this hill."

Her voice wasn't reproachful, but he felt reprimanded. He quickly signed, "I'll be back," and turned to face the gore.

You can't fight him. Nobody can. We can't, and neither can you. He balances both worlds. He's different.

The words echoed in his mind as he combed the hillside with Wallace and Valerie, looking for clues. He added little, finding only a few strands of hair near the corpse and something that looked like an old weathered piece of paper to their growing pile of evidence.

If it's him, how do I catch him? Worse, what if it's not, and I wind up chasing a ghost of a different kind? More than likely, it's a group of wannabe Satanists pretending to be a copycat of the Lightning Fork Killer. But…

His eyes swept over the field of blood.

But how can one psychopath do all of this?

*　　*　　*　　*

"What do you think, Hal? Definite similarities, right?" Valerie was glowing. Despite the grisly events of the evening, she was in her element, tracking a criminal and putting the facts together. Her face had that serious but happy cast Valerie got when she was certain her lead was solid.

"And that fork of lightning over the head can't be a coincidence," she continued. "You said it was tacky when Wallace QT'ed it. I wonder how long he'd been gone. Maybe the humidity kept it wet. Anyway, we're talking a signature here. It's gotta be. But you were there, you tell me. What's your take?"

Noah waited until he had the nose of the car headed to the station before he answered. The anticipation racked her nerves, and she hung on, although her instinct was to push him to say something. She wished she were driving. At least then, she'd have the car to control.

"I don't think we should assume anything yet," he replied. He paused, awaiting the inevitable tirade.

"*What?*" she cried. "I'd think if anyone would want to find the guy who did this, it'd be you. Especially since it might be the same guy who killed your—"

"I know what it looks like," he said. "And I'm not ruling that out as a possibility. We'll check that angle out, and any others we can come up with."

He's got to be joking, Valerie thought, positive she sensed smoke pouring out of her ears. But it was evident from the set of his jaw and the flint in his eyes that he was not.

She pursed her lips and fought the urge to cross her arms across her chest and pout. "What other possibilities?"

Noah shook his head. "See? That's what I was afraid of. Val, if we close our minds to the chance that it might have nothing to do with Lightning Fork, we may lose the actual perp."

"I'm simply asking. What other possibilities could there

be?"

"It's more likely the symbol might be a surname, like Storm, or Raincloud. Maybe our killer is Native American, and it's some sort of tribal symbol. Maybe it's a gang symbol, 'The Black Lightning's' or something. It could be several things instead of a sign that a killer who's been dormant for almost twenty years is back. We can't rule any of them out right now, not while the trail is so fresh that the shit on the wall hadn't even dried yet. And we can't rule out the remote possibility—very remote, I'll admit—that the killer didn't put it there at all. Maybe someone came across the crime scene and added it in an attempt to frame someone."

Valerie was, for once, speechless. She wasn't sure if the feeling she held for him at that moment was admiration or astonishment, and from the way he was avoiding her glare, he didn't want to know which it was, either.

Frustrated and biting back an argument, she pulled latex gloves over her hands and dug into an evidence bag, withdrawing the wallet they had found inside the purse. The smell of pricey perfume came with it. Fine accessories were not her style, but she was willing to wager from the way the soft leather felt, even through the gloves, that it was expensive.

She thumbed the clasp of the wallet open and leafed through it, searching for identification. She found a New Mexico driver's license behind a plastic screen, right in front of a Nordstrom's credit card. The photograph looked as if it had been taken by a professional; not one strand of hair was out of place, not one brush of makeup placed wide of the mark. She thought of her own disheveled-looking driver's license photo and smirked.

What kind of woman is this?

"New Mexico driver's license," she said, replacing the

wallet, "Wanda Murphy." She shook her head. "Sure came a long way to get killed."

*   *   *

Five-thirty a.m. Noah lay atop his futon, his feet dangling over the sides, his thoughts cartwheeling and discharging like an out-of-control fireworks display. He was supposed to be getting some shut-eye, having worked the case until four, but the sight of that poor woman's body torn to pieces on the hillside had brought back thousands of more memories than he'd admitted to Valerie. And now, as the golden morning sun attempted to sneak through the cracks of his thick blinds, he wrestled with demons he'd fought hard to convince Valerie he'd had no trouble exercising.

He pulled his feet onto the black mattress. His boots, worn Timberlands he'd had for years, added grass and soil that stood out against the white cotton sheet tangled around the soles of his shoes.

And if not for the shoe covers, they'd be coated in blood.

He covered his head with his right arm and gave the mattress a good thump with the other.

It didn't help. Shielding his eyes made it worse. Open, his eyes were free to explore his spartan apartment. Bare wood floors and undecorated, off-white walls were boring, but at least they weren't memories.

He never kept photos of his family where they were visible. Although he had a few photo albums tucked in a steamer trunk in the corner of the living room, he didn't need them. He wondered, sometimes, if that was a part of his gift—a memory that never let go of details. It was a boon to his detective work. It added repulsive details to his nightmares.

Detailed conversations, memories of victims, alive and dead, unburdening the terror they'd experienced, all of it festered in his mind until it exploded in graphic, lurid, terrifying night trips into both real and imaginary crime scenes.

It was one of the reasons why he never asked the dead their names. It was too personal. He knew everything about them soon; learning the victim's name was one of the first clues when solving a case. Still, it was easier to learn through the basic channels; a driver's license, a witness friend, a landlady.

He wasn't their friend. He was their justice, the only way some of them believed that right might come out of the wrong that had been done to them.

And after seeing that fork of lightning in still-wet paint, he was also scared stiff.

CHAPTER 10

Noah had gotten perhaps three hours of sleep when he walked into the station house, a light coat of sweat already shining on his forehead from the short walk he'd made from his car. Blanch had only to see the enormous Styrofoam cup of Mapco coffee steaming in his hand, to know he'd had another rough night.

"Should've gotten some sleep, Halabrin," she reprimanded.

"Sleep is for civilians," he quipped. He eyed the folder in her hand with curiosity. "What've we got?"

"Tox scan on that OD came back really quick. Must've slipped into the 'urgent' pile, but who'm I to complain? It was exactly as you called it," she said. She consulted the folder, but the peek was cursory. When the results had come back, she was so shocked at Halabrin's accuracy she'd stared at it for ten minutes. "Crystal methamphetamine and battery acid. Leno doesn't know why whoever dealt it to her bothered with the meth. It was almost strictly the other."

"Maybe to help pass some sort of taste test?" Noah speculated. His experience with drugs was nil. It was a shot in the dark, but he had to venture a guess.

Blanch shook her strawberry-blonde head. "Who knows? And at this point, that's all you need to know about that one. Congrats, you were right, point given. I've passed the case back over to Chartier for follow up."

"But—"

"No buts, Halabrin. I need you and Val on this new

homicide. As if you didn't know. You're too good to waste on what still looks like an OD until we can find a motive. You've already put in man-hours on the Murphy case. I heard Valerie thinks there might be a local family related to the deceased. She's here already following up that angle. You need to check in with her."

Noah paused, his heart racing in his throat. There was an issue he needed to make sure the captain had considered. He hated to ask, but he knew if he left the matter unuttered, he'd question himself later.

"You heard about the symbol at the scene?"

Blanch didn't falter. "Yes, I did."

"You don't think I'm too close? That the possibility it might be the Lightning Fork killer might cloud my judgment, make me too eager, prone to making mistakes?"

Blanch scoffed.

"To hear Acquistapace tell it, you haven't given the Lightning Fork angle of it enough of a chance. No, I don't think you're too close. I think you're the best I've got, and this is the bloodiest crime Leland County's seen in years. If I put any less of a DT on it, I have a distinct feeling it will come back and bite me on the ass. And Val's always been a good teammate for you. But promise me one thing?"

It was more of an order than a question, and Noah paused to hear her condition.

"If you do find this hitting too close to home, you'll tell me. I can't risk having a case this big fucked up."

Noah knew what she meant. It was no secret that Maribeth Blanch was the first female captain in the Leland County Police Department, or that it took her years to get a position that a male staff member would have achieved in less time, given her record. She knew that women were, at times, given less approbation than men in her position, especially in a state as backward in some ways as Alabama, and she wouldn't do anything to put her job in question. After working with her for the past few years, Noah knew and respected his commander, and he agreed.

"You got it, Captain."

She smiled and motioned her head toward the bullpen, the desk-filled room where Valerie awaited.

"Val's waiting for you. Go catch me a killer."

*   *   *

The second Noah saw his partner's face, he regretted not having the foresight to spring for a second cup of coffee. Valerie's hand supported a head of dark, disheveled hair lying askew in her bun in the way that it did after several run-throughs with her nail-bitten fingers. When she heard his footsteps, her eyes glanced from the screen long enough to notice his entrance into the cubicle, then returned to whatever had riveted her attention.

"Glad you could make it," she quipped. "What is that, decaf?"

Noah tipped her a quick, mocking toast with his cup. "Hazelnut Columbian supreme, I think. Sorry, I neglected to pick up one for you."

She scowled.

"You know I don't drink that pancake syrup. If it's not capable of removing the enamel from my teeth, it's not coffee. Now here, look at this." She moved a fraction of an inch to her right and pointed at the screen before her. Noah hunched down near her right shoulder, and as he did, he noticed how nice her hair smelled. Like lavender.

Wanda Murphy's bio, complete with picture, stared back. He leaned in and read aloud over Valerie's shoulder.

"Jesus, she's got her own website. Nineteen ninety Graduate of Gryphon High. She's a local, or was.

Valedictorian. Accepted at the University of New Mexico, graduated with a degree in Biochemistry and Molecular Biology... She was smart. But if she was so smart, what the hell was she doing in that part of town in what we can assume was the middle of the night?"

"Don't know why she was in that part of town, but she was in Gryphon visiting family," Valerie replied.

"What? Who?"

"It gets worse," she warned him. "I did a little research on the Murphy's, you know? Looked for an address and whatever so we can deliver the bad news to her family. Turns out, her father—Brogan Murphy—popped up on an unsolved from Kaiser from just a couple of days ago. He died last Friday after he left his job at the paper mill. The report said the company called it an accident, but the cops who arrived said there were suspicious circumstances. They mentioned a bit of graffiti involving lightning. Funeral's tomorrow. She was here for her father's funeral, Noah."

"You're shitting me."

Valerie grabbed her keys and stood, putting on her light-weight blazer with grace and pulling her long hair out from its bun, raking her fingers through and tucking it securely back in place with skill within seconds. Noah's heart skipped at the sight of her wavy tresses let loose, however briefly.

"No brothers or sisters," she went on. "The mother's all that's left. I have a feeling this is going to be more than a little difficult to break to mom."

Noah didn't speak, rendered speechless by his need to make his heart stop racing.

Valerie cocked her head and eyed him quizzically. "Are you driving, or am I?"

CHAPTER 11

The Murphy home was a modest white single-story ranch set well off the road. The walk was flanked by Chinese elms trimmed to thick shrubs that added color to the exterior of the house not fronted by the porch. An enormous magnolia in the backyard was grand enough to provide shade for a large family, and perhaps a swing or two. Despite the less than affluent neighborhood, the Murphy home looked inviting and comfortable.

Noah hated having to be there. He parked the car at the curb, allowing for the possibility that Wanda's mother—Brogan's wife, Katherine—might be expecting flowers or friends in the wake of her husband's recent passing.

"This is gonna suck," Valerie said from behind a hand that covered her mouth and muffled her voice. "That woman just lost her husband. Now she's lost her only child, too." She blinked back tears before they had a chance to swell.

"Remember we can't drag this out," he told her. "She's going to think we're here about her husband's murder. We can't give her time to get her hopes up that we arrested his killer."

She sighed, her chest rising and falling with the effort. Not that Noah was looking. "Ok. Let's do this. Do you want me to—?"

"I'll tell her," Noah said. It was more than his knack for delivering information that motivated him to offer to deliver bad news; Valerie was more of a softie than she let on. Noah knew it, but he never teased her about it because it was a quality he admired in her. He loved that years of detective work hadn't hardened her to the atrocities of human nature. If knowledge of her soft heart became known around the station, however, her reputation would suffer at the merciless hands of the stationhouse fraternity.

They took the narrow sidewalk, their arms almost touching. Noah imagined he sensed the sympathy radiating from Valerie already. He hoped she'd be able to avoid tears until they left the house.

The interior door was open, leaving no more than the screen door with a hook and eye lock between them and the Murphy household. A slow-paced piano inside played what sounded to Noah's untrained ear to be Chopin. He rapped the frame with a fist, and the piano halted.

"Trusting," Valerie said under her breath. "Her husband possibly murdered, and she still doesn't lock the front door."

A tall, sturdy woman with curly, dyed-red hair appeared at the door. Well-preserved, she could have been anywhere from forty-five to sixty-five years old. Noah knew from the information Valerie gained from the Kaiser police on the trip over that she was sixty-three.

"Hello?" she asked. Her voice was the slightest bit wary.

"Mrs. Katherine Murphy?" Noah asked. She nodded.

"Yes. Are you with the police?"

Noah and Valerie both provided their badges for her scrutiny as Noah continued. "I'm Detective Halabrin, and this is Detective Acquistapace. We're with the Leland County Police Department, ma'am. It's about your daughter, Wanda."

Katherine Murphy's hand flew to her throat; her chin shook in dread.

"Wanda? Leland County? What's—?"

"May we come inside for a moment, ma'am?" Noah

asked.

Her hand, thick and strong and, Noah had no doubt, normally steady, shook on its way to the flimsy lock. She pushed the door outward.

"Certainly, officers," she said. Her tongue darted out, fretfully wetting her dry lips. Noah accepted the door and held it for Valerie before following the women inside.

"Does this have to do with why she never came home last night?" she asked, leading them in more of a wander than a stride to the living area. "She said she was on her way to meet Shane. Her old boyfriend. They've been in touch over the years. He's divorced, now."

Valerie removed her notebook from her pocket and fished a pen from her blazer.

"Shane..."

"Shane Duvall. He's an engineer, he works over at Upton. He lives a few blocks over, closer to the factory area. They used to be playmates as children. I've often wondered what would have happened with them if she hadn't gone off to New Mexico." Her hand flew to her cheek. "Where're my manners? Would you like some coffee? Sweet tea?"

"No, ma'am. We're fine. Why don't you take a seat?" Noah motioned to the thick armchair behind her. Valerie sat at the same time Mrs. Murphy did, perching on the edge of a matching sofa. Noah sat next to Valerie, but nearest to Katherine.

"Mrs. Murphy, I'm sorry to have to tell you this, especially at such a bad time. Wanda... Wanda was killed last night."

The silence, already complete in the sleepy heat and humidity of the morning, grew until it became a physical presence in the room, stifling, smothering. Katherine Murphy's face grew slack, her eyes unfocused and unmoving.

"Wanda...killed..."

"She was attacked last night, perhaps on her way to or from her friend's house. I'm sorry."

A small gasp was all that Katherine uttered. Her mouth closed, opened, then closed again as she turned to Valerie for confirmation of Noah's message. Valerie leaned farther forward, her eyes conveying what she didn't have the heart to say aloud, that Noah was right, and her daughter was no longer alive.

"I'm sorry, Mrs. Murphy," Valerie murmured.

"I—who would do such a thing?" she asked. "First Brogan, now..." Her hands wiped the tears from her eyes before they had a chance to spill onto her cheeks, now ashy white with shock. They collected themselves above her bosom, clenching each other, the picture of a mother in grief. Suddenly, she peered up at Noah. "Do you need me to identify the body?"

"We've found out her identity from her driver's license, ma'am. We don't require a family member to identify the body but you can. I... I should warn you, it wasn't... Wanda won't look the same. I'm not sure I recommend it."

Katherine sniffed, and Noah withdrew a small package of tissue from his blazer and offered her one. She accepted it, dabbed at the forming tears.

"How did it happen?" she asked.

Noah had to admire the woman; she was handling it much better than he had expected. Perhaps the strength she was using to survive the death of her husband would carry her over until her daughter was buried as well.

"We believe the official cause of death was exsanguination," he said. "That means—"

"She bled out," Katherine finished. She breathed a quick scoff, and her eyes met Noah's once more. "I spent some time as an Army nurse. Not what you'd call battlefield stuff, but not far from it."

She picked a nonexistent piece of lint from the couch and wiped away another tear from the corner of her eye. When Katherine failed to speak again, Valerie took the chance to ask her questions.

"Mrs. Murphy, did your family, maybe your husband, have any... anyone who might want to harm you? Anyone in the neighborhood who might be stalking you, who had given you a reason to believe you may be in any sort of danger?"

Valerie poised the pen over her pad, ready to take down the answers. Her eyes were glassy, hovering on tears.

"No," Katherine replied, her voice devoid of emotion. "No one."

"Have you seen anyone in the past few days?" Noah added. "Maybe the past month or so, who was new to the neighborhood? Anyone unusual? Any salespeople, or people from a church who might have come to your door?"

"No one," she repeated.

Noah looked at Valerie. This was getting them nowhere. The poor woman was so distraught if the Flying Purple People Eater had come trotting down the center of the street at high noon, he didn't expect she'd remember it. It was pointless to continue the interrogation. Valerie put the notebook back in her pocket.

He reached for his business card holder and withdrew a single, white embossed card with his name and numbers, plus the Leland County Sheriff's Department number.

"If you think of anything, or if you need to talk, call me anytime."

There was an awkward silence as Valerie rose. Mrs. Murphy made no move to get up to walk them to the door.

"When can I... when will the body be ready?"

"The pathologist should be done with his work this

afternoon or evening. If you'd like to contact your funeral home, it should be ready by tomorrow," Valerie said. "But Mrs. Murphy… I'm not sure that would be a good idea."

Katherine accepted these words with quiet dignity. Her mouth puckered in a bitter frown, and she tore her gaze from the mental image that held it. For a moment, she was in her living room again.

"Thank you," she said. "You've been very… kind."

"We'll be in touch," Noah replied.

*   *   *

"One of us has to be there when Wallace examines the body," Valerie said. Noah hadn't spoken when she headed straight for the driver's side door after they left the Murphy home, which was good. One word from him, and she'd have broken down. She needed the distraction of the traffic to take her mind from the dismal expression on that poor woman's face.

"You want me to take it?" Noah offered.

"Naw. I'll do it. You take the boyfriend."

Noah gave her his arched eyebrow, surprised.

"It'll take my mind off it," she explained. "I mean… Not take my mind off it, but… I don't think I could handle the boyfriend right now, you know? Interrogation's hard when you're distracted."

"And the body's a no-brainer?"

"It's not like I have to pay attention to the body language when the body's not moving anymore. I'm afraid a real-life interview will need more attention than I'm able to give right now. The DB's Wallace's turf, and we know how good he is."

Noah shrugged in agreement.

"Boyfriend it is, then."

CHAPTER 12

Shane Duvall lived in one of the better areas of Gryphon, just outside the unfortunate part of town with the confused zoning board that had difficulty distinguishing between business and residential districts. His was one of the first blocks comprised of houses alone. Although the Dutch colonial home he lived in dwarfed the houses it flanked, it was far from large by modern standards. Two well-maintained pindo palms stood center in the yard on each side of the short walk. The yard was what Noah would expect from a well-to-do bachelor: simple, low-maintenance, but attractive.

Noah rang the doorbell and waited for over a minute. His finger was poised over the button, ready to push again, when he came face-to-face with Shane Duvall.

Duvall looked more prepared to step in front of a Hollywood camera than into an engineering firm. Noah had guessed that anyone who dated Wanda Murphy would have to be striking, and although he wasn't as good a judge of what makes up an attractive man as he supposed Valerie would be, he knew Duvall was handsome. Chocolate brown hair held in place with styling product, large, droopy blue eyes, a masculine dimple, and a grace that Noah detected from the simple act of opening a door; Duvall exuded confidence and poise. His button-down suit and slacks were midnight blue, his belt and oxford shoes dark brown. The man reeked class.

Noah discovered he was grateful that Valerie was willing to view the autopsy.

"Yes?" Duvall's voice, tinged with impatience, strained to sound courteous.

"Shane Duvall?"

"That's me. How can I help you?"

Noah showed his badge; Duvall glanced at it and nodded. Only the slight crease in the center of his brow gave away any sign of concern at the presence of law enforcement, but Noah had his attention.

The morning humidity grew by the second, and Noah wished for an invitation inside the air-conditioned home. Duvall showed no signs of welcoming him inside.

Noah decided the best approach would be a quick one. "When was the last time you saw Wanda Murphy, Mr. Duvall?"

Either Duvall was genuinely confused or a superb actor. His expression jumped to high alert.

"Wanda? What do the cops want with Wanda? She's not in trouble, is she?"

Noah couldn't meet his gaze. The man was truly upset; he'd have bet his paycheck on it. His stomach turned with the knowledge that he had to break the news for the second time that morning.

"I'm afraid so. Mr. Duvall, Miss Murphy was murdered last night."

"Holy fuck!" Duvall gasped, his breath gushing from his lungs as his posture slumped in distress. "What happened?"

"My partner's at the autopsy right now, finding that out."

"Autopsy." He washed his face with a dry hand. "Oh my god. I can't believe this. Her father just died, too. Last week." His palm paused on his mouth. Something dawned on him, and his worried eyes met Noah's. "Does Katherine know?"

Noah bobbed his head. "I just came from there."

"Holy fuck," Duvall said again. "I—I—I feel responsible." He let go of the door, and it started to swing inward. He caught it without looking in a smooth motion. After a long pause, during which Duvall's face grew longer and longer, he asked. "Why don't you come in, Detective? I'm gonna have to call into work if we're gonna chat. I'm supposed to be there in, like," a glance at his watch, "ten minutes for a meeting."

Noah motioned his consent and thought it must be pleasant not to report to work until most people are breaking for lunch.

Duvall led the way through a comfortable home with elaborate, masculine, Mediterranean décor: royal blue walls, arched windows, white tile floors with inlaid designs. In the living room, a spotless white couch and loveseat faced a white fireplace with wrought iron accents. The house was immaculate. Noah noticed Duvall didn't have a television. Noah thought of his own, tiny, dusty apartment and told himself he really should do better—at least get the dust kittens off the floor.

After a brief conversation using a sleek, silver phone in the neighboring kitchen, Duvall hung up, a dazed expression on his face and a dazed feeling starting to settle between his ears. Noah knew it was time to get him talking before the shock set in. It was best to start out with everyday conversation, anything incidental, to get his mind off why Noah was there.

"Nice place," Noah said. "Did you do any of the designing yourself?" He supposed at first the comment sounded flippant, but Duvall took it as it was intended, with a modest smile.

"Oh. Um, no. My sister." He laughed an embarrassed laugh, strode around the counter, and settled into the loveseat. Even in his grief, he moved with a sort of masculine elegance. "Well, sort of. She's got this friend that makes a living doing interior design. I showed him the floor plan, and he went bat shit. Did a good job, too."

Noah chatted with him briefly about the different features of the house, then his job, before working his way back to the purpose of his stopover.

"Mr. Duvall, you know I have to ask about the nature of Miss Murphy's visit last night."

"The nature of her visit," Duvall repeated, accenting every syllable as he contemplated his answer. A self-conscious expression crept back over his features. He paused as he searched for the right words. When he found them, he blurted them out, afraid he'd lose his courage to say them if he hesitated. "She wanted to get laid."

Noah acknowledged his words without response. He'd suspected as much. He waited, giving Duvall a chance to continue.

Duvall shifted in his seat. "She calls me whenever she comes to town. We used to date in high school; hell, I proposed on graduation night," he said with a bemused shake of his head. "She laughed, told me to get real. We went to different colleges; she went all the way." He stopped and smirked a little at the implications that sentence might have before clarifying. "In college. She went... she got the big degree, you know? I did all right. Hell, I'm still doing all right."

Noah nodded, feeling a little like a psychiatrist as he did so.

"But anyway, she calls last night. She's in town for her father's funeral. Said she needed some comforting. I knew what she meant." Duvall hesitated, wondering if he'd sounded pompous, his face saying he hoped he hadn't.

"You said you felt responsible?" Noah prompted.

"Why'd you say that?"

Duvall sighed and leaned forward, putting his elbows on his knees. "I proposed. Again. Last night, after we... after we were done. We were lying in bed and, I don't know. It just came out." His hands ran through his hair which popped back into place.

"What happened then?"

"She jumped out of bed as if it'd sprung a leak. Started grabbing her clothes, accusing me of pushing her, of asking too much. She got dressed and stormed out. I tried to stop her, but I couldn't find my pants. She'd had some wine, so I offered to drive her home. She digs in that expensive bag of hers, pulls out her cell phone, says she'll call a cab."

"And then what?"

He shrugged, a gesture that looked unpracticed on him.

"And I let her go. You don't understand; nobody stood in Wanda's way. She was a frigging firecracker. That's why I was wondering at first if she was in trouble with the cops. I thought maybe she'd driven drunk and hurt somebody, or maybe herself. Well, that and she said she'd felt creeped out lately like somebody was following her. I asked her if she'd seen anybody, but she said no, that she was just being paranoid, probably because her father had just passed away. He was killed—well, I guess you knew that already."

"What time did she leave? Do you remember?"

"About midnight, I guess."

"You said she called a cab? Do you know where her car is?"

Duvall's amazement was only overshadowed by his bewilderment.

"You mean it's not out there?"

Noah excused himself, raced to his car, radioed in, and put out an APB on Wanda's car—a black, late model

Mercedes Benz SL roadster convertible. So far, it was the only lead they had.

CHAPTER 13

The part of him that clung to the tattered remains of his humanity had a hard time parting with the idea that sleep was a huge waste of time. Nevertheless, he always was grateful when he awoke slightly more powerful than when he'd fallen asleep, more ready to take on the task of putting things right, of destroying the source of his miserable, painful youth and crushing the liars who'd humiliated him.

He rose from his dusty bed, asked himself if he was ready to begin the day, and discovered he was ravenous, a thought that brought a smile to his face. Food was one of life's few pleasures other than killing. The tastes and textures of varying cuisines reminded him of the spice of life, and most importantly, of the continuation of his life. The motion of spooning food into his mouth gave him fuel, power, strength. On top of that, if done properly, it tasted great.

He walked in the searing heat, grateful for the canopy of tree boughs above him that shaded him most of the way into town. Once he was inside the town limits, his overwhelming thirst drove him to the closest restaurant: a local chrome and red leatherette diner bedecked with vintage cola signs and servers dressed in uniforms suited for a bygone rock n' roll era. Aside from his dehydration, it helped that he was in the mood for grease and ketchup.

Cholesterol didn't concern him. With the gray man inside, no matter what he shoveled down his gullet, his arteries would remain as healthy as a marathon runner's.

Eyeing the menu, he noted that the cheerful atmosphere of the restaurant came at an exorbitant price. Dismissing the greed of humankind, he made a small shake with his head. Not that the prices were relevant—he never worried about money. The little plastic cards—which the gray man part of him thought of as novel instruments—never maxed out.

His wealth came with the sacrifice of the young couple on a hill whose blood was spilled by an assailant who still ran free, a young couple whose death he sought to avenge with every new drop of blood he spilled.

The chestnut-haired waitress who brought him his coffee found him attractive. She made the eraser of her pencil dance—*tap tap tap*—on her order pad, drawing his eyes toward her face. She cocked her hip his way and blinked her green eyes at him with seductiveness, a crooked grin on her reddened lips. She thought she was keeping her attraction mostly unnoticed; she didn't know about his command of the smallest of sensory output.

He told himself he should accept her subtle offer—the pheromones that traveled the air and tickled his supercharged nostrils told him that she was ready for him, that her body was his for the taking, should he want it. A part of him that was still very human stiffened, and he was grateful for the table that blocked the waitress's line of vision to his midsection.

He decided he didn't want to accept her unspoken offer. He needed fuel, and lots of it to keep his high-powered engine running at its peak. When he was alive, he'd have thought nothing of taking her behind her place of business and giving her what she asked for, heedless of the filth of the alley or risk of discovery. Now, his needs were greater than the joy to be had by spontaneous sex. He had a mission for blood. But not hers.

He placed an order for a large amount of food, gave her a wink, and sent her away. When she brought his order minutes later, her flirtatiousness was toned down to a bright smile and a bat of the eyes.

As he ate his pancakes, eggs, and sausage with a side of English muffin, coffee, and orange juice, he asked the gray man where to look next, where his next sacrifice lived. Was it the Murphy woman?

No, she gets to live, for now.

Delroy frowned, slightly disappointed that the easiest prospect wasn't the next in line. Then the gray man provided him with his answer.

This time, a family waits. They all die—all but the youngest.

A whole family. His grin returned. He decided they would wait until dark so he might kill them in their sleep. Maybe he'd even give himself a few days before they killed them, enjoy the suspense for a while. He had at least two days before he and the gray man had to rest again, maybe longer.

He smiled to himself, and from across the restaurant, the chestnut-haired waitress smiled back.

CHAPTER 14

Over the next week, the investigation didn't get much better. Valerie didn't learn much at the autopsy other than ascertaining the time of death, which had been probably less than two hours before she was discovered. This wasn't news. Sexual assault wasn't the motivation; the tests for semen or signs of abusive penetration came back negative. The depth and type of neck injury led Wallace to infer that a hunting knife, or similar tool, was used to slit her throat.

After consulting with the Kaiser Sheriff's Department, they learned that Mr. Murphy was not killed in a similar style. He had been hit on the head with brutal force, but strangely with a similar lack of evidence. No murder weapon had been found. There were no prints made by foot or finger to run through AFIS. After an extensive investigation, they discovered to their frustration that there was no blood, no skin under the fingernails, no hair, no spit, no semen. Nothing to run through CODIS. No signs of a struggle. As far as they could tell, nothing had been removed from the crime scene. The wallet and car keys were all accounted for.

Not to mention there was no motive. The styles may have been different, but the similarities were there.

Noah went through the file and tried to look for a common denominator, but nothing stood out. He asked the detective on the Kaiser case if the graffiti at the crime scene had been there before Brogan was murdered. Detective Aaron Masters—a man Noah pictured as very large and very black based on the bass tone and cadence of his voice—paused for a moment before responding.

"Naw. It was odd, though. Looks like someone left a little black rain cloud with a jagged fork of lightning comin' off it. You figure that means there's a storm brewin'?"

They cross-referenced crimes across Alabama to check for similar murders. Delving into the details of every murder committed in the state over the past few months didn't avail much, and the pile of murders in Alabama committed over the past few years was overwhelming. Birmingham alone was a stack Noah dreaded fishing through in the hopes that he'd find the one case that might offer them a lead. Still, he started with the local cases, rifling through pages of police testimony, searching for violent crimes that fit the profile, and hoping he might catch a reference to a piece of cloud-like graffiti.

Blanch rode his and Valerie's collective ass all week. Although they followed several leads to their unremarkable conclusion, Noah hadn't found the nerve to ask Katherine Murphy the one question he believed might tie them together.

Had they ever been to Lightning Fork campground?

Valerie spent the week biting her lip, dying to tell Noah to piss off, that she'd pursue the Lightning Fork angle on her own. But she knew that Halabrin was the best on the force for a reason; she wanted to trust his instinct on this one the way she had on so many other cases.

The problem was, she believed this time his instincts weren't doing their job. Either that or he was being deliberately obtuse not following the Lightning Fork angle. Still, it was better if they worked together on the leads he felt ready to pursue. Better to have them working together on the same case than working it from two different angles.

Two bodies, two clouds, two forks of lightning—an

obvious link between the cases. The symbol hadn't been released to the press after Brogan Murphy's death, so the odds of a copycat were nonexistent. But Noah struggled, incapable of making himself follow the one lead he knew might evolve into the case he'd been yearning to pursue most of his life. Whenever he thought about the idea that the murderer might be the creature that killed his parents—and dozens of others there that summer day, a chill caressed him like icy fingers stroking his skin. How could he explain to his partner, or to the captain, that the killer was a supernatural being? He couldn't explain it to himself!

He and Valerie chased every other lead or possible link that he came up with, even those he scraped out of the cold cases years past any hope of solving.

Valerie discovered a local gang—not much, less than a dozen local juvies—who called themselves the White Lightnings. Although the symbol left at the crime scene was black—a common paint sold in craft stores, as it turned out when the test results came back—they trailed the "gang" to their hangout at the local Wendy's parking lot.

They found the group hanging out on and around the hood of someone's ancient Camaro. Valerie half expected to hear Guns N Roses blasting from the speakers as they approached, a throwback to her personal experience attempting juvenile rebellion.

Noah and Valerie asked a few casual questions. Within minutes, they concluded that the White Lightnings were nothing more than a bunch of underage racist hoods that couldn't scare their way out of a shopping mall. When asked if they had a calling card, ten dull, pasty faces responded with blank stares and slack jaws. It was another dead end.

Next was the possibility the symbol originated with a tribe or cult. He and Valerie poured over books borrowed from the library, dug in police files, and checked the internet for countless eye-blurring hours. They found a few likenesses, most of them on meteorological websites, but nothing that matched the killer's handiwork. Noah's idea that maybe it was from a Native American tribe dissolved when he viewed the Indian's idea of lightning symbols. Most of them were more abstract than the illustration left at the crime scenes; many looked more like modern art than the black chicken scrawl they'd found.

They checked with the local gun and knife sellers to see if they had sold any large hunting knives in the past few months. Since it wasn't big game season, Noah hoped the sales would be few, and they were. They checked the backgrounds of those who bought with credit cards, and the most they came up with was a few traffic violations and a couple of DUI's. One man, Jeffrey Yeoman, had come up on a domestic disturbance issue, but further investigation showed that he and his wife had moved to Minnesota. He hadn't lived in Gryphon since March, which meant that unless they found proof that he'd come home in the past few days, he had a five-month alibi.

They compiled a list of names that might be related to the symbol and poured through local records looking for Storm, Raincloud, Rain, and Cloud. They found a John Storm, a few Raines and Raines's, and three Clouds, two of whom were female. Because Wanda was killed in the middle of the night, many of their leads had an alibi, however easy to debate: they were home. Owen Raines, a twenty-one-year-old white male, was a factory worker on the night shift during the murder.

Cold trail, everywhere they went.

Brogan Murphy had died on a Friday afternoon. The following Friday night, his daughter's life was taken. Then Friday dawned, one week since Wanda's murder. Noah

thumped his forehead later that he hadn't anticipated the
ticking clock.

CHAPTER 15

The air was fresh in the posher part of town, humid and laden with the thick smell of magnolia, jasmine, and chlorophyll from freshly-mowed lawns. It might have brought back fond memories of life with his parents in the upper-class part of town. If he'd had any.

Instead, it brought back a youth of abuse, of quickly being shuttled from a car, through the fresh air he craved, into an elaborate house, where his parents could watch and weigh his every move, usually finding him lacking before shoving him into the walk-in closet in his bedroom. The fragrance of mothballs and cedar might have stirred similar reminiscent feelings.

During the days, his mother, a large, dark-haired woman with a round face and onyx eyes, joined him in his closet sanctuary for their daily lessons. Among the coats, pants, and bags of sweaters, she taught him his daily lessons on math, grammar, and history. Most importantly, though, were his lessons on religion and his crucial role in it. Crucial, but not completely revealed.

The most love his mother revealed to him was the way her eyes glowed as she spoke of his importance.

"Delroy," she said, her hand sweaty and heavy on his forearm, "you are a terribly important element. Your father and I know that you are meant for great things. The world is too dangerous a place for us to allow you to roam free in it. Too much could happen to you. That is why we shelter you here. To strengthen your spirit, to keep you safe."

Her love for him that moment, and every moment she

revealed a sliver of his significance in the cosmic universe, was perfect. In those moments, his love for her became unparalleled.

Now, it was his time to avenge her once more.

He walked among the type of homes he and his parents had lived in before they were so pointlessly slaughtered—large three-story homes of brick, wide white columns, and ironwork. He strolled down the wide sidewalk that spanned under a veil of palm boughs as far as his eyes could see, his bag swinging by his knees. Despite the weight of the tools carried inside, it never grew heavy; on the contrary, the presence of its burden empowered him, reminded him of his holy mission.

He had decided to arrive earlier than he'd originally planned. The afternoon had grown late but had not yet reached twilight, much less nightfall, not time yet to expect killers at the door.

He smelled the thick night air. He was close. Because of the gray man inside, he could categorize not only the fragrances that hung in the heavy air but fragrances that were to come soon, like the metallic tang of blood. His heart raced with excitement.

When he consulted with the gray man outside a mammoth Greek Revival home, he discovered he'd reached the address they sought, the home where the traitors to truth lived. He considered ringing the bell but tried the doorknob instead. Sometimes the powers imbued to him by the gray man surprised him. As he'd hoped, the knob turned easily in his hand. Either the family had carelessly left the door unlocked, or he had discovered his newest ability.

They crossed the threshold. No alarms sounded. A positive sign.

Now inside the house, he paused, appreciating the pristine white that greeted him on the walls and marble floors, the white roses in bright white planters. The white was so stark, so clean and perfect, a part of him was surprised the home didn't smell of alcohol or bleach, like a doctor's office.

Yes, this place will look very nice in a short time. Very nice.

Where do I look?

Your sacrifices are already asleep, having gone to bed early in anticipation of an early airplane departure.

But what about the son? Isn't he visiting from another time zone? Will he be asleep too?

He's asleep, as well, the gray man said. *Jet lag. Flew in from... Italy. In town for a funeral for another you killed, a friend of his who had accompanied them to Lightning Fork that day.* A mental image of Parker Bates, a boy from a family two counties over, flashed across his memory. Delroy had dispatched him weeks before in an alley with a knife to his torso, severing him from navel to gullet.

Ah, yes.

He knew now what he must do.

They walked upstairs, where the gray man told him the bedrooms lay. Their sacrifices waited, unsuspecting, sleeping.

CHAPTER 16

The next call came that Friday night. Another murder, this time at Jefferson and Wabash—the pricey part of town. And this time, there was more than one victim. Three members of a family: the Harpers, mother, father, and son, had been slaughtered. The daughter alone had been spared.

Noah's heart sunk at the news, but at least now they had a pattern; the killer struck on Fridays.

"So much for TGIF," Valerie remarked, having also made the connection. She peeked at Noah from the corner of her eye as she drove them to the scene of the latest crime. He never took his eyes from the road.

"There must be a significance," he observed. "Maybe it's a ritual thing. A sacrifice every Friday for so many Fridays, and you get a prize from Satan's cereal box."

Valerie chuckled. "Or maybe it's somebody who lost their job on a Friday and decided to make everybody else hate Friday, too. We don't know anything yet."

"That's the fucking problem," Noah snapped, slamming his hand onto the dashboard. A second later, contrition spread over his handsome features. "I'm sorry, Val, it's just—"

"Just that we haven't gotten anywhere, and that's a feeling you're unfamiliar with, I know." She took a left onto Wabash under a canopy of magnolia trees. The road was lined with massive, swanky homes on two-acre plots with expensive landscaping. "Welcome to how the rest of the world lives," she announced.

At the corner of Jefferson and Wabash, she steered up

a circular driveway pulsing with red lights from the tops of police cruisers. She parked behind Dotch and Thomas's patrol car. Edwards and Wallace were already there, she noted.

"Oh, the locals are gonna love this," Noah said. "This is a three-ring circus to them."

Sure enough, a few neighbors were already gathering at the sidewalk despite the late hour, concern, or morbid curiosity on their faces. The police tape held them back. Valerie noted with satisfaction that one of the officers had the foresight to block the crime scene off at the sidewalk. That gave them several square yards with which to collect evidence. She hoped it was enough.

The lone surviving family member, a young woman with long, brown hair whose breasts and nose looked too perfect to be natural, hung in Dotch's powerful embrace. She sobbed, beat on his expansive chest, swung at his broad, dark face, and clawed at a uniform already streaked with her tears. Dotch was trying to coax her to the ambulance, where an EMT waited to treat her for shock, but her legs wouldn't hold her up; they wobbled beneath her like overcooked spaghetti. Dotch looked too afraid of the tiny woman to try to lift her.

Poor Dotch, Valerie thought. *He's got the hard job tonight.*

She heard a sound that drew her attention to the bushes outside the door. Sergeant Thomas was retching into the bushes.

Or, maybe not.

Inside, Edwards was snapping what she suspected was the first of many photos. Wallace crouched and labeled a piece of evidence—a severed leg—with a numbered plastic tent.

The house was beautiful, or would have been, if not for the gore. The vaulted ceilings, the beautiful art with baroque frames, and the vases and busts strategically placed on Greek pedestals registered in a small corner of Valerie's mind. What struck her most was the smell of blood and death, the horror of the murder scene that was the worst she'd seen in all her days with the Leland County Sheriff's department.

This was going to be a very long night.

To the right of the door, five marble steps led to a landing where one could head right, to a glassed-in porch, or left, up a curving flight of stairs that Valerie guessed led to the bedrooms. The stairs were littered with body parts that, from the looks of them, came from various family members. It was like they had exploded from the inside as they tried to flee down the stairs. Her gorge rose, but she managed to keep it down. Barely.

"Dear God!" Noah exclaimed, having come to a sudden stop behind her. His warm breath tickled the hair on her neck and sent a shiver down her spine. "What-what happened?"

Wallace shook his head, which looked uncharacteristically heavy with sorrow. Noah stepped around Valerie, and she made herself relax and focus on her breath.

"I wish I knew," Wallace said softly. "I've been tiptoeing around this scene for twenty minutes now, and I have to admit, I'm confused as hell."

"What do you mean?" Noah asked.

Wallace stood, so Edwards had an unobstructed shot of the leg. "It's the damndest thing I've ever seen," he replied. "Three bodies: mother, father, and son, older brother to the girl out there, in town for, of all things, a funeral. All torn to pieces. Yet, as far as I can tell, theirs are the only footprints. All of them were barefoot and in bed when the killer struck. There are footprints I can link to each of the victims, trails they left in the blood. Handprints that, I'd be willing to bet money, match the vics since they all seem to show patterns of struggling to get away. But no shoeprints, not even a gloved blood smear, nothing to indicate the presence of a culprit."

"Don't assume," Noah stressed. "Be sure to get them all."

"I will, I will," Wallace said, surprised at Halabrin's need to remind him. "You know that, Hal. But I have a feeling..."

"I do, too, Wallace," Noah said. The sight of the mutilated family saddened him. "If only we'd worked harder, maybe found the one clue that might have tipped us off on that Murphy case... maybe this all could've been avoided."

Valerie's head jerked his way at his admission and caught him with his head hung dejectedly.

He sounds so defeated, she thought. *Like he knows this is a no-win case. Why is he giving up so soon? That's not like him at all!*

Noah walked away, turning his back to her and Wallace. His hands started doing that twitching thing they did so often when he worked a murder case. He walked around the pool of blood, carefully positioning himself, so she and Wallace had no way to watch his hands.

Valerie asked Wallace if it was all right for her to enter the bloodier portion of the crime scene. Wallace nodded and pointed her to the gloves and foot protection, reminding her to keep her eyes peeled for evidence. He told her the path that he and Edwards had followed so she could do the same.

After wrapping her extremities in latex and plastic, she warily tiptoed around the pools of blood, striving not to disturb anything, alert for anything that might be evidence. In a house with as many housekeepers as this one must have, a piece of evidence was bound to leap out if it wasn't saturated under all the blood. She hoped.

She took the five steps to the landing and turned to the left. Her stomach clenched and threatened to revolt again at the sight of the body parts before her. A male head—the father, she deduced from the wrinkles near his gaping eyes—lay on its side, a quarter of the back of the skull gone exposing a hunk of brain tissue. Several more parts lay in jumbled heaps on the stairs.

Sweat sprung over her entire body, and she found her breath coming too fast until she was bordering on hyperventilating. She forced herself to redirect her gaze upward and to slow her inhales and exhales until she calmed down. The smell of the gore was nearly too much. Bile burned at the back of her throat, and she forced herself to swallow it down.

She took a few more stairs, heading deeper into the murder site, ever watchful, ever wary. She took the curve at a creep, her eyes never leaving her steps, the blood, and the bodies. When she rounded the curve, she looked down and saw that Noah was right below her, his hands flying. The motions his hands used looked familiar to her. For a moment, the bloodbath was forgotten.

Oh my god. It's sign language!

Valerie had been a faithful attendee of Faith Baptist Church of Gryphon for several years—a point of embarrassment to her devoted Catholic family and a heated subject of discussion at many holiday dinners. She'd tried in vain to explain to her parents that Faith Baptist had felt like home since the moment she sat in one of the padded pews. She especially liked the way they made a point to reach everyone who attended the services. Like the way they positioned a man who spoke sign language beside the pulpit at every service. She was familiar with the motions; she enjoyed how the translator's hands flew, swooping and fingerspelling with ease as he kept up with Reverend

Thorpe's message.

It looked like what Noah was doing right then. But if it was a sign, who in the hell was he speaking with?

Don't watch, she told herself. *It's not like you'll understand what he's saying anyway. He'll explain what he's up to when he's ready.*

But that was it. She wanted to watch, not because she believed she might catch a word, but because this was the first real insight she'd had to a man who'd been her partner—sometimes—for almost a year. A man who kept himself isolated, who was always courteous, but never let anything from his past slip. The only reason she knew what happened to his parents at Lightning Fork was her morbid fascination with the cold case that was the worst in County history. When she read the list of victims, she noted that two of them had the same uncommon surname as her partner. When she asked, he admitted they were his parents but said no more about it.

His reticence intrigued her. And now this mysterious aspect to his personality. What was he doing? Talking to himself? Possibly. It was the only thing that made sense.

She managed to tear her eyes away, and as she focused on the bloody scene before her, she noticed the biggest piece of evidence yet. It had been impossible to see before, as it was in the curve of the ascending staircase, unperceivable to anyone on the first floor. Although she had expected no less, the sheer size of it made her breath catch in her throat.

On the wallpaper, centered among the body parts chucked about without a care, was a four-foot black cloud with a jagged fork of lightning descending to the blood-stained baseboard.

CHAPTER 17

It wasn't much, but it was home. More like a granite cave, really, but it suited its purpose, kept him hidden as he recovered, and that was enough for Delroy.

The human half wasn't exhausted yet. The adrenaline rush from the slaughter still buzzed through his excited body, but it was time to rest for a while if he wanted to build his strength before the next kill. Taking out an entire family had been more physically taxing than what he was used to. His body was experiencing a strange combination of thrilled and tired, but it was a satisfying sort of exhaustion, the sort of drained but accomplished feeling that sets in after a long day of much-needed work.

He should have felt elated; it'd been years since he'd killed so many at one time, but his happiness was tempered by a new sensation: wariness. Tension had grown in the atmosphere. He sensed it in the muggy air he breathed, in the clothing he'd drenched in the Harper family blood, and in the way the gray man made him aware that his escape had grown narrower.

Now, even he sensed the presence of a hunter, a human who tracked his moves and sensed a supernatural quality to the murders. This someone knew what Delroy was, or at least understood in a way that most humans did not. There was a chance his supernatural hunter might cause him trouble and intervene with his mission.

He had the impression he might be running out of time.

But that was preposterous. No one, no human, understood what they were. Even those who saw the gray people wouldn't understand the true nature of their oneness. Their existence surpassed anything humankind knew, or would ever know. They were unique, they were unstoppable, they were perfect.

He ran cold water over his body, sluicing away the grime and blood that caked him. The water from the outdoor tap was icy, but there was nothing to be done about that. At least it smelled fresh, clean, and earthy. He used no soap, unconcerned about sanitation, simply about removing the possibility of odor. He took a towel from the bag and wet it under the spigot, splashing his arms and neck. Then, after removing his shirt, he splashed it over his torso and face as well.

His body was faultless: strong, muscular, and unmarred, save for the token scar on his lean face. He noticed his flawlessness without the affliction of vanity. One didn't have to be vain to recognize perfection.

The only factor that took away from his appearance was the presence of the gray man. He wavered back and forth within his body, there one second, seemingly gone the next, having blended perfectly with Delroy's corporeal body. The gray man never left—his moments of invisibility meant he'd hidden deeper within him. To the average human eye, Delroy walked alone. It took a unique perception to see the second being that shared Delroy's body.

He didn't bother removing the traces of blood from under his fingernails. He wasn't worried about the need to scrub DNA evidence from his body.

He often wondered why the gray man ensured that there was no trace of him to be found at the scenes of their crimes, though he left his body soaked with blood and all the evidence the police would ever need to pin him with their felonies.

It wasn't important. He enjoyed the smell of blood, both

fresh and browned, and the traces of flesh or other gore under his fingernails or hidden in the folds of his clothing heightened his desire to kill again.

Besides, no police officer would ever get close enough to extract that evidence from him. They would make sure of that.

CHAPTER 18

"Pamela, we need you to tell us what you saw. You don't have to do it right this second, but it would help us a lot if you can while the memory is clear. It'll help us catch who did this to your family."

Noah tried to sound soothing, like a confident friend available to hear whatever horror she had to share. If the ghosts he'd met inside the house were correct, he would be lucky to get anything he could use as evidence out of her—he'd be lucky if she was sane.

Valerie stood to Pamela's right, ready to lend a hand if she needed it. She considered taking out her notebook but decided against it. Standing before the girl with a pen in hand would only make her look like an overzealous reporter, and the last thing Pamela Harper needed right then was to feel as if she was being grilled for details. She already looked like a college coed who'd woken up only to find herself in the middle of a horror flick. Only for her, the nightmare had been real. She'd watched her family die, and for some reason, had been the only one spared.

Right then, Pamela was the calmest she'd been since they arrived. She sat on the lip of the ambulance door, her legs kicking listlessly. Judging from the droop of her eyelids, the sedative that the EMT had given her was taking effect.

Suddenly, Pamela's hands shook violently. The water in the small plastic cup clenched in her hands sloshed over the sides and down her tanned legs.

"You'll never catch them," she sobbed, her voice eerily

calm, the voice of shock. A second, less vicious tremor passed over her thin frame. She paused, closed her mouth, and collected herself before she spoke again. "You'll never get them. They—they aren't real."

You can't fight him, you know, Noah thought, remembering the words of the ghost in the tree from so long ago. *He's one of us.*

"What do you mean they're not real?" Valerie asked. "How aren't they real?"

"They... they're together. But they're both him. Only one of them's gray."

Noah's pulse took off at a race, his ears rang, and his mouth opened wide as Pamela's observation sank in. *She sees them too. My god, she sees them, too!*

"They look exactly alike. The gray man and the real man. And you can't kill them."

"What did they look like?" Valerie prompted, trying not to sound too eager. "Were they tall? Or big? Blond hair or dark?"

Pamela shook her head with her eyes fixed shut. The motion nearly knocked her over. The drug had affected her balance.

"No, no, no! They're the same man, only one isn't human. One is tall, dark, with a big scar," she touched her cheek.

Noah's heart leaped to his throat, hammering dangerously fast. His chest tightened, and he felt the throb of his pulse in his temples. He wished away the ringing in his ears, desperate not to miss any details of Pamela's description.

It's him! God in heaven, it really is him!

"The other isn't dark," she said. "He's gray. He's a... he's just like a freakin' ghost." A maniacal laugh escaped her enhanced bosom, and the Dixie cup slipped to the ground. Several ounces of water seeped into the dry ground in seconds.

"He's just like a goddamn ghost!"

CHAPTER 19

August 1987

Noah ran west, into the setting sun that glowed through the cracks in the tree branches above. Common sense screamed at him to stop, turn, and run the other way, but he had to get to the cabin. From his dream, he knew that his family met up in the cabin, and soon, the killer would be, too.

He came across the first mass of ravaged bodies and lost his footing, tripping over a root as his eyes stared, transfixed, at the horror on either side of the path. It was worse now that it was true. He felt his stomach clenching, burning bile rising in his throat, and was grateful now that he hadn't eaten.

He'd known his dreams had been real before but had had the luxury of being able to distance himself from them. The reality had been proven by headlines, news broadcasts, neighborhood rumors. Now, it stared him in the eye—a reality made horrifically tangible by its presence.

Piles of people—no, of humans, these weren't people anymore—scattered in a careless heap of darkening blood and severed flesh. The metallic smell of blood still lingered in the air. They hadn't been dead long; blood still oozed from some of the bodies. A few uncaring flies buzzed, and Noah winced, fighting the urge to shoo the scavengers away from what were, only moments ago, living, breathing campers.

It was when he saw the sightless head staring forever

into eternity that it suddenly hit him. These were people, they had been real, live people, and he'd let them die.

He should've said more, insisted harder. He should've acted sooner. He'd known, and he hadn't done enough. Instead, he'd stayed silent, foolishly believing that by the small act of mentioning his dream to his parents, he'd changed what would happen. It was his fault these people weren't alive anymore. And if he failed his family, that would be his fault, too.

A burst of energy sprung from guilt drove him toward his cabin with more speed than he would've thought possible. The sound of his footsteps drummed in his head along with the pounding of his heart.

At least I can save my family. I have to save my family.

He knew it was too late, but he pushed forward past the piles of mangled bodies to his left and right.

How did he kill them all so fast? Why didn't more get away? There's no way one man has the power to do this so fast!

Then, when his burning leg muscles were ready to fail with his next step, and his lungs threatened to give, the family cabin came into view at the bottom of a small slope. Pulling strength from a source he didn't know he had, he galloped toward it, his mind a movie projector playing out the scene he knew was about to unfold.

His dream had skipped this part—the part where he dashed down the hill, breathless, his side cramping with a stitch from lack of oxygen, his calf muscles taut and painful. Sweat trickled down his back, and he was certain that if his heart beat any faster, he'd die.

He began to round the cabin, heading toward the front door out of habit, and then remembered that doing so would be a huge mistake.

He's out there. He's outside the door, ready to come in the front door and kill them! He's RIGHT THERE!

The first story of the building had two doors on opposite walls. The first door, where they'd entered yesterday morning, was accessed from a broad field near the gravel parking area. This was where the killer was about to make his entrance. Toward the rear of the cabin, the second door gave a person a choice: the living area, the kitchen, or the spiral staircase leading to the bedrooms. It was through this door that Noah entered at a sprint.

He raced up the stairs to the landing outside of the bedrooms where his sisters and parents had gathered, terrified and babbling over one another in confusion. They'd seen the killer attack; they knew he had done impossible things, and they were paralyzed in their terror. Should they hide? Should they try to make it to the car and escape? Could he catch them before they did? Noah's voice joined them in their confused babble, and no one was hearing anyone at all.

As they struggled to decide, the killer strode through the door.

Tall, dark, with thick black hair and a scar on his left cheek, a straight, shiny, raised line that at one time had held stitches. The needle dots still showed, dots of scar tissue on either side of the line. He wore black jeans and a dark purple shirt. Every inch of him was streaked and spotted with blood. He carried a satchel confidently, as if he had all the time he needed.

Noah's jaw dropped. The ghost was right; this man was more than he appeared. While he looked human to Noah's family, Noah saw more—a black and white mist that flowed in and around him, that looked like a ghost of him, in him, and through him.

How is he doing that?

The killer dropped the satchel. Brittney and Ashley screeched in terror and grabbed one another's arms, not sure whether to duck into a bedroom or head for the door.

"Come on!" Noah hollered, pushing them down the stairs before him. "Run! Get out of here!"

For the first time since he could remember, they listened to him. They tore down the stairs and burst out the rear door before Noah said another word. He turned to his parents and knew now that they understood, knew they believed him. He also knew they planned to stay.

"You can't stay here!" he cried. "He'll kill you. Dad, I told you, he's got things in that bag—"

"Noah, go," his father said sternly. "We'll stall him so you and your sisters can get away."

"You can't—"

"*Go!*" his mother pleaded. Noah's eyes welled up with tears. He wanted to explain, wanted to grab their hands and drag them behind him and out of the cabin to safety. But there was no time. They were determined to stay, thought that they had a chance to save their children if they placated the monster downstairs. They didn't understand. And he had no time to explain. If he tried, he'd die, too—the weapon the killer was about to use extended far.

Besides, he already knew what was about to happen.

He never knew later how he got out the door and into the clearing, or how he raced to the parking lot where his sisters were putting the hidden spare key into the Blazer. He never recalled the trip to the police station or how they conveyed to the officers there what had happened. All he saw in his mind was his parents. All he felt was their fear. As he ran, he relived his dream in supercharged relief, his body somehow with his sisters and at the same time beside his parents as they faced their final moments.

He knew exactly what happened, how it happened, as it happened. He had lived it as surely as his parents were living it. Robert Halabrin and his wife stood before the door where their children had fled, blocking the way, their bodies positioned like defensive linemen.

The killer withdrew a weapon from his bag—a flexible, razor-sharp wire that had a reach of over fifteen meters. He began wielding his weapon, spinning it around his lean body like a martial artist, building momentum and length with every rotation. The wire flexed and contracted with every cycle, but to Jenny and Robert Halabrin, their killer wielded an invisible lariat.

He never took his eyes from Noah's parents.

"What if he doesn't see ghosts?" his father asked, realizing now that his and his wife's chances of survival were hopeless. It didn't matter if he charged or sat where he was; the man would use whatever invisible weapon he was manipulating and cut him down in an instant the way he'd killed the others they'd seen. "What if he was wrong, and all Noah sees are the echoes of people who once lived?"

Jenny turned to her husband with tears in her eyes.

"Then wave."

They waved, their hands limp and their faces pale and mask-like. Although Jenny expected this move to confuse their killer, he didn't hesitate but swung his wire in their direction with a confident arc.

Their final wave was frozen in time, a grisly final photo frozen forever in the mind of their son.

CHAPTER 20

August 2005

Valerie dismissed Pamela's babblings as the ramblings of a woman with post-traumatic stress. Noah knew better.

That Saturday morning, he took the mug books off the shelves and flipped through each one, simultaneously hoping and worried that there might be a photograph of the man Pamela said had murdered the Harper family. He suspected it was the same man he'd seen eighteen years ago. Noah knew a dark man with a scar was out there, waiting, a snake with a full belly. Waiting until Friday to kill again.

No luck. After hours of pouring over every book they had of Alabama criminals, he'd given up finding the mysterious killer with a scar on his left cheek.

What else was there? What evidence did they have? Were there any similarities in the cases, other than the state of the bodies?

There was the link that both Wanda and Pamela's older brother, Stephen—a big-shot editor who lived in Italy—had both been in town for funerals. They both were successful businesspeople, Wanda from a poor family, Stephen from a wealthy one. However, after re-examining the evidence, Noah found no relationship linking Stephen and Brogan Murphy.

This is ridiculous. There has to be something!

Valerie's worried face and uncharacteristic silence didn't help. He knew that the words "Lightning Fork" were dying to come out. He knew she was right.

He left the stationhouse under the premise of getting coffee better than stationhouse brew for the two of them, and as he walked in the blistering heat, waves of humidity made the distant air shimmer. With every step on the baking sidewalk, he thought about what he needed to do.

The killer was the same man, the man from Lightning Fork. There was no denying it now. He had to make a move, to close the noose on this man's neck before next Friday. Who knew how many victims this unstoppable ghost man would take? How many people did he plan to kill? And how was he choosing his victims?

Harder still, how was he, Noah, a mere mortal, going to catch a man who wasn't just a man? Who harnessed powers capable of making him strong enough to kill an entire family as if torn apart by a grenade without leaving a trace of evidence that he had been there? Not to mention nearly an entire campground full of people? And what about those unearthly weapons?

As he stepped into the Mapco, sweat that had collected on his back chilled his flesh in the wintry air conditioning. He poured two cups of coffee as if in a trance—hazelnut for him, black tooth enamel remover for Val—and paid for the coffee with change from his pocket. He laughed robotically at the clerk's comment about how it took a true caffeine addict to buy coffee in this intense heat and trudged back to the station.

Valerie leaped out of her chair as he approached her cubicle.

"They found Wanda's car abandoned outside John C. Memorial," she chirped. Noah was familiar with the cemetery, having visited there more times than he could recall. It was the same one in which his Uncle Trevor had chosen to bury his parents. He tried not to wonder too hard about why the killer might choose such a location to abandon the car.

Valerie continued despite Noah's dazed expression. "I might have another connection, too. There was a movie called Black Cloud that came out a couple of years ago about these Navajos. And there's another thing, a song called Black Cloud by a group called Crazytown—"

It was no use trying to pay attention to Valerie's hard research. Commonalities were adding up too fast. Too many coincidences, too many questions unanswered, too many years of wondering. Too long he'd been denying the obvious.

It was time to confront the demon.

"Take your coffee," Noah said, handing her the steaming cup. "We're going to Lightning Fork."

Valerie needed no further prompting. "It's about goddamn time." Snatching the coffee from his hand, she brushed past him, her backside an attractive blur in her haste to get to the car.

CHAPTER 21

It had been eighteen years since Noah had last seen
Lightning Fork Campground. In that time, the once-pop-
ular recreation site had turned thick with overgrowth; the
buildings now slumped, paint chipping, and covered in spi-
der webs. The formerly colorful snack bar and cafeteria
now missed its front door. It looked as is if it hadn't been
used in many seasons. The concrete block that housed the
campground's shower and toilet facilities appeared beyond
unhygienic. Muddy water trickled down its steps and into
a pool outside the door, and a few abandoned towels lay
on the ground at the entrance, undoubtedly serving as a
breeding ground for innumerable diseases.

Noah had heard that a few homeless folks had lived at
the campground during the off-season, but he doubted
even they would choose such depressing, unhygienic surroundings.

Before they left the stationhouse parking lot, Noah had
used his cell phone, calling to make sure someone would
be at the office once they arrived. Although August was
what had once been a peak season, he suspected the number of campers had plummeted since the slaughter. From
the look of things, he'd guessed correctly.

"Wow," Valerie murmured as Noah cruised past an aging Winnebago. A lobster-red man with a thick paunch sat
beneath its narrow awning, his weight threatening to col-
lapse the plastic chair beneath him. An ancient television
stood on a milk crate before him, its plug winding like a
long, thin serpent through the dust into the mobile home.

The lobster-man gave them a gap-toothed grin as they passed and waved.

"Friendly guy," she said. Noah gave a quick chortle.

Valerie shook her head faintly, and Noah wasn't sure if she was expressing disbelief or scanning for clues.

"God," she said, "this reminds me of that cult commune place that burned to the ground a couple of years back. Ever hear of it? Ugh, what a case."

Noah nodded. "Yeah, arson, right? Some crazy kid burned up a bunch of people trapped in the church or something."

"Yeah, I never believed that," Valerie replied. "I mean, how'd all those people get stuck in that one building if it started out as an itty-bitty fire? And the people—" she swallowed a huge lump in her throat. "Wallace said it looked like some of them lit themselves on fire, and others were broken, or half buried. It was weird."

Noah shrugged. Inside, his stomach felt full to bursting with churning acid. He recalled the last time he'd taken this road: fleeing in the opposite direction beside his sisters in a Chevy Blazer, his heart sick with the knowledge although he'd managed to save his sisters that his parents were dead, and damn it, he'd known it was coming.

The whitewashed office sat near the dirt road near the mouth of the campground, the only building that had received any care in years. Noah parked near the door, and a cloud of red Alabama dust engulfed the unmarked car. He paused to wait until the cloud settled, but Valerie burst from the car, eager to get on the trail of the lead she'd been most eager to follow.

She'd already knocked on the door when Noah mounted the three creaking steps to her side.

"Amazing, isn't it?" she said, surveying the area, one hand shading her eyes from the glaring sun. "This was once the hot spot for family fun. Now..."

"Now it's a ghost town," Noah said. As if to prove his point, two shadows—a gray young man and a little girl in a plaid skirt—emerged from the tree line across the drive. Their faces reminded Noah of late-night commercials pleading for money to help starving children in third-world countries. Their hollow, vacant eyes stared accusingly. He turned away.

"You all right?" Valerie asked. He bobbed his head silently and tried to swallow a lump that threatened to choke him.

A stout man in a Hawaiian shirt with hair that looked like a black Brillo pad yanked the door open and greeted them with a greasy smile that turned his cheeks into sweaty mountains.

"Come in! Come in!" he said, his Alabama accent as thick as the humidity. "You must be them. Detectives Halabrin and... "

"Acquistapace," Valerie offered.

The man with the brillo hair laughed too heartily at his faux pas. "George Bailey. My dad was a Bailey, and my mother's a big fan of *It's a Wonderful Life*." The line sounded rehearsed.

Bailey forced a chuckle again when they didn't respond. "We don't get too many visitors down this way no more. Mostly people with an interest with... well, you know. And a few ghost tours. We're on the Leland County Ghost Tour now. They come in buses." He made the last statement as if it was a point of pride.

He ushered Noah and Valerie in as if they were best friends back from a long absence. He poured them some sweet tea from the micro-fridge to sip while they sat in the one air-conditioned spot in the campground.

The office was square, with white walls and low shelves

cluttered with binders stuffed to bursting with papers. A beige metal wall locker stood behind the desk. Although the surface appeared clean, there remained a lingering smell of sweat and fast food. Bailey seated himself behind a desk cluttered with a blotter-sized calendar and numerous papers, most of them flyers. Noah caught the headline of one: HEARSE EXCURSIONS. He shuddered. *The man is making money off my parent's death.* His lip curled in disgust.

Bailey leaned forward, a dog panting at the chance to help. "Now, what can I do ya for?"

"Mr. Bailey, we have a reason to believe the Lightning Fork killer case isn't as cold as we thought," Valerie began. Bailey's amiable expression melted like ice in the Alabama heat.

"You mean he's back?" he said. "My God, it must be..."

"Eighteen years," Noah finished. Bailey swallowed.

"But why now? After all that time?" His eyes bulged as a thought occurred to him. "You don't think he'll be coming back here, do you? I mean—"

"He hasn't given us a reason to believe he will," Noah said, "In fact, we're not positive it's the same man. But you might want to evacuate the guests to be safe."

"Gosh, and it's the busy season," Bailey said. Noah thought about the not-quite vacant grounds and blinked. Bailey scoffed, but the sound was nervous. "I can't believe he's back. My uncle's gonna kill me if I shut this place down. It's almost belly-up as it is. If I empty it now...."

"You may save lives, Mr. Bailey," Valerie said. "There's no telling where the killer will strike next. He's left a symbol at each of the new crime scenes, a cloud with a fork of lightning coming down. That's why we're here. We're trying to see if there's some pattern, starting with the first known murders."

"The first known murders," Bailey said. He snorted.

"Makes sense to start here. Two killings between seventy-six and eighty-seven—the last one taking out almost the whole camp—and now this."

"Two?" Noah and Valerie's voices echoed in the tiny room. Bailey's expression changed from confusion to shock.

"You mean, you didn't know?" He sat back in his chair. "I thought for sure the cops would'a knew."

"We didn't—I mean, I..." Noah's cheeks flushed hot. He hadn't thought to check the history of Lightning Fork, and Valerie had been so busy being a tolerant partner and chasing his farfetched leads that she hadn't, either. When he'd finally mustered the courage to set foot on the land that had been the source of nearly twenty years of nightmares, he didn't want to hesitate. His single thought had been to get there before he had a chance to change his mind. "I'm sure it's in the files. I... we didn't..."

"Tell us about the first incident, Mr. Bailey," Valerie said, withdrawing her note-taking gear. Noah sighed and blessed her for her swift conversational gear shifting.

"Oh, it weren't like the last time," Bailey said. "Back in '76 it was only two people who died, not over..." He paused and dropped his head, seemingly ashamed to name the actual figure. Not that Noah needed Bailey to remind him that one hundred and thirty-six people had lost their lives and that his parents were the last two to die. Bailey raised his head, tried an apologetic smile, and continued. "Was a tragedy, though. A French couple, Jacques and Muriel Ducharme—"

"Who?" Valerie asked, her hand scribbling furiously on her notepad.

"Ducharme," Bailey reiterated, putting the accent on the final syllable and spelling it for her to remove any doubt. "They was killed over by the woods behind the family cabanas. You know, over on the west side?" His thick drawl turned the names Jacques and Muriel almost incomprehensible, but Noah worked out what he meant to say.

"What happened to them?"

Bailey sighed. "They was stabbed, both of them. That's all I know. My uncle Stepney managed to keep it out of the papers—"

"Stepney," Noah said. "Wait a second. Your uncle is Stepney Bailey?" Bailey blushed, turned acknowledgment into embarrassment. Noah choked back an incredulous laugh. "He owns half of Gryphon!"

"And Lightnin' Fork campground," Bailey added, suppressing a scowl. "Yeah. He talked to the cops, managed to get the whole thing kep' out of the papers. Didn't want the bad publicity to hurt his summer money from coming in."

"How did he manage that?" Valerie asked. "Someone must have found them."

"Someone did. Their son."

Both detectives winced. Noah did a double-take. "Wait a minute. They had a son?"

Bailey nodded. "Yeah. Delroy Ducharme."

"What happened to the boy?" Valerie asked. This was too good—something resembling a potential lead! She and Noah both leaned forward in their seats.

Bailey shrugged. "I asked my uncle what happened to the kid. I was worried about him. He stuck in my head, ya know? I guess it was him being 'bout my age and all. Last I heard, he was in an orphanage run by the Catholics. Um... St. Anne's, I think, over in Georgia, north of Atlanta. It's a ways away."

"I've heard of the place," Valerie said. "I have family over there. It's up in Bartow County."

"Mr. Bailey, I suppose it might be an odd question, but

do you still have a guestbook—or guest books—from nineteen seventy-six in your office or someplace?" Noah asked.

Bailey pondered the question with a hand over his mouth, scrubbing it with twitchy fingers. A finger shot up in an "aha" gesture, and he rolled his chair over to the binders on the shelves to his left. He consulted the spines for whatever detail he was looking for, and after a couple of nerve-racking minutes, he pulled a thick, black one out and heaved it onto his desk with a puff of dust.

"You don't happen to remember—"

"August 20th, nineteen seventy-six," Bailey said. "It was a Friday."

Friday. Chills set in on Noah's spine as he leaned in and flipped through the guest register. It started in January of that year and scanned pages with swift eyes until he found the page headed with "August" in bold type. He found what he was looking for, and though he expected it, the sight of the names toward the bottom of the page knocked the wind out of him.

"Murphy. Brogan, Katherine, and Wanda," he read aloud. His heart hammered in his throat, and he continued down the column until he reached the next family. "Harper. Stephen, Patricia, and Stephen Junior."

"My God!" Valerie cried, her voice thick with astonishment. "I'll bet you my next paycheck it's Delroy. He's killing everyone who was here the day his parents were murdered!"

CHAPTER 22

Your hunter is getting closer.

You're sure?

The silence that greeted his question was oppressive. The gray man didn't welcome challenges to his wisdom.

Delroy chewed his bottom lip and contemplated. The plan he'd followed was coming slightly unraveled, a snafu that shouldn't have happened; it perturbed him. He hated veering from a plan, especially one that had been working so well.

As soon as he'd bloodied that page in the book, he should have disappeared, vanished without any trace of having walked the plane of humankind, having been erased from the Book of Life. His sole connection to his past was his money, hidden in accounts in another country under the name Samuel Hain. That, and the memories of those whose lives he'd affected.

But now, his hunter knew his name as well. Delroy knew it as surely as he knew his heart was beating only with the help of the gray man.

The contract had said that no ordinary human would have the means to track him. Still, his hunter had found a way to learn it.

How did he do it? Had the name Delroy Ducharme survived on a piece of paper?

The man uses a counterforce we hadn't reckoned on.

A power as strong as the spells in the book I used?

Silence.

The book we *used?*

Doubtful. It would take a potent spell-maker to challenge our work. More likely that he uses a small crack in cosmic knowledge.

What does that mean?

But the gray man said no more.

Delroy found he was shaking and crossed his arms, warming himself as best he could with the heat from his body.

When his tracker had learned the name Ducharme, he'd found out Delroy's history, or at least the history of lies, the history that humans had told to explain what had happened that day. Using that account, his hunter might follow them to their next target.

This shouldn't be happening, but it was. He should have been protected from discovery, but it had happened.

What was a crack in cosmic knowledge? How often did this happen?

Delroy stood, pushed open the door to his shelter, and walked outside. The day was another bright, sunny one, the heat so powerful it was almost visible. He trudged over to the spigot and splashed himself with water, took a few swallows. The liquid felt cold, refreshing. He stuck his head underneath, saturating his hair, then stood, shaking off the beads of water like a dog.

He felt a little better. What was that expression? *No big whoop.* So, they had to move in a different direction, skipping this victim for the one after. Or another one on the list, it made no difference. They all faced death in the end. He'd see them all take their last breaths, take them all with his unstoppable hand or his otherworldly tools.

No one would bring this chase to a halt. No one could. Just because his hunter had managed to discover his name didn't mean he was cunning, aggressive, or had the upper hand. It merely meant he had an ability to access information, not a superhuman power. He wasn't invulnerable, the way Delroy was, just intuitive. He happened upon a crack in cosmic knowledge—whatever that was—nothing more.

He stretched. As usual, his muscles had grown more powerful as he slumbered. And he was famished.

His sleep cycles had grown shorter through the years as his body had grown stronger. With every death he offered the gray man, his body strengthened; with every sacrifice, he grew an increment more at one with the gray man inside. Soon, he suspected, his body would be a machine of perfect metabolic balance, in tune with the cosmic knowledge that the gray man now bestowed on him in small pieces.

They went over their checklist, the diminishing mental catalog of victims unknowingly waiting for his vengeance. Next had been Katherine Brogan, and then Sylvia and William Nobel. He'd skip them. If the hunter was following the list in order, he doubtless anticipated this attack, and he had no urge to confront him yet. He saw no need to disrupt his mission until it was unavoidable.

Who was next? *No, better yet, who was last?*

The hunter wouldn't expect that.

CHAPTER 23

"I'm not saying you're wrong," Noah said as Valerie drove them back to the station with her usual heavy foot. "In fact, I'd wager money that you're right. It's the best, most plausible lead we've had yet. But there's one thing about this that's bothering me."

"Why would Ducharme kill all those people at Lightning Fork eleven years later who had nothing to do with the death of his parents?" Valerie asked. "The day you and your family were there?"

Noah nodded.

Valerie's lips flattened as she considered it. "Well, I'm not a psychopathic killer, but I'd have to say it had to do with vengeance on the campground. The place where his parents died was still up and running and doing a wonderful business besides. Stepney Bailey squashed the story, so practically no one heard about what happened. George said they never caught anyone who killed Ducharme's parents, and eventually their deaths were ruled a suicide pact or something."

"Which had to hurt like hell," he said. "The idea that people believed his parents would kill themselves in a public place and leave their—what, eight-year-old boy?—all on his own."

"If you're gonna do it, better to do it where someone's gonna find your son and get him help."

"Do you think parents who'd commit to a suicide pact give a shit about their kid?" Noah asked.

Valerie shrugged. "I don't think they did it at all. I think there's a good chance they were murdered. It would explain the rage that's motivated him all this time. Maybe he didn't just find the bodies—what if he saw a man kill them or something?"

Noah winced, and then fell silent.

"What?"

"Just—I don't know. His parents die when he's eight, but he waits all these years to do anything about it? Why?"

"Well, he was a child for most of those years," Val said. "Hell, I've got a lot of unanswered questions, too. How'd he kill an entire campground full of people and not get stopped by even one? It's Alabama—surely *somebody* there had a gun. And how is he killing these people now and not leaving a trace?"

Noah turned to look out the window and said nothing.

*   *   *

Once back at the stationhouse, Noah and Valerie discovered, to no great surprise, there was no trace of a Delroy Ducharme in the phone directories. He also had no police record.

While they searched, Wallace arrived to confirm that their perp had left no trace at the Harper home, either. The lab had come through in record time, considering the urgency of the case.

"That's surprising," Valerie commented. She was standing in her favorite spot, near the air-conditioner closest to her desk, a mug of coffee in her hands. The side facing Noah read, "Screw 'em if they can't take a joke."

"No record at all, and then he kills all those people at Lightning Fork, all in one day?" She paused. "Do you think he had help? He had to have, right?"

They... they're together. But they're both him. Only one of them's gray.

"I think he had help," Noah admitted, but not explaining. "And you know, maybe it's not so surprising that he erupted all at once. He's probably a sociopath, well-behaved on the outside, but seething underneath, hating society and everyone in it."

"For not catching the guy who offed his parents?"

"Among other things."

Valerie sipped her coffee. "What I don't get is, why Wanda? She was, what, six at the time?"

"Why any of them? He's a killer. Our job is to try to catch him, not figure him out."

"Helps to do one if you can do the other," she said. "You know that. I'm really wondering how he knows who his victims are. And how is he finding them? You think he got a copy of the guest book?"

Noah shook his head and took a seat in her squeaky chair, tilting it back as far as it went, reclining and facing her as they talked.

"Bailey said that he had the only copy. We can call and ask if they'd had any break-ins, but I'd be surprised if they did. It's not as if they had a copier handy in a rinky-dink campground office back in 1987. How else is the killer going to get his information? Write it down by hand? Too time-consuming in the middle of a B and E."

"Well then, how?"

Noah finished his coffee and tossed the empty Styrofoam cup in a perfect arc into a trash container halfway across the room. Valerie offered a small smile of admiration, and his heart skipped.

"To know that, like you said, we need to know more about our suspect. We have to go to St. Anne's."

"What about the Katherine Brogan? And the Nobels? And what about the list?"

"We don't have enough evidence to say for sure that Ducharme is our guy, but let's get Robles and Telleman on it, ask them to keep an eye on the Brogan and Noble houses. If he follows the pattern, we've got until Friday. In the meantime, we've got to find Ducharme."

*　　*　　*

Meditation always helped him to stay focused on his objective. Closing his eyes, remembering the days of silence, of education. His early years were his childhood ideal. The idea of trading those hours spent in solitude to live like other children wasn't worth contemplating.

Delroy closed his eyes and brought to mind his fondest childhood memory. It began an hour or so after the bulb in his closet had burned out. He'd spent an hour in darkness, sitting on the thick carpet of his closet room, alone. No light came in from under the door. The darkness was complete. He had only the floor below him and the objects around him to orient himself.

Then, a line of light from around the doorframe. Delroy flinched in the glare. The door opened, and before him stood his mother, beautiful in her ceremonial robes of purple and blue. Behind her, his father stood, also robed.

"Come," she said, extending her hand. Delroy stood.

They brought him outdoors into the bright sunlight. In the center of the yard stood a square concrete altar, around which were three others dressed in bright robes as Jacques and Muriel Ducharme were.

As he exited the house, the others began singing in a language he didn't understand. His mother and father led him to the center of the yard, guided him onto the concrete slab where he was directed to lie down. Jacques and Muriel joined in the dance, and around they went. Delroy followed them with his eyes, not daring to move, hardly daring to breathe as his parents and their companions spoke in another tongue, waved their arms and hands toward him, and danced.

They worship me, Delroy thought. *They revere me. They have put me above themselves.*

Delroy's heart swelled.

In the gloom, now, recalling his mother and father's devotion to him, Delroy smiled.

CHAPTER 24

St. Anne's church lay outside the town of Cartersville, in a small backwater burg called Fenland that made Cartersville's population at 17,000 a metropolis in comparison.

The instant they caught sight of the church and its surrounding buildings, Valerie sensed an element about St. Anne's that gave her the willies. It wasn't that she was a lapsed Catholic—although she supposed flashbacks to her plaid-skirted, parochial school days might have had something to do with it.

Maybe it was the cemetery filled with old, crooked headstones that spread for two weed-infested acres behind the chancel. Or perhaps it was the scent lingering about it, reminiscent of newspaper, dirt, and mildew, that combined to give the place a feeling of disuse and death. The handful of children outside for recess didn't do anything to dissuade her belief that there was an unexplainable creepiness about the institution. The way they played without shouts, without jumping, just a handful of slumped shoulders and avoided glances made Valerie think of tiny zombies.

"Strict school," she observed. She was relieved to hear her voice didn't quake. Noah agreed.

Sister Paula, a tiny, gray-haired woman whose habit looked so large she could camp underneath it, met them in the narthex. She led them through the lobby to the hallway, a hundred-foot-long stretch of institutional gray and white that suggested a prison block. Valerie detected the unmistakable odor of Pine-Sol and the same gritty bathroom cleaner she used to scrub her tub. The familiar fragrances did nothing to help her feel more at ease; if anything, they struck her as alien, as if smells associated with home and comfort had no business in such a dreary, dungeon-like environment.

Sister Paula directed them into a closet-sized office the same gray as the hall. Noah and Valerie followed the nun inside since there wasn't room enough for her to squeeze in if they entered first. After she'd seated herself, they took seats across from the desk.

"I hear," she said, "that you're here to ask about Mr. Ducharme."

"Anything you can tell us about him would be helpful, Sister," Noah said. Valerie withdrew her notebook, and he followed suit.

Sister Paula gave a dry, eerie chuckle that made Valerie want to scoot her chair back. Sister Paula leaned forward and rested her weight on her dainty elbows. Her expression darkened, and she swelled like a cumulonimbus cloud prepared to flood the earth.

"I can tell you plenty about Mr. Ducharme," she said. "He came to us after his parents were killed. He was one of our longtime residents, staying on past his graduation for a few months as a groundskeeper. He stayed in a little apartment we created for him in the cemetery by walling off part of the tool shed and installing some plumbing."

"You don't sound fond of him," Valerie said.

Sister Paula sneered. "I'm not. I know I'm supposed to love all the children here. We are all God's children, and I suppose he was no exception, but sometimes I wonder. Mr. Halabrin, would you mind closing the door?"

Noah stood up and did as he was asked, moving his chair out of the way to make room for the door to swing, and feeling strangely like a schoolboy as he did so. Meanwhile, Sister Paula withdrew a pack of Winston cigarettes and a spotless ashtray from the top drawer of her desk. She lit up with a plain silver Zippo engraved with a cross which she closed with a practiced flick of the wrist.

Sister Paula slid her chair backward and opened a tiny window to ventilate the smoke. Valerie wondered why she hadn't noticed the faint, lingering smell of cigarettes before.

"He was a problem child, to say the least," Sister Paula said. The words plumed out in a cloud of smoke. "He fought with children, both big and small, male and female. He didn't care how he came away from the fights as long as he found someone willing to exchange blows with him. He didn't do his schoolwork often, but when he did, he did well enough to continue onto the next grade. It was frustrating; we all knew he was terribly smart, but he didn't care. He was caught smoking...." she viewed the butt in her hand. "Although I would do well to remove the beam." Valerie wondered if Noah caught the reference and made a mental note to ask him later.

"Did he have any friends? Anyone who would know where to find him, Sister?" Valerie asked.

"He had one kid, a Selena Dumas, who came to us during high school after having trouble with fighting in public schools. She was a real striver—latched on to anyone with a powerful personality, and Delroy surely had one. I'm not sure if she stayed friends with Delroy because he intimidated her, attracted her, or if she honestly believed he was going places."

"You think she might know where he is?"

"If anyone would, I'm guessing it'd be Selena," Sister Paula said. "She worshipped him. Of course, it has been almost twenty years since I've seen either of them, so I wouldn't get my hopes up."

"Why didn't Mr. Ducharme remain in your

employment?" Noah asked.

Sister Paula made a derisive sound and stubbed her cig-arette out in the ashtray. After making sure the embers were extinguished, she removed a tissue from the same drawer where she'd hid the cigarettes and wiped the ashes into a circular wastebasket next to her desk. As she did, her eyes danced from cigarette to ashtray to the detectives. It was obvious to Valerie she was stalling as she mulled over how much to reveal.

"There were two reasons," she said quietly. "And they happened the same day. I've often wondered..."

She lingered for a moment in thought. "The church doesn't ascribe too much to the premise of the devil. Some come away with their own theories: he's an entity, or per-haps he's a part of us. Everyone chooses their own way of thinking, despite what they teach you to believe. I believe the devil is real, and that one act of sin can lead to another, then another, like a domino effect."

Sister Paula contemplated the cigarettes and her ashtray, spotless once more, for a moment before grabbing another cancer stick and lighting up again. Noah noticed that this time, her hands trembled slightly.

Noah was growing frustrated. *What does the Devil have to do with Ducharme?* "Sister Paula?"

Sister Paula held up her hand and bowed slightly in apol-ogy. "He's no longer here because he had sex with one of the students. This was back in spring of nineteen eighty-six. April, to be exact, right after Easter."

One year before he killed my parents. Noah struggled to re-main impassive but had a feeling his pain was visible in the tightness of his face.

"You sound very sure of the date," Valerie said, noting the detail in her pad.

"I'm positive. I wrote it a thousand times on the

paperwork I dealt with that year. You see, it was the year St. Anne's was the temporary home to several artifacts on their way to the Vatican. These were items acquired from hundreds of museums across North America, all of them gathered in one of our storage rooms alongside the church."

"Why St. Anne's?" Valerie asked, her disbelief plain. "And why wasn't there a guard?"

Sister Paula chuckled, and Noah swore he felt spiders crawling up his spine.

"Would you expect to find priceless religious artifacts here?" she asked, waving her hand in the general direction of her office. Valerie had to admit the Sister had a point. "And there was a guard."

"Delroy Ducharme," Noah guessed. Sister Paula affirmed his words with a scowl.

"He'd managed to redeem himself by behaving for several months. He was a regular little ball of charisma then, but I didn't believe it for a moment. The Sister who was in charge then, however, decided it was time to reward him with some responsibility—an error that would never have occurred, had I not been hospitalized with a case of pneumonia. It turned out to be a hideous mistake. One of our senior girls ran into him in the cemetery while she was skipping class. He was always a handsome boy, and she had it in her head she was going to seduce him. Not that it would have taken much. He used his key to get into the room where we stored the relics, and that's where I gather they had sex. After they were done, he stole one of the relics and left. I've never seen him since. I suppose he wasn't exactly fired. More like vanished." She paused, considered her cigarette, and sighed. "The church hasn't taken lightly to the act."

Valerie thought of the run-down grounds, the worn

building. *They're choking off St. Anne's funding,* she thought. *They're killing one of their own churches!* "What was this young lady's name?" Valerie asked.

"Um, Madeline. Madeline Hundley. I think she's still around town, somewhere."

"Did you call the police about the stolen item?"

"Of course. The case went all the way up through the church, Vatican officials trying to hunt him down, and it was a madhouse around here for months. But they never found him. It was like he dropped off the face of the planet."

Noah and Valerie shared a worried look that said if an institution as immense as the Vatican couldn't track Ducharme down, what chance did they have?

Valerie licked her lips. "How important was this relic?"

"Priceless. It was one of two of the most irreplaceable items there. And if you do find him, we want it back."

"Of course, Sister," Noah said. "What was this item?"

"A book. A priceless book, black cover, centuries old. There won't be any mistaking it."

*　　*　　*

"A book?" Valerie asked. She flipped the pages of her spiral notebook with feminine hands, considering the notes she'd taken on Sister Paula's testimony. "What kind of book do you think it was?"

"If you wanted to know, you should've asked the Sister," Noah said.

Valerie sneered. "She wouldn't have told us. 'A priceless book, black cover, centuries old. There won't be any mistaking it.' Even though she obviously wants it back, she wouldn't tell us what it was called. She a: doesn't think we'd understand what it is or what it's good for, b: is afraid to tell us for fear we'd keep it if we found it, or c: she doesn't get it, either."

"You sound a little bitter. Harboring some resentment from your parochial school days?"

Valerie laughed. "I guess that place kinda got to me. Maybe I do have a few issues left with the church. I guess that's something I've got to work on."

"At least you're aware of the beam in your eye," Noah said.

Valerie smiled, and he had to smile back.

"It was creepy, though. Right?"

"As a haunted house," Noah agreed.

CHAPTER 25

It was a beautiful day. The summer sun shone on Delroy's skin as he exited his tiny hiding place and stretched in the glow, reveling in the feel of his strength. The wind blew through the longish grass, and he made a note to cut it soon as he ran a strong hand through his dark hair.

A glance to the fence showed that the car, as he'd suspected, had been found and towed, probably to the nearest police station. No matter, he didn't need transportation when he wasn't covered in blood. Walking to town on foot was a pleasant way to pass the time. He'd head there soon and find someplace to eat, but he wasn't in a rush.

He rinsed under the cold tap again and splashed some of the bracing water on his face and through his hair. Retreating into the dark of his granite hideaway, he noted that the pile of new clothes was dwindling. Time to buy more. He was running out of clothing free of bloodstains. It was a lovely day to go shopping. Maybe he'd buy some while he was out. Or maybe they'd continue to their next sacrifice. It was a gorgeous day to decide, a glorious day to walk, to be outdoors, to draw blood, and to settle scores.

They started to town.

As he walked, Delroy took in the sights of the trees, drooping and brown with drought. Although it was August, with fall at least a month away on the calendar, the parched trees were already losing leaves.

He breathed in heavy lungfuls of humid air. This summer, humid and scorching hot, was so similar to that summer. He tried to identify the various fragrances in the breeze and ignore the memories that inevitably tumbled through his mind like macabre clowns at a lurid carnival.

It worked at first when the walk was new, and his body was still alert, still buzzing with the bliss of his meditation. He was pretending to be one with his environment, that he was part of the dying, rain-starved flora that surrounded him, that his feet welcomed each beat of the roasting pavement at his feet. Maybe allowing himself to reach that oneness was his mistake—for what was he now, if not at one with the knowledge of the history, the present, and the future of the universe?

Sometimes, when he felt especially at one with the gray man, he was incapable of distinguishing the dividing line between the memories of reality, those of the ghost, and those of his nightmares.

The horrid memories that occurred most often, he suspected, were real. The recollections of an aloof mother and stubborn father. Parents who spent most of their evenings out and left him behind. Nights where he was allowed out of the closet only to be left alone with people he didn't know who regarded him with disdain.

They all said he wasn't good enough. He never asked for what. He knew. He had the scar to prove it.

"You were a great disappointment, Delroy," they said. "You aren't what you were supposed to be, and now your next life will be a great disappointment as well."

He didn't want to think that they were right. He had no memory of doing anything in a past life that deserved the treatment he received from the adults he knew in this one.

The idea of living another life like this one disheartened him. He thought of ending this life, of moving into the next existence. He wanted so badly to get his miserable days over with and maybe have the chance to start anew.

But the thought that stopped him was the idea that maybe taking his life was yet another sin he'd have to atone for. It might make the next life even worse than this one, if that was possible.

It had been so perfect for so long. What had he done wrong?

He knew that other children existed—he'd seen them on sidewalks, in cars, on bicycles. He wanted to talk to them, to ask them what they had done in their former lives that allowed them to roam without restraint, to grow up healthy and strong and free.

Why were they blessed while he was cursed? How can a person be punished for a life he didn't remember, for sins he had no way to recall?

He wasn't sure if it had rained many of those nights of his youth, or if that was an exaggerated touch of imagination. It seemed that whenever he tried to recall those nights, he remembered pressing his young face to a window streaked with raindrops, its touch on his face and hands cool from the night air.

His caregivers told him stories, and they all agreed on one thing. His parents were wonderful people, important people, people who mattered. He, on the other hand, was a disappointment.

"Why?" he would ask. "Why was I a disappointment?"

"Because you were rejected."

CHAPTER 26

Madeline Hundley lived in a white shotgun house in a row of small shotgun houses on a street with the misleadingly cheerful name of "Mystery Lane." Valerie laughed when she saw the street sign.

"Sounds right out of Nancy Drew, or maybe Scooby-Doo," she observed. "And what better place to hunt for clues?"

Noah pulled the unmarked car under a magnolia towering near the curb to thwart the muggy afternoon heat from claiming the car. It was the only foliage for blocks. Most of the patches of lawn nearby were small, square, and brown; most of the houses characterless. *These aren't homes*, Noah thought. *They're hotel rooms with mortgages.*

They took the narrow walk together, and Noah knocked on the screen door. As they waited, Noah noticed for the first time that day that Valerie was wearing perfume. It was a mild one, reminiscent of vanilla. He liked it.

After a long minute, Valerie said, "It's the middle of the day. Maybe she's—"

The door opened, and a middle-aged knockout of a woman stood before them.

"Can I help you?" Her voice was as thick and southern as the scent of jasmine and magnolias. A thin cotton blouse, tied under ample breasts, accented a flat stomach further exposed by low-hanging short shorts. Long, muscular legs ended in manicured feet with peach polish that set off a deep summer tan. Her wavy blond hair hung past her shoulder blades. Her green, catlike eyes met Noah's, and he noticed he barely had to look down to see eye to eye with her, an uncommon thing for a man his height.

Valerie caught the look she gave Noah, and she stifled the urge to bristle. *Professional, Acquistapace. Keep it professional.*

"Miss Hundley?" Noah asked.

"Yeah? What'chall want?" Her hand caressed the edge of the door.

"Miss Hundley, we're here to ask you a few questions about an old friend of yours. Delroy Ducharme?"

Hundley laughed a feminine tinkle that barely escaped sounding girly. Her hand swept through her hair, and Noah noticed her peach fingernail polish matched that on her toes.

"Honey, y'all still lookin' for that book? I'd'a thought you'd've given up by now." Hundley had a manner of speaking that used her whole mouth, drawing one's attention to her lips and tongue.

Valerie stood taller, her petite five-foot four-inch frame stretching to meet Hundley's.

"Miss Hundley, we're wondering if you've had any contact with Mr. Ducharme recently."

Hundley laughed again. "Contact? Delroy? Oh, no. He was just..." Her eyes danced over Noah's eyes, neck, torso, and pelvis. "He was just one of those things." Her eyes drifted back to Noah's crotch. Her bottom lip curled under a row of straight, white teeth. Valerie wanted to hit her. She forced her hands to relax, so her fingernails stopped cutting into her palms.

"Y'all want some tea?" Hundley asked. Her hand left the door, slid down her chest, and landed under her right breast, where she slowly adjusted a brassiere. A nipple appeared through the fabric, and then the other jutted out: a matching set of headlights. "I just made some sweet tea."

"You've had no contact with Mr. Ducharme in the past few years?" Noah asked. "When was the last time you spoke with him?"

"After we bumped pelvises. Why don't y'all come in? I have the coziest little places to..." she eyed Noah's face, especially his mouth, "... sit."

Noah turned to face Valerie, who looked like a cat ready to unsheathe her claws. "Sure," he replied. Valerie gave him an appalled *Why'd you say that?* look that made his heart drop a little.

They followed Hundley through the modest house to her living room, declining her offer for some tea. She was right about cozy; the only places in her living area to sit were a bamboo and white-cushioned Papasan chair and a daybed made up with a lacy coverlet. Hundley deftly maneuvered herself between the two detectives, forcing Valerie to sit in the Papasan or otherwise make a scene, while she and Noah took the bed.

"Could you tell us what happened that day, Miss Hundley?" Noah asked.

She smiled. "I could show you," she offered.

Valerie let out an exasperated sigh, and Hundley responded with an 'I'm sorry you ain't got it, sugar' glare.

"I was speaking more specifically about the incident involving the book theft," Noah said, trying to sound as businesslike as he could. "Do you remember anything about the book Ducharme took from the storeroom?"

Hundley sneered, a gesture that contorted her features, and then recovered with a smile. "I told those cops years ago I didn't know a thing. Of course, they weren't as good-lookin' as you. Or as polite." She shifted her position on the daybed, so her legs unfolded wide at the crotch, giving Noah an unobstructed view, should he want one. He made sure he kept his eyes above her collarbone.

She took a sip of a glass of tea and put it back on the wicker end table, leaning over and stretching like a cat as she did so.

"I suppose there are a few things I left out," she admitted, settling her glass on a souvenir coaster from New Orleans. She rested back and smiled at Noah as if he was the only person in the room.

"Such as?"

She sighed. "Delroy forgot all about me once we were done screwin' and he saw what was in that storeroom. It was as if he'd never been in it before that day. Once we finished messing around, he pulled up his pants and started browsing like a kid in a toy store."

"Do you remember anything about the items in the storeroom?"

"I sure do. Hell, I was as impressed as he was. Seems fuckin' wasn't the only thing we had in common. The place was full of statues, old figures, paintings, all kinds of crazy knickknacks. Most of them were of demons."

"You knew they were demons?" Valerie asked, making no attempt to disguise her misgiving about Hundley's knowledge on any subject.

Hundley smirked. "I was a Catholic schoolgirl out to piss off my parents, come hell or high water. Yeah, I knew they were demons. A few pagan gods and goddesses. Of course, a couple of 'em were the Christian sort: pitchfork, horns, goat feet, pointy beard. Most of them, though, were pretty rare. Baal, Camazotz, Yenaldlooshi, Gorgons, Hecate, Beyrevra, a tzitzimime demon... you name it, they had it. They even had the lost Kenneth Anger film."

Valerie tried to veil her surprise at the woman's ease at pronouncing such drawn-out words and failed. Hundley noticed, shot the other woman a patronizing glance, and continued. "There were demons there I'd never heard of, and I studied them the way most kids do the Greek and Roman shit."

"What about the book?"

"That? Oh, hell, I don't know. Delroy about jizzed his pants when he saw it, though. Called it... Oh, hell. Wait a sec, it's been a long time since I took any Spanish... *Libro de Muertos*?"

"Free the dead?" Noah ventured.

"Book of Dead," Valerie said. "Probably *El Libro de Los Muertos*." She said the word with such finesse Noah wondered if she spoke Spanish, or maybe Italian. Perhaps both. He felt ashamed he didn't know such an important detail about his partner.

"What is the Book about?" Noah asked. "Any clue?"

Hundley shrugged, her attempt at seduction forgotten for the moment. "He babbled on for a second when he found it. Something about the Spaniards in Central America recording the ancient tribal rites of an offspring cult of the Mayans that had found a way to balance life and death."

Yeah, but you don't remember much, Valerie thought dryly.

"What did he mean by that?" Noah asked.

Hundley huffed. "Beats me. By then, I'd figured he was a little nuts and I started getting dressed. He couldn't stop babbling about that book. He had this crazy grin on his face, kept turning the book over and over again, talking the whole time. He starts walkin' off, and I asked him what he was going to do with the book. He just says, 'You never know.' Then he puts the book in his shirt and walks out of the storeroom without locking the door, and there I was, half-dressed." She turned to Noah with raised eyebrows and a small smile. Noah pretended not to notice.

"What did the book look like?" Valerie asked.

"Old. Big, heavy." She measured out about eighteen inches square by four deep. "Dusty. Black cover, lots of pages looked about to fall out."

"Any writing on the cover?"

Hundley shrugged.

"And you've had no contact with Mr. Ducharme since then?" Noah asked.

"Oh, no," Hundley breathed. "I never saw him again." She fixed her eyes on Noah again. "I thought he'd be there the day they... bumped me from St. Anne's. He wasn't there. I was a little disappointed."

"Thank you, Miss Hundley. You've been too cooperative," Valerie said. She handed Hundley a card. "If he happens to contact you, please let me know."

Hundley cocked an eyebrow and accepted the card from Valerie, but never took her gaze from Noah. "Oh, my pleasure."

*   *   *

"God, I *hate* women like that!" Valerie seethed as she stormed back to the unmarked sedan. She threw her notebook into the backseat, jammed the key in the ignition, and barely made sure Noah had shut the door before she peeled from Hundley's curb.

"Throwbacks to an era of female dependency!" she exclaimed. "Treating sexuality like power. Has she never heard of Women's Lib?"

Noah struggled not to smile. He'd rather have died than say so—and if he did say so, the odds of perishing multiplied tenfold—but she was beautiful when she was angry.

CHAPTER 27

Noah keyed "Selena Dumas" into the DMV search and leaned back into his chair.

"Our luck, she'll have an address back in Fenland," Valerie joked with a glance to her watch. She hesitated for a moment, wavering on saying what was on her mind. Noah had been uncharacteristically silent on the drive back to the station, and she had spent far too much time wondering if he was thinking of Madeline Hundley or the case. She'd have been wiser to spend the time going over the case details herself.

Finally, her curiosity won out. "So, what'd you think of Hundley?"

He didn't blink. "I think she's well suited for a job as a call girl or exotic dancer," he said. He eyed Valerie with a grin that made her heart hesitate. "I also think you're a lot prettier."

As soon as the words escaped his mouth, he froze, putting his lips together seconds after an awkward silence. The monitor flashed as Dumas' information popped up.

"Selena Dumas, 313 Ringling Street, Apartment 3B, Gryphon," Valerie said. "Holy crap. She's a local."

"That's the first lucky break we've had this whole case." Noah stood and grabbed the keys to the Dodge, memories of Valerie's breakneck driving after they left Hundley's still fresh in his mind. "I'm driving."

*　　*　　*

Dumas lived in the middle-class section of Gryphon on Ringling Street, a name that always conjured up images of clowns and colorful canopied tents in Noah's mind. He and Valerie pulled up to 313 Ringling, an old, three-story walkup that strove to appear Italianate but merely succeeded in looking tawdry. Dumas' registered vehicle, a blue Honda Civic hatchback, rested at the curb with a flat rear tire.

The doorbell resonated through the oak door, a classic ding-dong that sounded homey and old-fashioned. Noah smiled.

"Just a minute," a male voice said. The detectives exchanged a slightly concerned look. The DMV files had said Dumas was single. Of course, that didn't eliminate the possibility that she lived with a man.

A short, wiry male answered the door, one whose description could best be said to be a photographic negative of Selena Dumas' DMV description. He cocked his head to the side and peered at them from behind wire-rimmed glasses. The smell of cooking Italian food wafted into the corridor from the apartment, and Noah realized as his stomach rumbled that he and Valerie hadn't eaten anything since their coffees that morning.

"Hello? Can I help you?" His voice sounded pleasant but guarded.

"We were looking for a Selena Dumas. Do you—?"

"Selena!" the man said, shouting the name behind the door and into the apartment. "There's someone here to see you."

"Who is it?" a voice shouted back.

The man cocked his head again. The gesture was starting to remind Noah of a curious dog. He and Valerie provided badges and introductions.

"It's the cops!" the man hollered, but without a lot of

concern.

"Shit," the distracted female voice hissed. Noah heard a thump as Selena dropped something soft. "Hold on. I'm nearly burning the garlic bread."

The man at the door motioned for them to come into the living room with another cock of the head. "I'd offer you dinner," he said, "But we weren't expecting anyone, and we didn't make enough for guests."

"That's all right," Noah replied. "We hope this won't take much of your time. We just have a few questions."

Selena Dumas emerged from a sleek kitchen much more modern than Noah would've expected from a building that had been so out-of-date up to that point. Maple cabinets and brushed steel appliances struck Noah as inconsistent with the exterior of the apartment complex. The living room in which they stood was much more traditional, decorated with colonial American furniture. The contrast between rooms was much like the contrast between Selena and her fiancée, whom she introduced with a pleasant smile as Rueben. Where Selena was on the tall side of average, Rueben was short. Selena was fair to the point of pale, with a smattering of freckles over the middle on her heart-shaped face, and she had straight shoulder-length red hair. Rueben was a dark-skinned black man with hair to match. Rueben's physique was trim and muscular; Selena was curvaceous, ample in the hips, and rounded in the shoulders and arms. They both wore a standard uniform of the middle-class American, though: jeans and printed t-shirts.

After hasty introductions and a few handshakes, Selena and Rueben invited them to take a seat. Her movements were graceful and elegant; she was the kind of woman Noah imagined riding sidesaddle. They seemed like pleasant folks, and he hated keeping them from their dinner, so he wasted no time in getting to the point.

"We were curious about what you remember about an old friend of yours. Delroy Ducharme."

The smile she'd had on her face until this moment evaporated. Selena hesitated for a moment; the light that had been in her eyes moments ago now gone. "Delroy? Wow, that's a name I haven't heard in a while." She hesitated. "What do you want to know about him?"

Rueben gave Selena a fleeting inquisitive look, which she returned with a small, loving smile that, Noah had no doubt, told him everything was all right. He took her hand, a gesture Noah found charming, and he noticed they already wore matching wedding bands, though they weren't married.

"Anything you can remember would be helpful," Noah said.

"Anything? Well, that's quite a bit. We were good friends back in school. We both went to St. Anne's, the Catholic School in Fenland. But I suppose you know that if you came here."

She tried to shrug, to relax her shoulders, but they tensed back up.

"Delroy was an angry kid. His parents had been murdered, and he said the cops wrote it off as a suicide pact. That made him furious, resentful, and very mistrustful of authority. He said some people saw knew happened, and that they didn't do anything. They didn't want to get involved. I find that hard to believe now, but at the time, it fit in with my whole need to hate the human race—especially adults. I was an angry teenager, too. It's what brought Delroy and me together."

She sighed, studied her fingernails for a moment. It was as if a weight had settled on her shoulders. The happy woman who came out of the kitchen now slumped in her seat, saddened and weighed down by memories.

Selena shifted her weight in her seat and looked at her fiancée. "Ben, do you mind if I...?"

"Not at all," he replied. He stood, kissed his fiancée on the forehead, and left the room without a trace of misgiving.

"Understanding man," Valerie observed.

"He's the best," Selena replied with a weak but sincere smile. Her pale cheeks had grown crimson, and Noah wondered why. "I had another life before I met him. I told him once that I want to keep that part of my life out of our life together, and he's never questioned it. He only asked me one question."

Noah took the bait. "Which was?"

A more genuine smile crept over her features. "Was I a prostitute?" She chuckled softly. "I said I wasn't, he knew I wasn't lying, and that was that. No questions asked."

Selena waited until she heard the click of a door down the hall until she continued. "Although, I do sometimes think that a prostitute might be easier to explain than some of the things I did do." She released a short, bitter chuckle. "I was a hellion. *God*, I was a hellion. I lit fires, I spray painted buildings, I knocked over headstones in the cemetery, I raised hell with the sisters... There wasn't a week went by that I wasn't sent to Sister Dougherty for misbehavior. And that was when I was a teenager. That I continued acting so stupid when I got out of school..."

Valerie leaned forward, ignoring the pad she'd removed to take down Selena's statement. Her warm brown eyes met Selena's tear-filled ones. "Everyone grows up at their own pace, I guess."

Selena laughed. "Yeah, and mine was set on crawl way too long. But anyway, where was I? Oh, yeah. Delroy and I moved in together after I graduated high school. He'd been fired for screwing some girl, an act he denied, and I believed him like the idiot I was. I thought he was the coolest thing since... well, anything. And I guess that mattered because I thought so little in life was cool. Drugs I liked. And alcohol. For a while, the list of drugs I hadn't tried was shorter than the ones I had. Then they came out with all this new stuff..." She blushed again and covered her mouth, and it occurred to Noah that she realized she'd shared more than she'd meant to with the police.

"Go on," Valerie said. "If it has to do with Ducharme, we need to know. He's been elusive, and anything you can give us on him would help."

"It doesn't," Selena admitted. "I just... It's been so long since I've talked about those days. About him. Now that I'm thinking about it, it's all coming back. But my partying had nothing to do with Delroy. He was the exact opposite; the man was a health nut. He had this obsession with immortality, beating death. If there was a theory out there about a way to live forever, Delroy tried it. Vitamins to undo cell damage, magnets, vampirism, the Fountain of Youth: and those are the few I remember. I'm sure there were more."

"Vampirism?" Valerie said, aghast. "You mean he drank people's blood?"

Selena nodded, her expression equally appalled. "He got really into the Gothic scene for a while. It was small back then. This was what? Nineteen eighty-six? Maybe seven? Most of the Gothic kids were into punk, industrial, or metal. Delroy talked the talk, and so he joined them to see if he could find someone willing to be his donor. Then he found out about AIDS and panicked. That stopped it quick."

"So, he wasn't your average health freak," Valerie said, biting back her urge to ask how a young man in the late eighties didn't know about AIDS. As long as Selena was gushing about her ex, they were gathering intel. Criticism might stop her outpouring.

"God, no. He was way more than that; he was obsessed, crazy with the idea of living forever. Sometimes I see an article on a new idea, someone's scheme on how to put off death, and—like the other day, I saw something on cryotechnology. I have no doubt Delroy, wherever he is, is on that bandwagon."

"Why did he have such a fear of dying?"

Selena's eyes darted back and forth a little, and she swallowed. Noah knew she was about to divulge what had made her so frightened.

"He wasn't afraid to die, although maybe I suppose that was part of it. I think watching his parents pass away affected him pretty badly, made him aware that he was going to die someday. But it was more than that. He didn't want to die too soon. He swore that he'd find a way to get back at everyone who was there the day his parents died, everyone who let it happen, and who let the killer get away. That year we lived together, he started learning all about fighting. He took classes in martial arts, sword fighting, fencing, boxing, you name it, he was all over it."

"Didn't he have to work?"

Selena scoffed. "No. When he turned eighteen the year before, this lawyer from Atlanta tracked him down and notified him that thanks to his parents, he'd recently inherited over three million dollars."

"Life insurance?" Valerie ventured.

"Doubtful," Noah said. "Most policies from that long ago won't pay on a case once it's been ruled a suicide."

Selena agreed. "It was a trust set up by his father when Delroy was a kid. He'd have collected it when he was twenty-one, but because his parents had died, he got it early to help him get started in life."

"Do you remember the lawyer's name?"

Selena gave a thoughtful sigh. "Yeah. I do, sort of. His last name was South. I can't remember the first name, though. Sorry."

"That should be helpful," Valerie said. "I'm sure the state bar has a list we can use to locate him. What about Delroy? Can you tell us what he looked like?"

"Tallish, about five-ten or eleven. Dark, curly hair, brown eyes. Great smile, but he's got a crooked tooth here." She pointed to an eyetooth. "Reminded me of David Bowie. Just one more of those sexy things. He was always in shape. He liked dark clothing and stuck mostly with blacks and grays. He also hated having hair on his face; he shaved every morning. As much as he hated it, I can't imagine that's changed. Oh, and a couple more things. He had a tattoo across his shoulder blades, a piece with storm clouds and this fork of lightning coming down to earth. Must have taken hours for them to do. And he has a scar." She traced a line along her left cheek from bone to her chin. "It made shaving a challenge for him. But it was yet another stupid thing about him that I found sexy."

"Is there anything else you can tell us about him?" Noah asked. "Did he have any other friends? Maybe one of the Goth kids he hung out with?"

Selena shook her head, and her thin red hair floated back and forth. "No, no friends. Back then, it seemed like it was always us against the world. He used to have an expression when something went wrong: 'If it's not you, and it's not me, it's OK.' I think he got it from one of those punk songs he liked. I thought it was stupidly romantic, and in a way, it was. At the time, he believed the whole world boiled down to us, and anyone else could go to hell. He didn't have any other true friends.

"As far as anything else about him... He's dangerous. I know that now. The man lives for the guilt he's kept inside, and to destroy those that he hates. He loves the idea of vengeance. He blamed himself for years for his parent's death, but it's like he... what's the expression? projects his feelings outward? He blames everyone he meets, mainly those people at Lightning Fork Campground that day. I don't doubt at all that he's the killer you're looking for."

"What about a book?" Valerie asked. "Did you ever see a black book that he maybe hid in the house somewhere?"

Dumas nodded. "Yeah. He had a lot of black books. There was one he studied a lot, though, more than the others. I didn't ask him about it, though." She turned her face away, ashamed at her meekness. "There was something about him when he read that book that scared me more than anything else he did. Sometimes I think that book—it was evil."

*   *   *

Noah and Valerie settled on having dinner together at a local Mexican restaurant that Valerie adored, and Noah tolerated called La Cantina. It was over sodas and complimentary chips and salsa that Noah spoke.

"Selena Dumas did a great job giving us a picture of Ducharme, but I'm curious why you didn't ask Miss Hundley about his appearance."

Valerie let out a long, heartfelt laugh that caught Noah off guard. When she caught her breath, she told him, "Never ask a woman what a one-night stand looked like. She'll always recall an image more flattering than the truth. Besides, Dumas had seen him more recently."

"What if we hadn't found Dumas?"

Valerie shrugged. "I didn't think Hundley was the most

reliable source for a physical description. Anyway, Dumas gave us a great one—ex-girlfriend and all, she's most likely seen him naked. Did you catch how she talked about him? Every other word was 'sexy,' or said with, like a reverence. I know I'm assuming the relationship was consummated, but I'd be shocked if it wasn't. Ducharme strikes me as a potent guy."

It was Noah's turn to laugh. "Oh?"

"Yeah, his whole fascination with life thing? What better way to live forever than to perform the act that creates life? To maybe create another little him?"

"Well, I don't know about that, but he is a sex and violence kind of guy if nothing else. For some men, there's a kinship between the two."

"That's sick. That's the sort of shit that perpetuates rape culture."

"That's testosterone overload," Noah agreed

Conversation halted as the waitress delivered their meals: shredded beef tacos for Valerie and chicken flautas for Noah. Valerie asked the waitress to wait and then asked Noah if he thought they were done for the day.

"It's seven-thirty on a Saturday. Our biggest lead is an Atlanta lawyer who may or may not still practice law and may or may not be in Atlanta. In either case, he'll be there tomorrow."

She opened her mouth to speak but dropped her finger as Noah continued. "That is unless you want to help me investigate the possibility that Ducharme may have signed up for postmortem cryo. Or maybe see if you can find out anything about the details about the Book of the Dead. Other than that—"

"I get it, I get it. The Dos Equis will have to wait."

CHAPTER 28

His food was bland, the Chianti dull and flavorless. Most days, his supercharged senses savored food with a palate more refined than a cultured chef. Today, his lunch of manicotti and salad merely helped ease his voracious hunger. Neither the thick pasta and red sauce nor the salad, with its balsamic vinegar and oil dressing, offered fulfillment.

Delroy put his fork down atop the basil garnish and sighed. An elegant older couple from a nearby table eyed him with concern, ready to offer their wisdom if he expressed an interest. He gave them a nod and turned up his lips at the corners in what he hoped was a grateful, but not interested, smile before turning away. The thought of having to interact with well-meaning people turned his stomach.

Don't worry. The hunter is no threat.

He heard the words but ignored them. It unnerved him that anyone had discovered as much as his hunter had about him. Every step the man took, everything the man learned, the gray man shared with Delroy since the gray man's finger rested on the pulse of all earthly knowledge. There was no way a human threatened them, not even an extraordinary human. Together, they had too much power.

So why did his food taste so flat?

Do not worry. He lives on one plane. Even if he discovers how we are linked, he still has no way to sever our tie. His human body is powerless to do it. We, however, have several ways to sever his. And we were

going to kill him, anyway.

We were?

Yes. He saw you years ago at the scene of your first sacrifice. He and his sister would have died at our hands soon. Now, he makes it easy by coming to us.

So why am I worried?

We aren't worried, simply preoccupied with this new knowledge and working it to our advantage. We are unstoppable, immortal. We are a creature more powerful than a demon, more tapped into the spring of knowledge than a river to the ocean. Without a spirit beside his own within him, the man who pursues us is nothing more than a mortal like the rest of your sacrifices. Sacrifices you easily slew.

Right. So very right. Nothing to fear. We—I am not afraid.

A handsome smile spread across his mouth, and he lifted his fork again. As he took his next bite, his food tasted better, as it usually did after a talk with himself, the dry Chianti blending well with the tang of the vinegar in his dressing.

His server came by, and he raised his finger. He ordered a second dry, red wine to complement his meal.

CHAPTER 29

"Anything?" Valerie asked, peering over his shoulder at the screen before him. On the screen was a smiling, handsome woman, advertising the purported advantages of cryotechnology.

"Exactly Jack diddly squat," he said. "Except for a few websites that ask visitors to sign their guestbook, none of these places have anything usable to trace our boy. And, of course, all the labs themselves are closed for the weekend. I've sent a couple of e-mails to a few 'Contact Us' links, made a couple of calls when I was able to get some phone numbers. All cold. You?"

Valerie cleared her throat and ruffled through some papers obtained from internet research, holding them before her as though she was preparing for a rehearsed speech.

"Okay... According to what I've found, the history goes something like this: The Spanish invaded Mexico in the early 16th century, frequently sending missionaries to convert what they considered the "pagan" Mayans. At first, they were charged with documenting the culture while at the same time converting them to Christianity. So, they kept codices on things like the calendars, counting systems, logograms, hieroglyphics—that sort of thing.

"Some of the Spanish missionaries apparently grew fascinated by the Mayans—the gold, the architecture, the culture, even the religious beliefs. Two of them in particular—Bishops Rodrigo Pascuale and Janucho Calderon—became involved with a rebellious sept of the Mayans the Spaniards called, *'Los Muertos Fuertes,'* or 'The Strong Dead,' under the guise of recording their rituals for posterity. Apparently, this sept wasn't happy with the current beliefs on the Mayan gods, umm..." she consulted her page, "*Itzamná* and *Kinich Ahau*. They decided to turn them into gods in need of blood and sacrifice. The compilation of these records became *'El Libro de Los Muertos*,'"

"Our Book of the Dead," Noah said.

"You got it," Valerie affirmed, glancing up from her page briefly. She lost her spot and retraced the lines of the printout with her finger.

"Okay, so moving right along... It says here..." she consulted her print-out, "Blood sacrifice was nothing new to the Mayans, they sacrificed to their gods to maintain a balanced cosmos, they believed that the blood of their rulers was the best of all—"

Noah made a face. "Ugh. And I thought we were hard on the president."

Valerie laughed. "Well, these *'Muertos Fuertes'* took it a step further: they sacrificed the blood of their enemies to bind themselves to the dead, becoming, they believed, almost undead themselves, balancing life and death.' The members of the *Muertos Fuertes* believed that, depending on the quality of their sacrifice, they had the potential to become immortal, nearly impossible to kill.'"

"They believed they were undead?" Noah asked. "Like vampires or zombies?"

"Uh, not really," Valerie said with a shake of her head. "The undead have to die first, if anything I've learned from the horror flicks has any basis in actual legends. I never read where the *'Muertos Fuertes'* had to die to get their power. There is one thing about self-sacrifice, something about people offering their blood, but I didn't know how reliable that website was, so I skipped it."

Noah swiveled back and forth in his chair, his fingers

extended and pressing against one another, deep in thought. Valerie thought the furrow of his brow was simultaneously pensive and adorable.

"Fits right in with what Dumas was saying about Ducharme," he said.

Valerie blinked. "Oh," she said, "One more important detail: they also gained the ability to," she scanned the page again, "'stalk and kill their enemies using the body of a ghost within their own, leaving no traces of themselves behind.' Weird stuff, huh?"

An indecipherable look crossed his face. "Looks like the *Muertos Fuertes* had a lot in common with our killer," Noah said.

CHAPTER 30

Delroy sat up, his heart beating wildly in his chest. Instead of sleeping, his body had assumed a new, trance-like state, recuperative hypnosis, riding the alpha waves of relaxed awareness. While he did, he found them viewing a new type of dreamlike sequence. These weren't hellish recollections. No, this time, he lived actions that were to come.

A smile crossed his face; this was a good sign. Not only was his physical body improving, but his psychic power seemed to be growing as well! In the twenty years that he had shared his body with the warrior, never did he have any indication that the power of the warrior within him had any more spiritual gifts to give. This new revelation was exciting. The abilities he'd been blessed with seemed endless. Better yet, he had an eternity to uncover all the possibilities.

The premonition had shown him a glorious scene from his future, a scene he ached to fulfill soon. Not one coated in blood—yet—but they were inflicting pain to humans on both emotional and physical levels.

His hunter. The man he'd been killing in the dream was his hunter! He felt it in the marrow of his bones.

He saw them confronting his hunter on the grass before his parent's mausoleum. The human had found a source of power, but a pitiful source, a gray one not trained in human warfare or any other, and female besides.

The hunter faced them, his features painted with fear and confusion. The gray one within him braced herself, but for what she didn't know.

How had this pitiful human expected to fight? He had no weapon, no tool, no knowledge, and very little power. He was dead for the taking.

They didn't have to attack him with any tool in their arsenal. This "supernatural" challenger needed no supernatural device to be killed. Delroy and the gray man merely reached forward and pulled the beings up by their frail necks and choked the life from the human carrier. His enemy tried to swing, to strike them, but his attacks were feeble and ineffectual.

A human female friend of Delroy's challenger sat on the ground, alive but unwilling to help him. She paid him no attention at all but sat on the ground unmoving, unblinking. Had he already taken care of her? He must have.

As the haze of the trance had dissolved, Delroy rose with a smile. He had told himself correctly; his hunter was nothing to worry about. He had seen the future, and it was death.

It was easy. It was going to be so easy.

Still, it wouldn't hurt to speed things up a little ahead of schedule.

He gathered his bag. He was ready to kill again.

CHAPTER 31

Noah's dream had the usual template of fog, mystery, and a terror that was a sure sign that it was a premonition. The difference was, for the first time since he'd dreamed of his parents' deaths, he was back in his own body.

And once again, the villain was Delroy Ducharme.

Noah found himself dropped into an assault without a clue as to how he got there. His feet dangled inches above the ground; his body hung suspended at the end of Ducharme's spiritually enhanced arm, his neck held tightly in the crook of the murderer's hand, cut off from its oxygen supply. Noah swatted at Ducharme's forearm, kicked with what little energy he had left, but it was useless. His strength was gone.

Where am I? How did we find him? Where is he hiding?

But trying to study his surroundings while he was on the verge of blacking out proved pointless. Pinpoints of light danced in his vision, blocking anything that might have given him a clue. Still, Noah strained his eyes to the edges of their perimeters. Behind Ducharme stood... a small building? He couldn't tell, and the harder he tried, the more his vision worsened. He turned his eyes to the left, the right. All he saw were gray and black lumpy objects on the ground and grass. Rocks? Could he be hiding in a park? Somewhere near the foothills of the mountains farther north?

He heard Valerie's voice droning nearby and was shocked that she did nothing to help him. He caught a glance of her from the corner of his vision. She sat on the ground before the small building with an object in her lap, her voice emitting steadily, soft and monotonous, in a language that sounded like Latin. She was chanting.

Why is she chanting? Why isn't she helping me? What is wrong with her? Is she possessed or something?

Then came the most startling revelation of all. Ashley was there! He knew she was there, though he couldn't see her. His dead sister was trying to help, but she couldn't. Worse, he knew that she shared his pain, that she was aware of every ache, small and large, that whatever Ducharme inflicted on Noah, he delivered to Ashley.

What in the hell is going on?

He strained to scream, to cry out, and to beat the arm that held him with such force Ducharme would have to release him...

He woke up in his bed, screaming, swinging, and covered in a thick sweat reeking of fear.

CHAPTER 32

Delroy's new shirt had picked up a damp ring of sweat under each arm. A puddle of sweat had also collected on his back and chest. No matter. It wasn't as if he had to worry about evidence. He was as untouchable and unobtainable as a ghost.

He *was* a ghost, at least partly.

It had taken over three and a half hours to cover the distance to his next victim's home on foot, but he wasn't tired; the early morning warmth didn't rob him of strength. He drank from the Gatorade bottle in his right hand. His left carried his satchel.

Delroy reached the doorstep of the squat white house of his next sacrifice and paused. Overgrown weeds, grass, and bushes gave the yard a jungle-like feel. He shook his head as he set the bag onto the welcome mat, an ugly, sand-covered brown thing with what he assumed was supposed to be ivy coiled around the frayed edges.

He grasped the doorknob and let himself in, creeping with inaudible steps into a shadowy, corn-yellow kitchen. Heaps of dishes surrounded and filled the sink. Grease spots and multicolor spatters hazed the color of the stovetop. The linoleum suggested dirty, dun-colored brick. A refrigerator peeked from behind numerous Crayola artworks held in place with magnets from destinations like Graceland, Dollywood, and the Grand Old Opry.

A waist-high bar and overhanging cupboards separated him from the living room—another home decor monstrosity in muddy browns and algae greens—where he peeked in on his victims.

The older couple sat on a squat couch together, their pasty faces white in the backwash of a television set. The wife had short, messy white hair. The glasses perched on her nose bore a tacky faux pearl chain. He wore a sweat-stained tank top and washed-out trousers. His white fringe of hair strove to reach Einstein proportions. A bowl of popcorn rested between them, half the kernels curdled with butter, but they were either done eating or disinterested.

Pathetic duo. He was doing them a favor. For a moment, he considered if killing them was the worst thing he could do. They already seemed lifeless, their existence devoid of pleasure.

These people were at the campground the day your parents died, and they did nothing! Kill them. Let the sun god deliver them into their next existence. He will justly determine their fate.

He leaned over, rummaged softly in his bag, and withdrew his weapon—his favorite of all of those given to him from the otherworld: a cord, thinner and more transparent than fishing line and sharper than glass. A small metal handle on one end served as a sheath; a weight on the end helped pull the cord out as he worked momentum by swinging the tool from side to side.

Delroy swung the wire around his body, building force. The bleary-eyed couple paid him no more mind than the breeze generated by the fan beside the couch. In seconds, the momentum was high enough, and he stepped around the bar, gave the cord one final, powerful swing, and struck. Or, rather, sliced.

They didn't have time to gasp. Their bodies fell apart, sliced in two with such heat and energy they barely bled. An initial splatter covered the front of his shirt. He inhaled the metallic scent and sighed. It was over so quickly.

After performing the necessary tribute, he gathered his weapon, left the house via the back door, and placed his tool into his satchel on top of his collection of implements and the book.

It was a beautiful morning, sunny, with no clouds. The heat was starting to build, but it wasn't stifling yet. A good day for a stroll.

He rounded the house to discover there was a new car in the driveway.

When Delroy had arrived, they'd noticed the old black Cadillac to the side of the house. Now, a blue Ford sedan had parked behind it. One with lively occupants on the way to the front door.

No matter. He continued down the drive.

"Hey! Hey, you!" a resolute voice cried, taking a few bold steps in their direction. They paid him no mind.

"Tara, get in the car!" the voice barked. The man who'd addressed Delroy dashed to the Ford. Both doors to the car opened, and the female slid into the passenger seat, slamming the door behind herself. The taller human, the male, ducked inside for a moment, grasping something from within the car and then chasing after Delroy again. It didn't take long before he caught up since Delroy was in no rush.

The human froze in a shooter's stance, hands grasping a shiny, black object held at eye level.

A crack shattered the dawn. Delroy paused a second as a white-hot pain entered his chest, then stopped just below the sternum. He turned to face the man who'd shot him.

The shooter's jaw dropped. "What the—?" He raised the gun again, a determined crease in his brow.

Another shot penetrated Delroy's chest. A fiery pain once more, then, again, nothing.

"What *are* you?" the man asked, fear bleaching his

features.

Delroy paused, looked at the man. Tall, white, with blue eyes and short brown hair. He wanted to rush at the man, to tear his heart from his chest for trying to kill them, but decided not to. It would ruin the pattern.

"Two more down," he said. He cocked his head. "Don't stand in my way. I have no grievance with you."

CHAPTER 33

Early Sunday morning, as Valerie searched the computer for the address of Ducharme's lawyer, Mr. South, Noah took a call from the neighboring town of Kaiser's Detective Masters.

"Looks like your boy's stepping up," Masters said. Noah's heart dropped. "Almost in time for the Sunday papers. Another murder, a middle-aged couple here on Parkington. Name of Pilgrim, Walter and Naomi. Restaurant owners. Had a little rib place over on Peekskill. She ran the restaurant, he worked as a meat cutter to supplement their income and get a discount on some material. Found this morning by their neighbors who came over for a cookout."

"Time of death?" Noah asked.

"Our best estimate, going by liver temp, this morning, ten o'clock. The young neighbor couple got a peek at our killer this time. Caught him as he was fixin' to leave, but it didn't stop him from goin' anywhere. Guy pulled off a couple of shots, but our killer kept right on going. We would really appreciate your help on this one. Not enough similarities for the feds to jump in yet, but..."

"We'll be there as soon as we can. I've got some info we've unearthed on this end. Might benefit us both to share anything new we've thought of or come up with."

"Sure, if you don't mind a little speculation," Masters said. "Little warning, though: the press is all over this place, practically set up a little campsite outside the perimeter, drawing parallels, claiming police incompetence. Frankly,

I'll be glad to get all the assistance I can get—anything to close this case ASAP. I'll be at the crime scene here all morning." He gave the address, and they agreed to meet within the hour.

*   *   *

Valerie expected yet another blood bath in the Pilgrim home, but the weird, one-story foursquare had relatively little blood around the two corpses. The couple had been sliced into two almost perfectly severed pieces. So had a fan on a metal pole. On the wall behind the couch loomed another cloud, its fork of lightning zigzagging down to what would have been the heads of each victim.

Noah's complexion paled, and his eyelids fluttered, didn't want to stay open. He heard a ringing in his ears as he wavered on his feet.

For a second, Valerie was certain he was going to faint. She reached out a hand to steady him and noticed his pulse jumping in his neck.

"What's wrong, Noah?" she asked.

"Heat," Noah said. "I need to get some water. I left my bottle in the car. I'll be back."

He turned, feeling as if his muscles had seized up as he marched, stiff-legged, for the door.

Detective Masters of the Kaiser Police met her in the living room as Noah headed out. Squat and black, Masters filled every inch of his suit with what looked like former muscle gone on the soft side. His boxy face was heavy in the jaw and forehead, with his eyes, nose, and mouth squeezed in the middle. He extended a hand, and Valerie gave it an affable shake.

"That Halabrin?" Masters asked, motioning to the shutting door. Valerie said it was.

"I don't know what got into him," she added. "He's not usually like that. He saw a hell of a lot worse at our last crime scene. At least with this one, the scene's fairly clean."

"The definition of cut-and-dry," Masters said. "We've been trying to figure out what the killers might have used as a weapon, but short of hauling in a powerful laser, we're drawing a blank. Not to mention the fact they don't look as if they've moved—the bodies are still upright. That's part of what's so weird. And, just like the last one, no evidence to collect that we can find. We did find a dirt sample for the crime scene analysts to work on, but there's no telling if it came from our suspects. This house is such a mess, it's probably not. This is the wackiest thing I've ever seen. Ever."

"Our techs should be here any minute; they left the stationhouse right after us. What else have you got so far?"

Masters smiled.

"One thing we've never had before. Survivors. The crazy part is, the male says it was only one guy that walked out of the house. Covered in blood. He also thinks he shot him."

"He shot him, but you said no evidence. You didn't mention any blood from the killer," Valerie observed, "No spent casings from the shooter."

Masters shook his head. "That's because we didn't find any."

*   *   *

Rich and Tara Martinez waited outside at their car, a Ford 500 parked beside the Durango, within the rope of yellow tape that kept the gathering crowd of newspaper reporters at bay. At the edge of the driveway, she saw Wallace and Edwards arriving in Wallace's gold '65 Pontiac

Tempest.

"About time," she murmured.

As she approached the witnesses, pad in hand, Noah stood from where he'd been resting in the passenger seat of the Durango. She watched him put the bottle of water back onto the floorboard, his visage pale and anxious, and then she noticed a bowl beside a pile of what looked like a mayonnaise-based salad in the grass to the right of the walk.

"You all right, pard?" she hollered. He jiggled his head in what he hoped resembled an affirmative gesture. She responded with a curt nod and approached the couple.

"Mr. Martinez?" she asked.

"Right here," Martinez said.

With a name like Richard Martinez, Valerie had expected a dark-complected man, and she was taken a little aback when he faced her full on. Tall, with an average build, Martinez was as white a man as she'd ever seen; in fact, he was fairer than most. His hair was brown but a lighter shade, cut into a high and tight fade, and his eyes were a beautiful, light shade of blue. His wife, Tara, sat on the hood of their Ford, a blanket under her backside to protect it from the scorching metal. They looked to Valerie to be in their twenties, and she wondered how they'd struck up a friendship with a couple who were decades older than they were.

Noah joined her as she got within conversational range of the Martinez couple. He still looked a little green around the edges.

"I understand you believe you got a shot on the killer," Valerie said. "Mind explaining what happened?"

Martinez glowered. "Man, I already told that Masters dude everything that happened," he said, emphasizing his words with emphatic hand motions. "We came over to visit the Pilgrims like we always do. Every other Sunday, we come over and cookout, have since Walt and I met. We work together at the Best Foods over on Clark," he said with a wave in the general direction. "I stock shelves, he cuts meat. We got to talking on our breaks a while back, and he's a cool dude, gave me some tips on how to handle the management. They're—" he waved, his hands saying negative words his mouth did not. "I got out of the service a couple of months ago, and I wanted a little money while I wait to get on at the academy. I was about to quit workin' at the store, but Walt told me how to deal with managers."

"You put in for the police academy?"

He nodded. "So today, as we're fixin' to start coming up the walk, this dude comes runnin' out the door... well, not runnin'. More like... ambling." He mouthed the word as if he felt a little uncomfortable saying it. "He's got blood on his shirt and pants, so I know he's gotta have hurt 'em at least. Tara tossed her casserole—" *The salad,* Valerie thought, "and ran for the car. I usually keep my piece in my car, just in case—we're not that far from Atlanta, you know, we drive there sometimes—"

"Are you familiar with Georgia and Alabama State laws regarding concealed weapons?"

"Yeah. I know I can carry a loaded weapon in my car. I read the laws. It's cool. Dude, you don't even need a permit or license to buy a gun in this state." He hesitated. "I do have a concealed weapons permit, though. I keep it in my glove compartment."

"Concealed weapons?"

"Yeah. I used to be an SP in the Air Force, had to get out because of a bum knee, but I got the permit."

Valerie raised her eyebrows. Alabama state law typically requires that concealed weapons permits only be issued in the interest of public safety. A guilty expression crossed

Martinez's face; it was the first time he didn't look on the defensive.

"I know, but I just keep thinking it's just a matter of time before I'm on the force—"

"I'm not worried right now about the specifics on the legality of your weapons possession. What I want to know is why you shot the man coming out of the Pilgrim's house."

"Dude, he was covered in blood!" Martinez exclaimed. "I asked him what the fuck he was doing—pardon my language—and he gave me this real creepy look and says, 'Two more down,' and starts talking about having a grievance. What the fuck—" his hand went halfway to his mouth. "Sorry, ma'am. What was I supposed to think?"

Martinez hesitated, and Valerie knew from his wrinkled brow that he was mentally going over the scenario, for the hundredth time, trying to figure out if he'd done anything wrong, or if he should've acted or spoken differently. Despite the impression Hollywood tried to present of middle-class America, it wasn't every day that a civilian, even a civilian who used to be a military cop, shoots another human being. Although the killer had gotten away after killing his friends, walked away on his own accord after Martinez believed the bullet had hit him, he was dealing with feelings of guilt and responsibility inherent with such a life-threatening act.

From the look on Tara's face, she was also having difficulty coping. Of course, her stressed expression might have been grief for the loss of her friends.

"So, you took the gun from the glove box..." Valerie prompted.

"Right. I took the gun out, and I aimed. Now he's just..." Martinez gauged the distance from the car to where the killer had stood, "Fifteen? Ten feet away?"

"And you're sure you hit him?"

"Twice. Practically dead bang. I've always been a good shot. I've had lots of practice."

"Where?"

"Where did I practice?"

"Where'd you hit him?"

Martinez flushed. "Oh. In the heart. I hit him in the heart."

Valerie tried not to appear dubious. "Are you sure? Moving target and all. And he walked away."

"I'm sure. I watched the bullet go in! And if that wasn't enough, I got him again in the sternum." He pointed, in case Valerie had any questions where on the body that was.

"And he strolled away? He didn't attack you for trying to shoot him? He must have been armed." Valerie almost finished the sentence with, "judging from what he did to your friends," but caught herself in time.

"I'm sure. I saw the bullet hit home. Twice. And the motherfucker strolled it off like it was nothing. Pardon my language. Even if he had a vest, he would have flinched or something. Gettin' hit with a vest on still hurts like hell."

"Show me where he was when you hit him."

Martinez took Valerie to the place he'd eyed moments before, a flat, clear section of the driveway. Valerie examined the spot, her hand ready to grab the gloves she'd stowed in her pocket. Noah joined her, and they circled the area. There was nothing; no blood, no discarded weapon, no bloody bullets, no casings. Nothing.

Once again, the Lightning Fork killer had vanished, leaving no trace behind.

*   *   *

When Noah found his voice, the questions came

tumbling out, eager to be heard like those of a rookie cop who believes he's on the verge of his first big break.

"Did the killer have a vehicle?" he said to Martinez, whose head jerked in surprise at Noah's sudden verbal explosion. "Did you get a license plate number? Did you see where he parked?"

Martinez studied Noah as if he'd grown another eyeball amid the two he currently had darting madly around the yard, searching for a clue.

"Naw, man. I told you. He just... ambled off."

"He strolled away, covered in blood?"

Martinez nodded.

"Did he have anything on him? A gun? A bag, maybe, full of weapons? A book?"

"A book?" Martinez snorted. "What the fuck dude gonna do with a book?"

Noah's face grew hot, and he knew he looked like a fool. At this point, Valerie interceded, saving Noah from further embarrassment.

"We think the killers may be involved in some cult activities. The book might contain their rituals."

Martinez indicated that he understood with a small "Ahh," and Noah was once again grateful for Valerie's incredible ability to save him from looking like an ass.

"Naw. No book. He did have a bag, though. This ugly brown thing with handles."

"A suitcase?"

"No, just a..." he moved his hands, indicating a rounded shape, "a big bag."

"Canvas," Tara said. Three heads swiveled toward the blond perched on the edge of the hood. "It was canvas. And it was full," she made curved motions with her hands as well, "Really full, you know? I'll bet it's where he held...." She broke down, her face contorted into a mask of grief.

Martinez turned from the detectives and took his wife in his arms.

Noah and Valerie exchanged a wordless and brief exchange of glances that said, "We're done here."

CHAPTER 34

Noah overheard Valerie's pithy conversation with Wallace. He had found a possible clue from a fiber at Wanda Murphy's murder: a fiber from an uncommon fabric used by few designers to manufacture business suits. *Which might be potentially useful, but I'd be willing to bet it matches one of the outfits in Wanda's suitcase.*

Since they'd left the Pilgrim home, he and Valerie had opened every file on the killings they now believed most likely occurred at the hand of Delroy Ducharme. The description of the Pilgrim's killer given them by Richard Martinez matched that of Selena Dumas exactly, right down to the scar on his cheek.

They poured over every detail, from Brogan's attack to their speculation that Wanda had left her car after realizing she was too drunk to drive, to the Harper slaughter, and now the Pilgrim couple. Noah turned over every clue left at the crime scene for what must have been the hundredth time, wondering about the relevance of each and praying that the lab found something they could go on soon.

That piece of old paper I found at Wanda's site, he thought, *I wonder if that was part of the Book of the Dead? Hundley said it looked as if it was falling apart.*

Noah doubted the fabric held a connection to the Lightning Fork killer and told Valerie to pursue the lead on her own. After a brief meeting with Richard Martinez and the station's sketch artist, he headed into the evidence room and extracted the box from Wanda's crime scene. Several pieces of potential evidence, none of it useful, had been cataloged, and he rummaged through until he found what he was looking for—the worn piece of paper he'd found.

Hurrying to the table a few feet away, he carefully placed the plastic bag underneath the fluorescent light. The paper was old, alright—older than he'd realized in the dark under the streetlights. Yellowed and crumbling, it was difficult to make out any of the contrasting marks on it. Squinting, he brought it up to his face trying to decipher it.

This could be anything. What a waste of—

His eyes adjusted to the brightness of the overhead bulbs and his fingers traced the plastic cover. He couldn't make out any words, but one illustration was barely discernable on the worn parchment. A pair of legs attached to a torso made of two human shapes.

This is too much. How much more proof do I need?

He needed to track a more direct route.

At two o'clock, he arrived alone at the Harper home. He'd made a few phone calls; Pamela had been prescribed a heavy-duty sedative and would be staying with her aunt for a few more days. With the rest of the family gone, he'd have the house to himself.

With the exception of the deceased Stephen Jr.

Although Mr. and Mrs. Harper had gone on to whatever world lay beyond this physical plane, Stephen had stayed behind. The Pilgrims had chosen to move ahead as well, or else he would have interviewed them since they were the most recent victims and therefore more apt to point him in the right direction.

The Harper home had already been cleaned and cleaned well. According to Rita St. Julian, Pamela's aunt, it would also be painted before she would allow Pamela to come home. It was easy to see why. The clean-up crew provided by the county was good, but even combined with the efforts of the Harper housecleaning staff, most likely the best money could buy, there remained faint traces of blood in the white carpet and the matte white paint on the staircase wall.

Stephen Harper sat on the steps, his translucent form hunched over. His roundish head looked bulbous, mounted on average shoulders. Although he was in his twenties, his hair had already thinned and receded. When Noah opened the door, he looked set to die a second death of ennui.

"Hello," Noah signed. Stephen gave him a halfhearted salutation, a wave of an arm that could have been misinterpreted as a shrug or perhaps a dismissal.

"You look bored," he motioned. Stephen's shoulder jerks and weary grin told Noah he was laughing.

"Nothing to do," Stephen replied. "I wish I could read books. So many books here, but I can't touch them."

"Why are you here, but your Mom and Dad gone?" Noah asked.

"They wanted to go. I am here for Pam," he said. Noah indicated that he understood. He'd suspected as much. Although Pamela wouldn't be able to talk to her brother—at least at first—it might help her to know he was there. That is if it didn't drive her completely mad.

"You see the killer?" He asked. Stephen nodded. "What'd the killer look like? What'd the killer do?"

Stephen winced a little and turned his face away. Noah waited to see if the specter would face him again. He did, but his face had grown older in the short time since he'd looked away.

"Scary," Stephen said. "Two men in one man. One is a ghost, one alive. I saw the dead one after..." His face screwed up as he tried to find the words to convey what he meant. "I saw dead one after I was dead, too."

"The live man was possessed?" Noah asked.

"I don't know, but I don't think so."

Noah hadn't thought so, either. Whatever forces Ducharme had channeled to give him this incredible killing power, it wasn't by accident. He had a mission to kill everyone who'd stood in Lightning Fork campground the day his parents died and had somehow used the forces of a dead man to do it. The question was, how? The book had taught him something, but what? The church wanted it back badly; they said it was priceless. The Book of the Dead.

Noah withdrew the sketch he'd had gotten from the sketch artist, and Stephen's eyes widened. It was all the confirmation he needed. He put the paper back in his folder.

"Did you see a book?" Noah asked. Stephen's head dipped in confirmation.

"The living man had a bag." He shuddered. "Tools he used to kill my family. The book was in the bag."

"I'm sorry," Noah said. Stephen gave a wan smile. Noah decided a change of subject was in order.

"How long are you staying?"

"Until Pam is okay," Stephen said. His eyes flitted to the staircase where his family was found. The bloodstains, though indistinct, screamed at Noah, and he didn't doubt they cried out in voices nearly unbearable for Stephen to hear.

Stephen's somber face frowned. "I'll be here a long time."

CHAPTER 35

The memory dance descended on Delroy again.

Since they'd been so successful recently, and his prophetic dream loomed so imminently, Delroy had hoped he wouldn't have to rest after his latest sacrifice. However, the damage to his torso the young man's bullets had inflicted made another hiatus necessary. His body, while immortal, had to heal.

Thus, he slept. And as he slept, memories and things like memories mixed and dissolved together in a solution so complete he could not separate the two without shattering the whole. He dreamed of a time a generation ago, of a journey of another young man with a chaste heart and a confused mind. A journey that led to darkness.

Within a building made of gray cinderblocks and concrete, a child cowered between the figures of two adults, one male one female, as they crossed the threshold to a strange and eerie meeting place. Torches chased away the gloom in a losing battle to conquer the dark. From the corners, enormous brass burners emitted fragrances both mysterious and thick with ominous enchantments. The smoke they gave off danced and bulged into forms that disappeared before their shapes were fully realized.

A bright, intricately-patterned carpet separated the room into halves, each half-lined with murky figures in headdresses and bright clothing. The figures on either side of the carpeted aisle appeared bold and enormous, their chests puffed out, their hands clasped behind their backs.

The child's teeth chattered with cold and fear as his

parents led him down the carpet to the head of the room. On an ornate wooden throne, a faceless man in black sat, so cloaked in shadows that they seemed to comprise his shape. At the crown of the throne, a golden sun blazed.

Drums beat in the distance, a soft tempo akin to marching feet that made the young man's skin crawl.

"We present you," his father said, "with the gift of our son."

Delroy shivered and dropped his head as he'd been taught. Necklaces of colorful flowers adorned his neck and waist. The fragrance, combined with the potent incense, made him want to vomit.

It was time. The moment for which he'd been born had arrived. He only wished he knew what was expected of him. A lifetime of silence, of isolation, of brief, pressing lessons on frightening subjects all culminated into this moment. Back when he'd been locked behind the walk-in closet door, he'd have given anything to be beyond it, to be in this moment he'd heard alluded to so many times. Now that the moment had arrived, he wished for the safety of those close walls.

Sensing that someone was watching, Delroy raised his head. His mother gave him an insistent look that pleaded with him to cooperate. How could he? Aside from the fact that he had no real idea why he was there, Delroy did not *want* to be there. This place, these people, the man on the throne, all of them seemed to be studying him, analyzing him. He wanted to be home, to be alone with his books or his few toys or his nanny, alone in his closet with the door locked and the lightbulb burned out, if need be, but not here. Anywhere but here. This wasn't at all what he expected—the penetrating looks, the ominous sense that the man in the headdress gave him, it wasn't right.

The smoke curling from the drums took the shape of

macabre faces screwed into grotesque, hungry grins.

"Do you come willingly, young man?" the man in black asked, amused by his own question. He pulled the cowl to his robe back and revealed both a human and a diaphanous gray head adorned by a bright white headdress. From under his robe, gray, transparent feet overshadowed the corporeal ones clad in a pair of colorful sandals.

Delroy's heart threatened to freeze in his heart as icy blood pumped through the chambers at record speed. Should he answer the ghost-man honestly? He'd believed, until now, that honesty was always best. Until that moment, however, honesty had been the easy route to take. His parents always seemed to know when he'd lied; at best, he'd get a scolding. Often, they hit him, but he'd grown used to that. A stinging blow faded with time. Bruises healed.

Here, he suspected the worst was much worse.

"Yes," he fibbed. "I come willingly."

The relief on his parent's faces made the lie worthwhile. The ghost-man in the black cloak stood and withdrew a dagger from his belt, a long, obsidian blade, half-buried in his massive hand. He drew the cutting edge across Delroy's cheek in a swift, calculated action.

Delroy screamed in surprise. The pain from the deep cut felt both hot and cold. Blood ran down his cheek, and he felt the liquid flow in warm rivulets. The anger he felt drowned out his hurt. Had his parents wanted this? What did the man wish for him? Was he going to die?

The cloaked figure studied the blood on the blade. After a careful inspection, the dagger fell to the floor behind him with a heavy thud and clatter. His mother gasped.

"He is neither worthy nor willing," the man said with a wave of a powerful hand. "He did not come of his own accord. You have disgraced me. This child has no understanding of the exchange of life for life. He does not know what you ask of him. More than that—you have disgraced yourselves. Breeding a child for sacrifice! And what sacrifice? He is unhealthy. He is barely educated. This boy is no better than cattle. Do not insult me again. Leave. Now."

His parent's contrite wails and pleas for a second chance faded as Delroy fled down the brightly colored carpet out of the concrete cavern, clutching his lacerated face in his young hands.

CHAPTER 36

The hillside where Wanda's mutilated corpse was found looked and sounded much more desolate in daylight; the fences more rusted, the gravel road dustier. The riverbed was nearly dry after yet another week without rain; a brave dribble of water struggled along, its weak trickle drowned out by the nearby factories hard at work.

The corrugated tin buildings across the road had to feel like a sweatbox on the inside, Noah thought. He made out the tune of saws and die-cast stamps, as well as a churning sound from a machine he was unfamiliar with. Massive air-conditioners and fans struggled against the feverish weather. Not even the sweltering weather stopped Gryphon's factories. He wondered how often they suffered from heat casualties.

As he exited the unmarked car, he saw Wanda's ghost sitting at the edge of the gravel road, her long legs disappearing in the sharp saw grass. Her gaze never left the dribble of dying stream. She looked like a woman contemplating a walk into the ocean, never to return.

If she heard Noah's approach, she didn't show it. Neither her head nor her body pivoted, which made it difficult for him to understand when she asked, "You catch him yet?"

Noah stepped forward, crouching beside her, so she saw his hands. He had half a mind to speak, knowing her supernatural ears heard him, even if he wasn't attuned to her otherworldly wavelength. It always felt weird doing that, though. "No," he motioned in answer to her question.

Wanda turned, her once blond locks falling over her shoulder and onto her collarbone. Her expression showed no accusation, simply disappointment.

"I know the man is free," she said, her face contorted, distraught. "I feel him. He is out there, killing. I feel their deaths, like mine." She put a hand on her chest, and the sadness in her eyes clawed at Noah's heart.

"I'll catch him," Noah said. "I'll find a way." She smiled a feeble smile that reminded him of Stephen Harper, and he knew they both doubted that he'd bring their killer to justice. Her blue eyes looked on the verge of tears. He swore to himself that he'd prove them wrong.

"Wanda, when the killer was here, did he have a book?"

Wanda's distress fled momentarily as her eyebrows scrunched in the middle in thought, her lips puckered as she gave Noah a shake of her head.

"Book? No. He had a bag."

Again, with the bag. Does he always keep the book in the bag with his weapons? Does he need the book to kill, or is he maybe protecting it? What if we're completely off?

He let out a heavy breath, but his heart felt no lighter for it. He stood. "Thank you, Wanda."

He turned from her and continued down the gravel road, studying the long grass as if expecting to find a clue. A small breeze stirred, blowing the grass into a frustrated, oscillating dance.

A few paces farther, and he noticed for the first time a tiny building sandwiched between two factories. The confused Gryphon zoning board had struck again. At the edge of the chain-link fence, beyond the brick wall that signaled the end of hovering industrial buildings, stood a tiny purple-paneled building with a hand-painted sign: *Madame Ubora's Insights and Sounds*. In the center of the lettering, a hand with an eye in the palm.

A psychic in this neighborhood? Noah thought. *It's a wonder her business survives.* Though he supposed the reason Madame Ubora survived at all was due to her discreet location. Northern Alabama harbored some staunch Fundamentalists—outspoken, God-fearing folk who didn't look lightly on those who spoke with the dead or claimed to.

The hours on the door said the shop was open from 3:00 to midnight.

It's not my job to care if she chats with dead folks or demons. But I wonder if she saw anything the other night?

*   *   *

Judging from the low-rent neighborhood where Madame Ubora's shop stood, Noah had expected a disorganized store filled with shadows, festooned with beaded curtains, burning candles, and reeking of sandalwood or patchouli incense. Instead, Insights and Sounds gleamed. Fluorescent lights bounced off polished metal, mirrors, and long wooden shelves. Bags of incense lay in ordered piles next to aligned candles of various fragrances. Short daggers and long swords hung from the wall to his left. Wind chimes decorated a wooden frame near the window. Books and gemstones made up the bulk of the aisles in the center. In the rear of the store, a curtain with a large hand on it had been swept to the side, prepared to hide a table flanked by benches. In the center of the table, a crystal ball rested in a tripod gold stand.

On entering, he surprised himself by feeling a much happier mood than the gloomy one he'd experienced outside. He supposed it was the sunny ambiance of the shop.

A rod of incense burned in a clear glass holder atop a glass and chrome counter. Its fragrance reminded Noah of something wonderful, but he couldn't place the scent.

"Is that fresh-cut grass?" he asked the braided woman behind the counter. She turned from her book—an enormous tome with a purple leather cover—and smiled, a gorgeous straight white grin that lit up her dark face.

"When's your birthday?" she asked. He thought he detected a hint of an island accent, but at the same time, she sounded almost British. Noah chuckled; a strange laugh that welled up from inside, impossible to stop.

"December twenty-second," he said.

Her smile, if anything, grew wider. She slapped the book shut and sat up. "Capricorn," she said with a snap of her fingers. He wondered where she was born. *Somewhere in the Caribbean, maybe?*

"Might have known it," she added. "You earth elements are all alike. Smelling those earthy scents. In answer to your question, if you think it's fresh-cut grass, it *is* fresh-cut grass. It's a mutable fragrance."

"I'm sorry... mutable?"

The woman beamed. "It is an incense that has been enchanted to become what you want it to be the most, your favorite scent. It changes in the olfactory glands of those who inhale it. For me, it's lilac, or sometimes hyacinth. I love florals."

Mutable. What a novel idea. Of course, the truth was probably more like a new shipment of incense that she was trying to unload. He didn't believe in mutable fragrances, but he had to admit, it sounded good. Then again, he'd never said his favorite smell was fresh-cut grass. She'd had no way of knowing that. Was it a lucky guess?

"What sign are you?" Noah asked.

"Virgo. Another earth sign," she said with almost a hint of sheepishness.

"Are you Madame Ubora?"

"I am. You'll be wanting to know about that woman

killed down here the other day. Why don't you go ask her what happened, now?"

"Huh?" Noah asked.

Madame Ubora chuckled. "You got the gift, right? The sight? I got it, too. All kinds of duppies showing up in here all the while, wanting to talk to me, all chatty chatty, telling me what to tell their loved ones when they come by for a reading. Sometimes I can, sometimes I can't. But I do what I must, same as you."

Noah's jaw fell so hard he felt it. For the second time since this case opened, he'd met someone who saw the shadows—and what's more, she knew he did without him saying a word.

His stomach clenched in a knot. Her conversation had been light, but it confronted him with more guilt than anything Valerie had said or done since he'd first arrived at Wanda Murphy's crime scene. It was as if Madame Ubora had taken one of her mirrors from the wall and held it in front of him, demanding that he admit to what he saw in the mirror every day: a man terrified to speak the truth, to admit to his gift, and to use it to catch the killer he knew was out there. A police officer who, for the first time in his career, was denying the truth to himself—that he knew who the killer had been all along and had only postponed the inevitable—at the cost of the Pilgrim's lives, maybe even the Harper's. And if he didn't step up his pursuit, Ducharme might once again get away with murder.

His breath didn't seem to want to come. As he struggled to pull air into his lungs, Wanda Murphy strolled through the wall to Madame Ubora's shop, followed by two other specters, a young black man and a tall white man with lank hair and a dour expression which looked vaguely familiar. From the rear of the store, another ghost materialized, the junkie whose body Noah had seen at the warehouse up the street, the OD he'd had to pass on to Chartier because of the Lightning Fork case.

Madame Ubora watched with great interest as Noah gasped like an asthmatic and viewed the "duppies" about her shop with nothing short of shock and amazement. She hadn't been lying. The woman was a genuine psychic, and what's more, she knew about his gift and how he used it—or, rather, how he hadn't been using it.

He found enough air to speak. "How—how do they know to come here for your help?"

Madame Ubora waved a hand about. "Look around you. It's what I do. It's how I live. I got the gift, and I use it. You do too. Tamara here—" she motioned to the junkie, "told me how you told your lady cop friend she didn't die on her own. That's important. What you do, it's very important. To us and to them."

"How do you talk to them? Do you use—?" he motioned to the crystal ball. Madame Ubora shook her head.

"They hear me talking, and I read their lips. Sometimes, I hear them, too."

"You can *hear* them?" Noah felt a twinge of jealousy that surprised him. Madame Ubora leaned over the counter, her head bobbing in affirmation, braids swinging. She leaned her elbows on her counter.

"A few," she said. "But enough about me. You're here about you. You need help, and I can point you to your help. You need to understand the *Libro de Los Muertos*, the source of your killer's power, and I know just the duppy to ask."

There seemed no end to her knowledge of his life. Had she seen him in her crystal ball? Did she read minds? Did her ghosts tell her about him? He tried not to be too flustered, but he wondered what else she knew about him and how. "He honestly gets his power from the book? This killer I'm after?"

"Yes, man. And you don't need to worry about chasing the wrong man. The man you're after, he is the killer. French name... Ducharme, or something, right?"

"Yeah. Ducharme. Delroy Ducharme. I—know. I—" He pulled his sketch from his pocket and unfolded it. "This is him."

Madame Ubora waved her hand at it and looked away. "Don't show me. I don't need that face in my head. Draw all kinds of bad energy here. Put that away." After Noah put the page back in his pocket, she turned around. "The man you need to ask questions, he's locked up in a cage at the psychiatric hospital. Name of Brad Gardner. He'll tell you what you need to know."

"You mean in the Acorn Institute?"

Madame Ubora chuckled. "Yeah. I bet it was some white man who named a mental hospital after a nut."

Noah had to laugh along. Despite his slight feeling of unsettledness, her pleasure was contagious.

Then it hit him.

The tall ghost with the lank, white hair was Roger Canon, a man whose killer Noah had brought to justice two short years ago. His wife had stabbed him in his sleep; the wife had cried burglary gone wrong. Noah had made sure she was arrested and brought to trial. She was convicted of murder and sentenced to twenty years.

As Noah gave Canon his full attention, the man gave him a vague, approving smile.

As he stood and watched, others came. A young woman found dead on a hiking trail; a boy poisoned, then brought to the hospital by his mother who suffered from Munchausen syndrome by proxy; a woman whose father "accidentally" killed her while cleaning his gun. They entered, floating through walls and doors, gliding up the aisles of mystic merchandise until the tiny shop was full of people he'd helped see justice during a career of police work. He was surrounded by his dead, those whose afterlife was—he hoped—maybe a little better because of the work he'd done.

It was then that he realized the young black man who'd come in with Wanda was a male counterpart to Madame Ubora, most likely a son. He was also a young man killed in a drunk driving accident whose killer Noah had put away back in his beat cop days.

"You be careful, Halabrin," she murmured. "This world can't afford to lose a man like you."

He'd never told her his name.

CHAPTER 37

"... And the fibers—get this—are found only in suits made in Korea," Valerie said with a flourish of her hands. She'd been speaking for several minutes now on her research, but to Noah, it was lost in the buzz of the stationhouse mechanics: keyboards clacking, voices murmuring, the ring of a telephone, the jingle of keys.

"Guess who is known for buying suits made in Korea?" she went on. "Military guys. They go to these little tailor shops—"

"I don't think that's what we need, Valerie," Noah said. He placed his coffee down on his desk and found a chair to sit in. It was easier for him to tell someone he respected that he disagreed with them when viewing them eye to eye. Alas, the stationhouse had a shortage of seats. There wasn't an unoccupied chair in the room. He picked his mug up again and took what he hoped looked like a pensive sip.

Valerie's face colored with indignation.

"What do you mean, 'I don't think so?' It's a great effing lead. What did you find out in your little expedition today?" She ended the question with her hands on her hips, ready to take Halabrin down, pin him, and slap him stupid if he gave the wrong answer.

Noah sighed. He'd known, on some level, for days that it was going to come down to this. At one point in the investigation, he had to either clue Valerie in on the truth about Ducharme and his link to Noah's past or bury his head in the sand and let Ducharme flee to God knew where. Neither prospect sounded painless, but the idea of letting Ducharme get away with all those murders… *No. No way.*

How to tell her, though? Valerie was about as down-to-earth a person as he'd ever known; it was part of what he loved about her. Her ability to use logic to work out the facts of a case more often than not matched or surpassed his, although her impetuous urges to follow those facts led some to believe her head wasn't screwed on as straight.

He braced himself and somehow found the nerve to speak. "There was this shop down on that gravel road where Wanda Murphy's body was found. A woman, um, Madame Ubora—"

"Another witness? Great. We've already got one. He even claims he shot the killer in the—"

"She says she knows someone who can answer some questions for us."

Valerie frowned and paused for a moment to digest what Noah had told her. As she did, a cynical expression crossed her face. "Did you say *Madame* Ubora?" she said, making no effort to mask her sarcasm. "What is she, a psychic? Or does she run a bordello? Great witness."

Noah's eyes dropped to the floor. He'd known this wasn't going to be easy, but he hadn't known how hard it would be. "She's a psychic."

Valerie's mouth flapped for a moment before she found the words to speak. "You're continuing our investigation on the advice of a psychic? Have you lost your ever-loving mind? I mean, how desperate are we to find the evidence we need that now we're following a psychic? What're you going to tell the captain?"

Noah avoided looking at her. "I didn't plan to tell her anything yet."

"And when were you going to bring her up to speed?"

Noah's silence, compounded by his guilty expression,

said everything Valerie needed to hear. She put her hands on her armrests and looked ready to leap out of her chair and start a shouting match. Just as Noah braced himself to undergo a barrage of logic and probing questions he wasn't ready to answer, her mouth closed. Her brown eyes studied him, the beautiful brow above them furrowed in thought.

"I won't tell Captain Blanch what you're up to, and I'll give up my trail so we can follow whatever lead you're on for one day—twenty-four question-free hours—but on one condition. You answer one question of mine, and honestly. No ducking, no beating around the bush, no ostriching and sticking your head in the sand, or acting like you don't know what I'm talking about."

"Anything," Noah said.

It was Valerie's turn to brace herself. She took a deep breath, her tongue running over her front teeth for a moment. "Why do you use sign language at crime scenes? And why some and not others?"

Noah's head swiveled around the stationhouse, his face a guilty, concerned mask as he hurriedly searched for anyone who might have overheard. Although the rest of the bullpen had their faces buried in paperwork or computer monitors and were otherwise occupied with their cases, he wasn't about to air his secret in a place so ripe for gossip fodder. He checked over his shoulders, trying not to look as if he was engaged in a clandestine affair and failing.

"Halabrin?"

"Let's go get some coffee," he suggested.

She paused. He didn't seem as though he was avoiding the question, just putting her off until they found somewhere else to discuss his answer. "OK," Valerie agreed, "But it better be decaf this time, or I'm not going to sleep for months."

CHAPTER 38

A small *plink* echoed quietly off the smooth stone walls of his shelter, but Delroy heard nothing, his psyche buried deep in his healing trance. Before his chest, the small, squashed shape of an expended bullet coated in blood now lay on the floor. Though his body had expelled the bullet seconds before, the torn fabric of his chest had nearly healed; the traces of his injuries reduced to two small, jagged, red circles fading to pink as he slumbered.

Delroy dreamed, or perhaps remembered, a six-story building years ago, in the middle of a cloudless night. He recalled the curious stare of the lady behind the admission counter who saw no justifiable reason for a boy so young to be brought in with such a severe trauma in the middle of the night. He remembered what it was like to hold his face in his hands as warm blood streamed down his forearms and dripped on the white tile floor.

A friendly hospital worker in white scrubs with pink elephants brought him back to an examining room where she gave an injection of something she said would help with the pain. As he waited for the numbing agent to take effect, he drew a small, black book embossed in gold from within his jacket. He tried to make out the title by sounding out the letters. Although he was well beyond the start of what should have been school years, the boy didn't read well yet. Still, there were pictures for him to study, diagrams he hoped would help him understand certain parts of his confusing life.

"How did this happen?" the woman in pink elephants

asked, threading the needle with surgical string. Her face expressed concern—perhaps too much.

She tapped his face, and when the boy didn't flinch, she brought the needle to his flesh and pierced the cheek, looped it through the cut, and tugged. He winced more at the thought of what she was doing than discomfort.

He evaded her eyes, not willing to tell her the truth and afraid she would read it there the moment the falsehood left his mouth.

"I fell. On some glass," he mumbled. It was a bad lie, but he didn't want to think too long for a better one. If he'd hesitated, she'd have known for sure. He turned a page, trying to portray the air of a disinterested and tired young man, desperately wanting the conversation to end. He had a feeling this book had the answers he was looking for.

Breeding a child for sacrifice! ... He is unhealthy. He is uneducated.

"Hmm," she replied, looping the thread through his face once more. He risked a glance, tried to tell whether she believed him. "Lucky thing the one cut was all you got. And I'm glad your hands are okay."

Her eyes were brown. Pretty. The rest of her face was round and pockmarked, but her eyes were pretty. Although her words held no accusation, he knew what she was implying. He wanted to bash her face in.

This boy is no better than cattle.

He didn't answer but instead turned another page. He resolved to tune the nurse out. He needed to pay attention to the book—this was important stuff. Uneducated? He'd show them.

Maybe his parents didn't know how to teach him well. Maybe he wasn't a good "sacrifice" because they lacked something. But he knew he was smart. He'd teach himself all he needed to know. His parents had plenty of books, and he knew how to read a little. Enough to teach himself the rest. It was time to take things into his own hands.

"Well, maybe from now on, try to choose safer places to play."

"Hmm? Oh, yeah. Safer."

She needed to shut up. He was having a hard time focusing on the book.

He'd found the book in the back of the car on the ride to the hospital and had stowed it under his shirt to read when he had time away from his parents' analytical stares.

Like now. His parents waited in the other room as his face was tended to. It was no surprise they hadn't come into the examining room as he was treated. He suspected they were ducking confrontation with any other adults, trying to avoid too many questions. Smart, really, but he'd hate to find out later that he'd contradicted whatever story they'd told the hospital people.

It didn't matter. The book was enough to keep him occupied. He'd finally figured out the title to the book, no thanks to the troublesome nurse. In glossy embossed letters on the cover, the title gleamed; it seemed even more beautiful now that he understood what it said. *The Sun Dance of Offering.*

"Good book?" the nurse asked. She'd barely glanced at it. He knew she was trying to make conversation to keep his mind off the needle, but he still wanted to scream at her to be quiet.

Delroy nodded slowly as she pulled a suture closed, his eyes fixated on the page.

"I'm learning a lot."

CHAPTER 39

Steaming cups of decaf cappuccino clasped in their hands like security blankets, hunched over the table that separated them with intense expressions on their faces, Valerie supposed that she and Noah appeared to many like a couple out for a date after work. The way her stomach quivered might have led her to the same conclusion, but she knew the real explanation for her nervous stomach.

Not that the idea of a date with Noah was bad—unprofessional, maybe, but not bad. But it wasn't the notion of a date with her partner that made her heart flutter like a woman on a first date. She was thrilled that now she was about to know the reason for Noah's infamous eccentricity. He was finally going to let down one of his many walls for her, and from the way he'd gone to such lengths to hide it, it was a wall comparable to the legendary barricade in China.

His eyes darted, fearful of being overheard even in the shop packed with a bustling after-work crowd.

"You know I've never lied to you, right?" he asked.

It was a strange way to start, but Valerie was determined not to do anything to undermine his decision to share his secret with her. She shrugged.

"Not that I'm aware of," she said, her voice as offhand as possible. Noah's face grew dark as if the weight of the world had depended on her response to this simple question, and now, based on her flippancy, he was hesitant.

She tapped her short nails on the side of her mug and bobbed her head side to side. "Okay, no. I don't believe you've ever lied to me, Halabrin. You don't strike me as the type."

He leaned farther forward, and the table leaned slightly in his direction. "What type of person would you say I am?"

Valerie inhaled as she considered her answer.

Sexy. Mysterious. Attractive. The kind of guy I normally chase until my legs wear out from fucking him and my brain goes kablooey.

Instead, she said, "I'd say you're responsible, ethical. A good cop and a good friend. Although I can't say how you are with animals. You've never owned a dog—"

"Valerie!"

"All right, all right. What'dya want from me?" Valerie raised her oversized mug and prepared to take a sip.

"Would you say I'm prone to flights of fancy?"

The mug dropped back to the table without touching her lips. Her face was incredulous. "Flights of—Halabrin, what are you getting at?"

Noah ran his hand through his blond hair, an action that Valerie had done herself countless times in her dreams. It distracted her a little, and as his green eyes met hers, her heart stopped for a second. *Get it together and stop dicking around. This is important!*

"I see..." his voice trailed off, and his face pivoted toward the far wall as if he was studying the blackboard drink menu. Any nerve he'd had back in the station had fled, leaving him with a nervous stomach and a pounding heart.

"Halabrin, if you say 'dead people,' I'm gonna have to contact Shyamalan, 'cause you'd be plagiarizing."

He didn't say anything, but his eyes never left hers. A chill swept down her spine as Noah's unspoken confession dawned on her.

"My god, you think you do."

You think you do, Noah mused, *as if there's room to doubt a statement I never even spoke aloud. Oh, God, now I'm thinking of the way she views my words as a "statement"—as if I was a witness or a suspect to a crime. Or maybe a nutcase ready to check into the Acorn Institute.*

The words he'd struggled to put into perfect order were gone, rendering him incapable of discussion. Valerie was a straightforward woman in a career based on logic, and more important than logic, she required evidence. He had none.

"So," she said, struggling for a casual tone after taking a sip of coffee, "you're talking to ghosts? Is that it?"

Noah pressed his eyelids under his fingertips and indicated to the affirmative.

"Do they come to you... or...?"

"No. No, they don't come to me, and I don't ask them to appear to help me out. They're there only because they died recently. You'll notice, I normally sign where there's a death involved. Sometimes it takes a while for the spirit to leave, to move on after it dies. I can take that time and find out what happened to them, discover if there was any foul play involved."

Valerie waited. She took another sip and put her oversized mug down gently as if she were handling Noah's fragile state of mind instead of a piece of stoneware.

"What do they look like?"

He shrugged. "Like the stereotype, believe it or not. Transparent, gray, and white. Shadowy." He knew he was temporizing until his thoughts fell into order, stalling until he regained solid reasoning that would prove that he wasn't crazy, that this was reality, and not some childish daydream carried over into adulthood. But his mind had turned into a jellyfish, floating in a sea of uncertainty and vulnerability. He'd exposed his most private part to the woman—no, fuck that, no denying how he felt now, the person—whose opinion mattered most to him. If she refused to accept this—his innermost secret—as a fact, it would shatter him.

Her hands danced to her face, the table, the paper placemat under her mug. She sniffed. She made uncomfortable faces.

"Do they all know sign language?"

It was a question that shouldn't have sounded doubtful but did, at least to Noah's ears. He fought the urge to sigh with resignation, exhaling his breath with deliberate control. He wondered if it looked to Valerie like he was struggling to keep his temper. He suspected it did.

"The first time I tried to talk to one, I was about ten years old. I ran into him while I was walking in the woods one day, and no one was around, so I took the opportunity to talk to one—a ghost—for the first time in my life. I spoke to him, and he tried to speak back, but it didn't work. I didn't hear him. He tried to explain why his voice was inaudible to me using his hands. Not sign language, then. I didn't know sign. I wanted him to try to use a simple form of sign, you know? Well, he did. I took his motions to mean that while I was stuck on this plane, he was capable of moving within planes, or dimensions, or whatever. We chatted the best that we could with our hands. That night, I asked my mother for sign language lessons."

"Why?"

"I guess it had to do with the way the old ghost said he could move between dimensions. In my ten-year-old wisdom, I took that to mean he had access to all kinds of information in all sorts of places. And on top of that, what did I have to lose? Turns out, my logic might have been a little immature, but I was right. Even if a person doesn't know sign when they die, they can access the knowledge of how to do it after their death."

"So, we can get our hands on all kinds of knowledge

after we die. Neat idea," she said. Her countenance froze as she realized that her statement reflected an overt doubt of his story. Her eyes fluttered, and she stammered as she continued. "So... is there any way you could—"

"Prove it to you right this second? No. Even if there was a ghost in this room right now, how do I demonstrate to you that it's there? Ask it a question about your life? What would you have me say to it?"

She didn't believe him. Not that he'd expected her to. But he'd hoped.

"Come with me to Acorn Institute," he said, his voice pressing.

"The nuthouse? Why would you—?"

"That's where Madame Ubora said I'd find the answers I needed. She said there's a man there that talks to ghosts, too. That he knows about the *Libro de Los Muertos*. Maybe if you see... maybe it will help you understand what it is I do."

He gave her what he hoped was an honest and very sane expression that pleaded with her to give him a chance. Valerie's face scrunched up as she argued with herself on the wisdom of going with a man who may be crazy to an institute full of people whose sanity had already been decided and found short.

"Look at it this way," he said. "If it turns out I'm not on the side of the fence you think I should be on, I don't have far to go to my padded cell and brand-new white coat with reeaallly long sleeves and lots of buckles."

She laughed, and the sound made his heart sing.

"So, you'll come?"

She eyed him heavily, but the expression wasn't as critical as it had been moments ago. He could have leaped over the table and kissed her.

"I promised you a day, Halabrin," she said, "and if

nothing else, I keep my promises. When do we go?"

Noah eyed his watch. "It's almost six now. By the time we got there, it'd be too late to get anything accomplished, not to mention I'm not sure what time lights out or visiting hours are. Tomorrow morning, bright and early. Meet me at the station at six. We'll be at the Institute by seven-thirty."

Valerie stood. "Deal." She picked up her purse and sorted through it for her keys. "And let's pray Ducharme doesn't strike again tonight."

CHAPTER 40

Delroy awoke in his gloomy, dank quarters and sat upright on the floor. His head whirled, still reeling with foggy images just out of reach as it often did after long rests filled with dreams, memories, or peculiar combinations of both. Only wisps of what had surfaced remained this time: images of fire, anger, profound disappointment, and fear.

Now, more awake than asleep, strong, and full of the power of the gray man, he feared nothing. As long as they shared this human body, they both lived, unstoppable. They used the same body to fulfill their needs for life and blood, for violence, and—sometimes—what one of them viewed as justice.

Stretching, he slowly became more alert, his mind more capable of coherent thought. They considered moving on to the next sacrifice on his list. It was sooner than usual, but it already felt like a good day to kill again. Regardless of what the gray man said, Delroy couldn't rid himself of the thought that he was running out of time.

He straightened his spine, assumed a comfortable cross-legged posture for meditation with his back resting against the wall, and communed with the oneness of himself, the elegance of his strength and bottomless power, and the fury that drove him to continue his mission. He reached inward and saw in himself the source of his power, the ancient being that shared his body, the warrior, corrupted with power, blood, and knowledge no one on earth was meant to find. They saw the silver cord that joined them, and the blood in his veins sang.

He knew that it was in them to provide perfect sacrifices to the Sun King. His death had made him perfect, and they would live forever, as long as he continued to offer the blood in exchange for life.

Before his bloody hand had ever touched the page and made the contract that bound them eternally, he'd known who would die so that he might live. His first offering to his cohabiting spirit was so large, so gruesome, and so full of emotional and physical pain, he'd swelled with power mere hours after sealing their bond. The gray one was pleased—and Delroy was unstoppable.

He felt no grief for his actions. Remorse for a human? Not possible. Liars, all of them capable of deceit and hatred, there wasn't one human worth saving, not one worth protecting, not one he wouldn't kill if it meant that he might live.

People were such disappointments.

As he dwelled on these thoughts, his body hummed with the energy of the *Muerto Fuerte* within, charged with the power of the negative thoughts he gladly harbored as fuel for his mission.

As he did, data from the fountain of all knowledge came to him. He decided against the pursuit of another kill.

The hunter would be arriving soon, and they wanted to be sure to be there when he did.

CHAPTER 41

The phone on the other end rang monotonously, a dull, listless sound that made Noah think it might be drugged. After several pathetic rings, as he was about to hang up, the other end was answered.

"Hello?" a feminine voice said.

"Brittney?"

"Noah? What're you doing?" From the sound of her voice, chances were good she was drunk or exhausted; with Brittney, either was possible. He prepared himself for a complicated conversation impeded by alcohol, sleeping pills, or some combination of both.

"I just got off work. How've you been?"

There was a pause as Brittney swallowed on her end. "I'm doin' all right. Been better."

The conversation lagged, and Noah questioned his motives for calling. What had he expected to tell her? That he was on the trail of the man who'd killed their parents, who'd committed the violent murder spree that led to their sister's mental breakdown and suicide? That he'd dreamed he was as good as dead himself? *Gee, Britt, thought I'd call and let you know which drawer I keep my will in. Just in case, you know? Get real, Halabrin!*

"Noah?"

"I'm here, Brittney."

"What's the matter? You sound gloomy." Her voice was clear now. He wondered if she was waking up or if he'd scared her into sobriety with his silence.

"I'm always a little on the blue side. You know that.

Comes with the job."

Another sip, this time he thought he recognized the sound. A coffee mug? She did the familiar exhale Brittney used when drinking a hot liquid. He smiled. She was waking up.

"How's the joe?" he asked.

"How do you do that? Jeez, you never stop detecting. How'd you know I was drinking coffee?"

Noah laughed, and it felt good. His tension loosened a little. "I know you, Britt. You always make this funny little breathing sound when you drink something hot."

Brittney laughed. "Busted. Yeah, I wanted to wake up a little before I... I had this crazy dream, and when I woke up, I thought... Well, never mind. You'll think I'm crazy."

"Try me," Noah said, trying to keep the curiosity from his voice.

"I... I dreamed I graduated from college. With honors. And you were there, and Valerie was with you, and Nick was there."

"Nick? Your ex?"

"Yeah, crazy, isn't it? But he was there, and he was so proud of me. When I woke up, I thought, 'What the hey?' and started filling out this application I've been sitting on for a couple of weeks. Maybe I'll get back into that nursing degree."

"You're going back to college? Wow, Brittney, that's so great! I'm glad to hear it."

"Well, don't get too excited. It's only an application."

"Still, it's a step. I think it's awesome."

"Yeah, yeah. You're making me blush. Enough about me. Why'd you call?"

Keep it steady, don't worry her. "What do you mean?"

"Noah, you've been my brother for... what, twenty-eight years now? You never call unless you're either checking up on me or you've got some major bomb to drop. What's up?"

He licked his lips. "I think I may be on the trail of something big. A huge case. One that could change our lives."

"Our lives? And since when do you tell me about cases you're working on? You always said you can't talk about a case while you're working on it."

"This one... I have to, Britt. You need to know. In case... in case something happens."

This time it was Brittney who paused. When she spoke, her voice shook. "Noah, you're scaring me."

"I don't mean to. And I'm sorry for bringing it up now when you're so... when things are starting to look up for you. God, why'd this have to happen now?" He searched his ceiling for answers. Finding none, he continued. "Listen, I think I may be tracking the man... the thing that killed Mom and Dad."

Dead silence, save for Brittney's shallow breathing.

"Thing? What—Noah, what're you talking about?"

"Brittney, do you remember that story I told on the way to the campground that time?"

Hard, stressful breaths came through the phone. "Yeah?"

"I wasn't lying, Britt. I wasn't a crazy kid trying to get attention that day. I wasn't crazy. I have the dreams—the ones that see the future. And I talk to ghosts. Always have."

He waited to see if she said anything, but she didn't. He went on. "You probably knew that since it happened. You saw that it happened. You know I was right. But I didn't fight hard enough to get us all out of there, and we all paid the price—Mom and Dad most of all. I've had to live with that my whole life. Now I think I'm tracking the same guy. All the signs are there, and it looks like—"

"Did you have a dream? You know, like you said you do? Did you dream it was the same guy? Is that why you think you'll die?"

He wanted to lie. He wanted to tell her that yes, he'd had a dream, and it was the same guy, but he came out all right. He wanted to lie, but he couldn't. She had to know the truth. She had to be prepared.

"Yes, I had one of those dreams. I saw a man in it with me. It was him—the guy who killed Mom and Dad. It wasn't good. He—he was strangling me."

Brittney sighed. He heard a quiet sob and knew she was struggling back the urge to cry.

When she spoke again, her voice was as grave as he'd ever heard it, on the verge of a breakdown, a scream, or maybe both, and uttered from between clenched teeth. "Get him, Noah," she said. "You have to make this right for us. I don't care how you do it. Find him, track him down, and do whatever you have to do. And when you do, kill him. 'Cause if you don't, if he hurts you at all, I swear to God, I'll hunt him down and kill him myself."

CHAPTER 42

The Acorn Institute had been founded, Noah discovered as he surfed the net the next morning, ninety-six years ago, by a man named Sturgis Wells, a magnate of the tobacco industry. Wells founded the Institute after the diagnosis of his son, Patrick, with a severe case of dementia praecox—the term then used for schizophrenia. Wells was a rich but sensitive man who learned quickly that for many outside his financial circle, funds were not available to care for those whose disabilities, while mentally debilitating, were not deemed medical emergencies.

Named by Patrick, whose favorite tree was an enormous oak outside his bedroom window, the Acorn Institute had now been in business for over a hundred years.

The greatest irony of the Acorn Institute's history, though, was that an institute founded on the needs of the underprivileged now housed the mentally challenged of the richest families of Leland County. A dozen rooms had been more than enough to house those with mental challenges at the turn of the twentieth century. Now, a dozen rooms weren't nearly enough to hold all of those in the county in need of care. Due to limited space, it now housed the mentally disordered elite.

Brad Gardner was such a man. Noah punched the name into his favorite search engine and discovered—after sorting through a dozen or so unrelated pieces about men with the same name—that the Brad Gardner he sought was the great-great-grandson of Sturgis Wells. He, like Patrick Wells, had developed schizophrenia at a relatively young age and had made quite a few headlines six years ago, when his relatives uprooted a longtime resident from her room to put Brad in the family institution.

"How's it going?"

Noah jumped in his seat. He'd been so entranced in his research he hadn't heard Valerie approach him. She smiled a shaky smile, and he tried to grin in return.

"Fine. Doing a little reading on our guy."

"Brad... Gardner. Schizophrenia, huh?"

"Yeah. Let's hope after this morning that you don't feel I belong in a room across the hall."

She laughed. "No way you're getting in there on a cop's salary, anyway."

*   *   *

The Acorn Institute was an antebellum mansion on an indeterminate number of acres—indeterminate because it utilized no fences and rested in the heart of Leland County's least populated and most overgrown swampland. The driveway had no parking slots, but they weren't at a loss for a place to put the unmarked sedan. A wide, circular drive left ample room for visitors, and a handful of plain vans Noah guessed were used for institutional purposes.

Although Acorn employed no fences, the front door did have a telecom system used to identify visitors at its locked doors. Noah introduced himself to the man at the other end of the speaker and explained that he had an appointment while extending his badge in the camera's direction.

Within a minute, a flustered-looking man in his mid-thirties pulled the door open. He was dressed in Levi's, a cream button-down shirt with the tails out, and white Adidas sneakers. His auburn hair was tousled on top, but it was difficult to tell if the look was intentional or if he'd merely had a rough morning.

"Come in, come in," he said with a wave of his hand, which he then extended, first to Noah, and then to Valerie. "I'm Dr. Ian Matheson. Mr. Gardner's regular Doctor is Vincent Morgan, but Dr. Morgan is... calming another patient." Noah wondered if the patient currently being "calmed" was the cause for Matheson's agitation.

The interior of the Acorn Institute was homey—if one's home was a mansion. The white marble tile floor extended to a curved marble staircase to his left. High ceilings held ornate fans lazily stirring in the heavily air-conditioned foyer. Polished windows were hung with sheer draperies that Noah wagered cost more than all of his living room furniture combined. To the left, inside the door, stood an unmanned antique walnut desk with a marble nameplate that matched the floor, which read: Gina Hathaway. All the furniture—the chairs flanking the windows, the console table holding the guest book and plume pen in its silver nest, the jacquard print living room furniture that gave the foyer a cozy look—appeared antique and expensive but comfortable.

"Can you tell me anything about Mr. Gardner, Dr. Matheson?" Noah asked.

Dr. Matheson paused. "May I see some credentials? Up close, I mean," he asked. Noah and Valerie apologized and withdrew their badges.

"Sorry," he added after a quick inspection, "Just precautions. Vince... my partner... would be upset if I dumped information too liberally on strangers. You see, I don't work here. I'm on a social call."

"Your partner?" Noah asked. "I thought the Acorn Institute was a family-run business."

"I think he means domestic partner," Valerie interjected. "Am I right, Doctor?" Matheson nodded. Noah wished he could slap his forehead; instead, he repeated his question about Gardner. Matheson indicated his compliance with a dip of his head and proceeded down a long, white, tiled corridor to the right. Noah and Valerie followed.

"Mr. Gardner came to us at the age of eighteen, diagnosed with acute paranoid schizophrenia. He has constant psychotic episodes. Auditory and visual hallucinations, mostly. In most instances, schizophrenia takes time; the onset can begin in the teens, but it takes years to develop. Not so with Mr. Gardner. His was an almost instant full-fledged and chronic onset." He paused outside a white door and made no motion to open it.

"Can you tell me about the hallucinations?" Noah asked.

"What is it you would like to know?"

"Are they repetitive? I mean, does he see or hear the same type of thing over and over?" Noah's stomach churned; he already knew the answer, but he had to hear it, had to let Valerie hear it from the doctor.

"Are you asking me if his delusions are constant versus the hebephrenic type?" Matheson asked, his expression revealing respect at Noah's insightfulness. "Well, yes. Mr. Gardner believes he is the victim of persecution at the hands of ghosts. He says they talk to him constantly. He claims that they won't stop talking to him, that they torment him. Something about a deal that he backed out of—some sort of contract with the dead. It's a complicated delusion, but it stays amazingly consistent."

There but for the grace of God, thought Noah.

"I should warn you," the doctor continued, "that his family has requested that Mr. Gardner not be medicated. I feel it's a ridiculous measure on their part really, but so far, he's shown no tendencies to harm himself or anyone around him, so it's not a matter of safety. Still, if it makes you feel more at ease, I can ask if he minds being restrained."

"Restrained?" Valerie said, a sudden wave of hesitation setting in. "Are you serious?"

Matheson ran a strong hand through his auburn mop; creases formed at the corners of his mouth. "He tends to lash out at the ghosts he sees. He hasn't harmed anyone yet, but he does get very angry, full of rage. He doesn't have many visitors, though, so he probably wouldn't mind it—"

"No," Noah said. "That won't be necessary. Mr. Gardner is fine how he is."

Matheson's lips turned up weakly at the corners. "As I said, he doesn't get many guests, so he might be very glad to see you."

Valerie wondered whom Matheson was trying to reassure. He pulled a key ring from his pocket and unlocked the door.

It was all Noah could do not to scream in terror at the sight that awaited him inside Gardner's room. Pacing, playing, scowling, and otherwise keeping themselves occupied were more specters than Noah had seen in one place in his life. And the center of all their attention, in a chair in the heart of the room, sat Gardner, curled up and shivering.

CHAPTER 43

He looked nothing like Noah expected him to. Noah had supposed that even a great-great-grandson of a powerful man like Sturgis Wells would have a presence. Instead, Gardner's scrawny frame sat hunched, his arms crossed protectively over his lean chest as his slate-blue eyes darted from figure to gray figure. His ashy hair had been cut in a style so short as to almost appear military. Gardner's closest thing to a powerful feature was his jaw: it was square and slightly protruding. As Noah watched, one of the specters dove at him maliciously, snapping his transparent teeth in front of Gardner's face. Gardner let out a feeble whine and flinched, then wrapped his arms around his legs and rocked back and forth, back and forth, back and forth.

"You're doing the talking, right?" Valerie whispered as she entered at Noah's heels.

"Of course," Noah replied.

They stopped before the chair. Valerie stood a little behind him almost as though she sensed, somehow, the presence of the malicious ghosts in the room. Noah wondered if she planned to use him as a shield if Gardner attacked.

Noah stood before Gardner for a moment, wordless, wondering where to begin. Would Gardner know that he and Valerie were there as friends? Or did he suspect, after years of persecution at the hands of phantoms unseen by anyone else, that all humans thought he was crazy?

"Mr. Gardner?" Noah said. Gardner stopped rocking but said nothing. His gaze never left the ghosts before him.

"Mr. Gardner, I'm Detective Halabrin. I'm with the Leland County Sheriff's Department. I was wondering if you'd help me by answering a few questions."

"Help?" Gardner snapped. "I need help, too. *Always* need help. No one helps me. You're not here for me? You didn't come to lock me up double?"

Their voices were impossible for him to hear, but he knew from the way they threw their heads back that several of the ghosts laughed at Gardner's gibberish.

"I'm sorry," Noah said. He crouched before Gardner's chair, so they were face to face. "I wish there was something I could do." He nearly jumped up again as the door behind them shut, leaving him and Valerie alone in a room full of spiteful ghosts and a man society had deemed insane.

Maybe it was the tone of his voice, but Noah expected that it was more than likely the way his eyes followed the ghosts darting around them. Gardner sat up, his fear forgotten in his excitement. He watched as Noah's eyes darted around the room and pointed a trembling finger at Noah.

"*You!* You, you, youyouyou see them *too!*" he exclaimed. "The ghosties. They're—they're everywhere." He slumped back down and began scratching at his forearms. "They're everywhere." Red welts materialized under his fingernails. "They're everywhere. I didn't know. I didn't know I didn't know I didn't know...."

A gray arm shot between Noah and the madman and swiped at Gardner's face with an ineffective hand. Another leaned over and whispered in his ear. The words were inaudible to Noah, but they had the desired effect on Gardner. He pulled his legs back up to his chest and wrapped his bony arms around them with a whimper. Noah shivered in sympathy for the man.

"You hear them?" Noah asked. "Why is it you hear

them and I don't?"

"I'm more alive. I'm more alive than dead. I'm more alive."

"You're more alive than I am? How's that?"

Gardner shook his head, a motion that must have soothed him because he continued the action for a full twenty seconds as he spoke. "I'm more alive than I was dead. I'm more alive than dead when I signed the book. The book is dead. I'm alive. I should be dead, but I had the power. I had the power, and it was good, but then it turned bad, and I didn't want the power, and now I pay the dead." He stopped shaking his head, but the motion moved into his torso, which rocked back and forth again.

"The book—the book of the dead? The *Libro de Los Muertos*? You had power from the book of the dead?"

"Borrowed a page from the crazy man," he said with an angry chuckle. "Borrowed a page. He promised me power. Made the bloody signature. Had the power... the power... But then I wanted the power to go away, and it leaves, and I'm like this, and they're here. Always here. They're always here."

He stopped rocking and looked Noah full in the face, and for a moment, Noah saw the handsome young man Brad Gardner used to be. A smile wobbled over his thin lips as a light bulb went on in his head.

"You... you know the crazy man," he said in a singsong that chilled Noah's skin. "You know him. He's stuck you. Right here." He pointed at his temple, "and here," he gestured at his heart. "He stuck you, and now you're stuck. You're stuck, and he's the gingerbread man."

Noah hoped it wasn't a sign that he was unhinging that he followed this nonsensical talk.

"That's right, Brad," he said. "The crazy man is the gingerbread man, and he's out hurting people, and no matter how fast we run, run, run, we can't catch him. That's why I'm here."

Gardner bowed his head as if it made all the sense in the world.

"You need the book," he said. "You need the book. See the book, you know the sign."

"Tell me why I need to see the book, Brad. Explain about the sign."

"You see the book, you'll know how unbeatable he is. If he is like I was, he is mostly alive. If he's mostly alive, you're fucked. No killing him. No killing him. He lives and lives and lives—"

"And if he's mostly dead?"

"You'll know. You'll know. If he's mostly dead, he was dying. He was dying, and he signed the bloody signature. He signed in red, and then he lived again, and he's more powerful than I ever was, and he holds on to the silver string, and the ghost-thing lives with him, and he lives and lives and lives and kills and kills—"

"He holds the silver string?"

Gardner nodded. "The silver string is what holds him here," he said, pointing to his chest. "You snip the string— poof!" His hands fanned out like a magician showing his hands were now empty.

"Snip the string? That's all?"

Gardner laughed a short, deep, eerie chortle and gave Noah a somber frown. "That's all, but that's all. As long as he kills, those souls pay for his. He won't die, but his debt is paid, and he stays alive as long as he keeps new souls coming in his place."

In other words, that's all, but...

"How will I know if he's more dead or more alive?"

Gardner shrugged and once again started his self-soothing rock. "Get the book. See the book. See what page he signed. It's a contract, he signed with blood. You get the book, you see where he put his signature, you'll know if you can kill him." Gardner sat up and put his hands on his knees. The ghosts around him had, for the moment, fallen silent, their amusement satisfied at the moment with the conversation between Noah and Gardner.

"I'm not alone, am I, Noah?"

The sound of his name startled him like a splash of cold water. He hadn't told Gardner his first name, but Gardner knew it, just as Madam Ubora had known it. Maybe the ghosts had told him, but he doubted it. It hadn't occurred to him until now, but he'd known before she'd spoken that the woman behind the counter at Insights and Sounds was Madame Ubora. Did they all know one another, somehow? Were they all linked?

No. Pamela Harper hadn't known I could see. Unless she was too shocked to notice. And I couldn't tell about any of them until they said something. Still, he wondered what made Madame Ubora and Brad able to hear and know things he couldn't.

"No Brad," he said soothingly, "you're not alone." He wanted to put a reassuring hand on the man's shoulder, but he refrained, not knowing how Brad would interpret his gesture or if it'd be welcome.

Noah turned around and motioned to Valerie that it was time to go. As they approached the door, a thought occurred to him. He turned back.

"Mr. Gardner, why don't you have the power anymore? You said you had the power, that the book gave you power like the gingerbread man. What happened to it?"

Gardner hesitated. "I got tired of washing my hands," he said. His hands twitched in his lap, and his head fell forward. "Now, they own me. Now they own me. Now they own me."

Gardner repeated the sentence for as long as it took

them to leave, and Noah wondered for days afterward how many minutes or hours passed before the poor man finally stopped.

*   *   *

It was a long ride back to the stationhouse.

The air-conditioner tried its hardest to push cold air out of its vents, but it was a losing battle. The freon had done double-duty that sweltering summer, and at nearly noon on a late August day, it was struggling to cool the SUV. Valerie didn't notice; the chill that had set in the moment she saw the tormented Gardner hadn't left.

She sat in the passenger seat, watching the dry horizon pass by but not seeing it. The trip they'd made that morning gave her a lot to think about. She'd never had a reason to visit a place like the Institute before, and the feeling it left in her heart was far more disturbing than the many visits she had made to her late grandmother's nursing home. At least her grandmother gave the family the impression that she was at peace there; she said the people were kind and that she was well taken care of.

The idea that Gardner's family had opted not to medicate him, not to give him some serenity, was unfathomable to her. She wondered if the reason they'd chosen to leave him unmedicated was that the drugs didn't take the ghosts away. Perhaps his wealthy family didn't want to live with the notion that Brad was beyond help, hated the idea that others knew about his lack of response to medication, and therefore chose to let him live in his private hell. The idea sickened her.

Gardner lived in a constant state of torment because he thought ghosts hovered around him; he heard them harassing him all the time. How did he differ from Noah?

What made Noah able to deal with the ghosts he saw when a similar conviction broke Gardner into a crazy shell of a man locked away from humanity?

"So, what do you think?" Noah asked.

"About what?"

"About Gardner."

Valerie shrugged, more a helpless movement than a resigned one. "What I don't get is... why wouldn't his family medicate him?"

"They probably did. At first."

Valerie guessed his implication. "You don't think it helped."

Noah's face revealed little, but she noticed slight stress lines around his eyes and mouth. "It must have scared them to death," he said. "Giving him all the meds in the world didn't take away what everyone else thought were hallucinations."

It was then that Valerie understood the emotion Noah was suppressing. It was fear. Seeing Gardner had given him an insight into a life he'd escaped, a life of white walls and placating voices and weekend visits.

He abruptly changed the subject. "So, what's your take about what he said?"

Valerie hesitated. "I'm not sure I get what he said. And I've been wondering why you brought up the Book of the Dead in there. Where did all your interrogation skills go? Don't you know never to provide a person with the answer you're looking for?"

Noah shrank from the force of her words. "Yeah, I did do that. I'm sorry. I should've let him bring it up himself."

"If he would have. There's no telling now. You gave him the answer you wanted to hear, and he ran with it."

"Maybe he did. I don't think so, but you may be right. But he said, 'the book is dead.'"

"All books are dead, Hal."

Another uncomfortable pause.

"There is one thing that I'll admit, though I'm not sure what it says about me. You two were watching something. It was as if little birds were flying around in the room, and only you two could see 'em. The way both of your eyes followed those... whatever they were. I don't know. It was creepy. And I don't know how he knew your name. You didn't tell them, did you?"

"I told them I was Detective Halabrin."

"No one there knew you as Noah until Dr. Matheson saw your badge right before we saw Gardner?"

Noah shook his head. Valerie slumped in the seat, her hand at her mouth the way it did when something puzzled her.

"Does this mean you believe me?"

"Let's just say I'm not as inclined to rule it out as I was yesterday morning," she said. She checked her watch. "I told you yesterday at five-thirty that I was going to give you one day to prove to me that you see ghosts. That means twenty-four hours. It's only eleven now, so that gives you another six and a half hours to have me fully convinced. So, now what?"

"Now we go back to speak to the ghosts that I know will tell me more. If they're still there."

"Who's that?"

"The ghosts of my parents."

CHAPTER 44

If Lightning Fork Campground had been empty before, it was nothing compared to the desolateness that had settled over it now. There were no cars, no campers, nothing to indicate the campsite had included human life—if barely a handful—two days before. Even George Bailey's office was deserted, his sense of self-preservation winning over his need to make more money for his already wealthy uncle.

Noah kept his eyes on the uneven ground as he steered the Durango down the weed-eaten drive—more of a wagon trail than a road—and headed to the far rear of the campground. To the right, what had once been a softball field was now dense with wildflowers. Two ghosts glided through the thigh-high foliage like waders in an ocean of green and yellow. To his left, a forest bordered the path. New growth had flourished over the past twenty years. What had once been a fun area to rest in the shade now looked likely to veil lost children or perhaps swallow them.

"Where are we headed?" Valerie asked. Her voice was small, like a child's, and he knew the eerie atmosphere that loomed over Lightning Fork had touched her, too.

"The family cabanas in the back, on the hill."

"Where Jacques and Muriel were killed?"

He'd made the connection before but had chosen not to tell her. How ironic that his family had stayed in the same area as Ducharme and his parents. He wondered if they'd shared the same cabin. The feeling that had until that moment merely tickled his spine now drenched him in a nervous sweat. It seemed that every event from the moment of Jacques and Muriel's deaths had spawned a strange, irrevocable circle that was destined to include him. His dreams. His premonition about his parent's death. His ability to see ghosts. All of it tangled up with the life of Delroy Ducharme in a loop closing tight enough to suffocate him.

The muggy air in the unmarked was thick as quicksand. Noah tried to crank up the air, realized the dial was already on full blast, and slapped his hand back on the steering wheel in frustration.

"My family stayed there, too," he said. "Most years, we'd stayed in separate cabins—my parents with the adults, and me and my sisters with the youths—but that year we shared a cabin, because..."

The sentence died in his throat. Valerie turned to see why he stopped. The expression on his face was so racked with guilt she longed to reach out and touch his hand, his face, anything to give him some small measure of comfort, but she knew she shouldn't. It was unprofessional.

To hell with unprofessional.

She reached over and grasped his right hand, gently pulling it from the steering wheel, so it rested intertwined with hers on the seat between them. He shot her a startled look but joined his fingers around hers, nonetheless. She expected him to give her a squeeze and pull away; instead, he gripped her palm like a lifeline. Agony painted his face, not from her touch, but from the memory that had died in his throat, cutting off his speech. He might not have caused his parent's death, but he was lugging around some serious guilt, nonetheless.

Why would he—?

"You knew, didn't you?" she asked, her voice barely more than a whisper. "You knew that day was coming.

That Ducharme was coming to Lightning Fork. You knew, and you blame yourself for your parents dying that day."

Lines of stress emerged at his eyes and mouth. Valerie saw his Adam's apple bob as he swallowed a hard lump in his throat.

"I tried to warn them," he said. "That's why we were all together that day. They were placating me. I told them I had a premonition. I get those, sometimes." He scoffed. "You must think I'm nuts now. Ghosts and precognition. Who do I think I am? What right do I have—?" His voice choked off again, and he swallowed a sob like a hard knot in his throat.

Valerie said nothing, and Noah turned to see her face. He expected to see disbelief, or worse, pity. He saw neither. "They put us in a cabin together," he said, "and told me that nothing could happen to us if we were all in the same spot. It was their way of giving in to what they saw as my little... outburst. I tried—"

"Then it's not your fault."

"*I should've tried harder!*" he cried, pulling his hand away and banging his fist on the steering wheel. "I should've thrown a royal fit, broken windows, or screamed or cried or hit something—or someone. I should've tried harder, begged them to listen, I should've made them listen..."

My God, he's starting to sound a little like Gardner, Valerie thought. But, unlike Gardner, she didn't fear him. She knew that if she'd lost her parents, especially if it had happened the way it had with Noah when she was a child, she would've been driven out of her mind. He was insane with grief, but not insane. She wondered again how he held himself together day to day, literally living with ghosts and figuratively seeing the ghosts of his past. Even if the ghosts he spoke to were all in his head, the ones that lived in his memory were more than enough.

He pulled in front of the second to the last cabin in a row of neglected gray A-frame cabins and stopped the car. The dust settled, and his eyes bugged as he focused on a point straight ahead. She guessed that in Noah's mind, someone stood there that her humble eyes didn't see.

"Noah, what is it?"

"It's Ashley. My sister's here."

"Why is that so surprising?"

"She died in her apartment. Ghosts don't usually leave the place they died unless..."

Several seconds passed. Valerie spoke the notion she suspected had occurred to Noah.

"Maybe, to her, this *is* the place she died. If not literally, then spiritually."

Noah agreed. "That must be it. It would certainly explain why she haunts here instead of the place... where she hanged herself."

It was the first time he'd shared any details of Ashley's death. A hush settled between them, and the silence in the absence of the car's running engine was absolute. Valerie was reminded of the vibes she felt in church as a child, as if she was in the presence of a powerful entity; she felt awed nearly beyond speech. When she did speak, it came out in a whisper.

"Hal, do me a favor. Speak aloud as you do your thing, so I can follow. OK?"

Noah consented, and they exited the car. Even in the heat, the air in the back of the campground closest to the woods smelled green and fresh.

Ashley was the most beautiful spirit Noah had ever seen and, even in the gray, translucent quality of death, one of the most handsome women. Her long, blond hair shone ghostly white now, and her skin appeared to be a light gray, like other spirits. Her clothes were the same as the day he'd found her; Levi's and a fashionable, dark V-neck shirt. Then it had been blue. Today it looked charcoal gray. Her feet bore white socks, no shoes. She'd chosen comfortable clothes to die in. He wondered if it mattered now, if she noticed her attire at all, or if it was a manifestation of her thoughts, or his.

"Hello, Ashley," he motioned and said aloud for Valerie's benefit, although the signs were obvious. No sense leaving any part out.

"Hello," she said. Noah repeated it. Valerie stood almost on her toes, straining to see what Noah's eyes saw, but there was nothing. Nothing but air and the cabin. She gave up and paid attention to Noah's movements.

"How long have you been here?"

Ashley shrugged. "Off and on, since I died."

"Why here? If you have a choice, why come here?"

"I knew you'd come someday. I am surprised it took so long."

Noah frowned and dropped his head. He'd thought of coming thousands of times over the years to see if his parents were there, to talk to them, and to tell them he was sorry. All that time, he'd had no idea that Ashley waited for him. Yet another item to add to the mountain of bad moves about which he felt guilty.

"I couldn't do it," he replied. "I told myself that they're the type who moved on immediately. That they didn't stay for me. For us."

Ashley smiled. "You're right. They didn't stay. They moved on like they should." Her heart-shaped face dropped down, looked at the translucent sock on her foot. "I stayed. I couldn't go. Not until I talked to you."

"Why? Ashley, why stay for five years? You should move on. Go to Mom and Dad. I'm sure they're waiting for you." His hands waved vigorously as he emphasized his point, and knew he looked like a crazed conductor.

"What's five years in eternity? Mom and Dad are patient. They'll be fine. You need my help."

Noah's hands stopped flying long enough to digest the meaning of that statement. His head tipped to the side.

"You could've come to me at any time. You know I can see you. Why wait?"

"But you couldn't, Noah," she motioned, her face pained and her actions punctuated with wild movement. "You can see me now because you're ready. Before, you couldn't. I tried!"

She'd tried? When? How often? Shame colored his features. All this time, he had it in his power to solve the crimes, but he'd been ignorant because of his inability to face his parents' deaths.

"All right," he said. "So now I'm here. Now I'm ready. What can you tell me?"

"Ducharme—the man who killed them—he started eighteen years ago when he made this contract."

"Yes, I know. The Book of the Dead. He signed his life away to trade for eternal life."

"Right. And soon, he came here. Killed dozens of people, wanted revenge on Lightning Fork, on the owner, but most importantly, he wanted to kill people. He'd wanted that for years. Noah, he's so evil."

Maybe it was Ashley's expression. Maybe it was the way Noah spoke the words he signed. Valerie shivered.

Noah continued translating: "These deaths also gave him great power, which is why he killed so many at once. Afterwards, he went..." her hands paused, then she finger-spelled "dormant," an action Noah found funny since it showed she knew that he didn't know a sign language equivalent. "He had to sleep. He has to do that sometimes, to keep his body strong, to live forever."

"Is he vulnerable when he is sleeping?" Noah asked.

"No," Ashley said. "He's never easy to kill."

"Ashley, why now? After eighteen years? Why'd this take so long for him to do?"

Ashley gave him a frustrated look. "I told you. He sleeps, he wakes up, he kills, he sleeps again. In large time amounts. Sometimes he sleeps for months. Besides, he didn't start killing locally. He chased down the far away ones first. Then he worked his way back. The people he kills now are all that's left of those here the day his parents died. After this, he starts killing those who were here the day he first killed, soon after he signed the contract."

"You mean—"

"You, Brittney, and anyone else who managed to escape twenty years ago." She hesitated, her face a reflection of sadness. "Not many of those."

"How does he find them? How does he find his victims if they're all over the country?"

"It's the ghost inside. The ghost is part of him now. It taps into the knowledge we share, like that Jungian thing. The collective unconscious."

"There's a ghost inside him?" Valerie interjected. Noah glanced her way before returning his attention to Ashley.

"I understand I need to find out if he's more alive or more dead. Can you tell me that?"

Ashley shook her head. "No. The contract is supernatural; I can't see it. Gods and demons are the only beings that can tell that without seeing the book."

"What do you know about how to stop him? Can you help me?"

Ashley's guise reflected surprise at the question and maybe a little insult. She stepped closer to him. Her see-through arm floated to his shoulder, where it perched without passing through. Coldness seeped through his clothing and into his skin, but it was a sweet feeling, like a cold drink on a sweltering afternoon.

"I'll do whatever I can, little brother."

Then, from the shade of the woods, from behind the cabins and out of the tall grasses, shadows of specters arose, the ghosts of those who died at the hands of Delroy Ducharme. The ghosts of those he'd failed to save. His hand, now mute, flew to his mouth as his eyes filled with tears. The spectral eyes held no accusation, only sadness and perhaps a little weariness. They looked like people who'd overstayed their welcome involuntarily and were ready to go home. He longed to help them, to free them from the grief and the feeling he knew they carried with them that something wasn't put right that needed to be. He was determined to do whatever he had in his power to alleviate their need to see justice done.

Ashley turned her head and regarded her companions. Without a word, they spoke; no sign of conversation took place: no moving lips, no hand motions. Still, Noah saw the understanding pass between them, though the words were inaudible to human ears.

"We'll all help," she told him

CHAPTER 45

For the first time in days, the sky above loomed sorrowfully with the burden of impending rain. The humidity, which had been heavy enough to make clothes stick to the skin, now also made it difficult to breathe. Valerie peered at the clouds through the window of the car and cringed. Noah understood why. It didn't bode well that the weather chose this day to unleash a violent summer storm. It seemed the gods were against them, the pending storm a harbinger of celestial wrath.

The gods, he thought. That was the phrase Ashley had used: gods and demons. He hadn't questioned her about it—it hadn't struck him as a time to discuss semantics about philosophy and religion. Now, however, he wondered. If it boiled down to it in his final battle with Ducharme, did it matter to whom he directed his prayers? Or would he have time to pray at all? He'd never feared death before. The shadows had proven to him that life went on after death. After his recent dream featuring Ducharme, however, he feared the pain that most likely awaited him before crossing over into that plane.

"What's the rush?" Valerie asked as Noah tore down the road, fishtailing in the dry Alabama gravel.

"I need to talk to someone else now," Noah said.

"Who?"

"Madame Ubora."

"The psychic? Are you going to ask her how to find Ducharme? Do you think she'll know?"

The tone of her voice spoke volumes, tomes of

volumes, and every syllable lifted his spirits. If her doubt hadn't dissipated, she was willing to put it aside long enough to give Noah his shot at finding Ducharme his way. Either she'd come around or was caught up in his enthusiasm; he didn't care which, as long as it gave him time enough to find the shadow they were hunting.

"God, I hope so. I'm not looking forward to going back to the station and explaining to Captain Blanch how we spent our day unless we can give her a productive answer. Are you?"

*   *   *

Madame Ubora's stayed open until midnight. He knew that from his last visit. His hurry was borne of an eagerness to find and confront Ducharme, preferably before the storm. Now that he'd found the intestinal fortitude, he was afraid to slow down for fear he'd never start again.

"Detective Halabrin," Madame Ubora said as they entered, "How nice to see you! I knew you'd come back." She placed her book down and came out from behind the counter to embrace him like an old friend.

"Of course, you did," he replied with a smile. "Our grapevine is more reliable than Bell South." He introduced her to Valerie, who also felt the cheerful glow within Insights and Sounds affecting her mood. Despite the horrible time they'd had tracking down Ducharme and the odds that faced them now, a smile now played at the corners of her mouth. She accepted Madame Ubora's hand with a genuine grin.

Madame Ubora released Valerie's hand with a little reluctance, her knowing eyes darting from Noah to Valerie and back.

"You'd do well to look into this, Mr. Halabrin," she said

with a knowing glance to Valerie. Noah's face grew crimson.

"We're uh... we're here because we—I mean, that is, I—was hoping that maybe, Madame Ubora... About some help. I was helping you'd hope me. Hoping you'd help me."

Madame Ubora shook her head, her expression struggling to be blank, but her eyes still held a twinkle.

"You can't?"

She threw back her head and laughed; her laugh roared through the shop, bounced off the walls, and startled Noah.

"I can help you, Detective Halabrin, but only with Ducharme. And my insight on him is limited—he's got some mighty strong forces working for him. The rest is up to you."

"Anything. What've you got?"

Madame Ubora strolled to a shelf in the center of her shop. Valerie and Noah followed, and Noah observed two ghosts as they walked through the aisle partitions and tailed along like a little parade.

Madame Ubora removed a book wedged between a horizontal stack of books and what Noah guessed to be a male fertility statue based on a generous appendage dangling between his legs. The book's cover was faded brown leather, and from the condition of the worn yellow pages, mildewed at the spine, it was an antique. Embossed in gold on the cover were the words, *"To Run with Spirits."*

"You must be joking," he said, suddenly wary. "Another book? I hope you're not thinking that I'm going to make a contract the way Ducharme did. I'll wind up in a padded room like my friend Gardner! Who told you that this book is the key to my success?"

"He did," she said somberly with a gesture to one of the

spirits behind him. The ghost of Madame Ubora's son stood behind him, a pleading expression on his handsome face. His eyes, dark in death, motioned to the book with a bow of his head as if to say, "Take it, please."

Noah frowned. He wanted to argue, but he had no alternatives. If a spirit said the answer lay in the volume in Madame Ubora's hand, who was he to argue? He took the book.

Madame Ubora's son looked relieved but also a little tense, as if he wanted to tell Noah a lot was riding on his ability to utilize the book.

"I don't know what this book will tell you," Madame Ubora said, "I have not read it. I but I know this. No man-made tool is going to kill that thing. Your police batons, your mace, your guns—all worthless. You might as well leave them at home. The answer you're looking for to vank your duppy is in there. I trust Peter, Detective Halabrin. My son's never been wrong. Not since..."

A silence fell. The only sound was the lonely drumming of the long-awaited rain as it fell on the roof of Insights and Sounds and pattered on the windows.

So much for beating the storm.

"Now what?" Valerie asked.

"Now we have to figure out where to find Ducharme," Noah said.

Madame Ubora watched the conversation but said nothing. Noah wished she'd offer some of the "Insights" her shop name promised but sensed that despite the help he'd received thus far, in the end, this was a battle he fought alone. Whatever happened, the fates wouldn't lend a hand. It was his job to find the killer—his, and Valerie's.

"Ashley said something about him having to sleep for a long time so he can live forever, right?" Valerie said.

"Yeah?"

"So, I've been doing some thinking. Where does a person sleep for a long time? A perfect place where it's quiet, and people tend not to disturb things? A place where he wouldn't have to worry about paying rent when he's off tracking down his victims on his killing sprees."

Noah shook his head. "I don't see what you're getting at."

"Where did he live when he worked at St. Anne's? And where did they find Wanda's car? A cemetery!" she exclaimed. "His parents—they were rich, right? I'll bet you ten to one that they're in a huge mausoleum in John C. Wright Memorial. Think about it. Big cemetery, way out of town. I'll bet you it's where our man is hiding."

Noah's jaw dropped. Of course. It made so much sense now. He was more dead than alive when he signed the contract; he lives and kills to give souls to the dead, souls he despises along with the rest of humanity because of the death of his parents. And Wanda Murphy's car had turned up outside of John C. Memorial. My god. Why hadn't he seen it before? Where else would a man like Ducharme spend eternity than beside the very parents he sought to avenge?

Madame Ubora caught Noah's gaze, the slightest upturn at the corners of her lips telling him all he needed to know.

He turned on his heel and dashed for the door. With a wave of the book in Madame Ubora's direction, he shouted, "Thanks!"

"Bring my book back!" she returned.

If I live, Noah thought.

CHAPTER 46

Hunkered down over the monitors as they were, the detectives didn't hear the stealthy approach of their captain until she hovered over them like the rain clouds looming in the sky outside the station. Although they'd called and asked to speak to her to update their captain on their investigation, she managed to catch them both off guard.

"What's crackin'?" she asked. "Tell me you have news. Tell me you have a clue. A lead. A witness. Something. But don't tell me you're back here and starting from square one, or that you're sitting here hoping for the phone to ring with a lead you can follow. And don't tell me that you've been failing to report because you've been chasing your tails like a couple of rookies. If you are, I'm going to have to get the feds involved. This had gone on too long as it is."

"We have a definite lead," Noah assured her. "In fact, we think we may know where the killer is hiding."

"You've narrowed it down to one person," Blanch said, waving her hands the way she tended to when she became displeased. "Great. Scientifically impossible, according to Wallace, but I'll bite. And who is this killer? You know, you two haven't exactly been keeping me updated on this investigation. It wouldn't do to have you off questioning a suspect only to find he's our 'killer'—our one killer—and my two detectives get killed by some psychopath. There I sit, having no idea where you are because you're off gallivanting all over Leland County without bothering to check in. So please, Detective Halabrin, Detective Acquistapace.

Clue me in. I'm *only* your superior officer. I *only* hold your jobs—and, at times, your lives—in my hand."

Noah took the verbal blows without a duck or block. He deserved them, every one, and he knew it. He would be lucky to escape this investigation without a reprimand, not to mention his life, but he wasn't about to see Valerie catch some shit because of what he knew his captain would view as a wild goose chase.

"Captain Blanch, it's my fault," he said. "Valerie was humoring me on a few leads, and as it turned out, they panned out okay. It's one of those leads that we're following tonight. Turns out, there was another murder at Lightning Fork Campground a few years before the one... the one that made the papers twenty years ago. Two people died, husband and wife, questionable circumstances. They had a kid. We're following up on the kid, a Delroy Ducharme. Maybe it's a shot in the dark, considering the time lapse involved. But it's a start, and it makes sense."

Blanch followed them both with her eyes, checking to see if they were trying to snow her. Their steady faces showed trace amounts of guilt, but no bullshit. Satisfied with Noah's explanation and Valerie's subtle gestures of accord, she calmed down. Slightly.

"You're following this Ducharme. Where do you think he's hiding?"

Noah pointed at the monitor. On it, the obituary of Jacques and Muriel Ducharme glowed brightly in the storm-facilitated dusk inside the station. Burial took place on August twenty-second at John C. Wright Memorial Cemetery. There had been no church funeral.

"I don't get it. It's an obit, Halabrin," Blanch said.

Noah agreed. "We suspect he may be hiding in his parent's crypt."

Blanch made a sour face. "Well, that's disturbingly

morbid, isn't it?" Her mouth turned down further as she continued to contemplate the particulars. She made a disapproving sound and then brightened. "Well, if you think you've found our man, you might as well take back up—"

"It's just a suspicion right now," Valerie interjected. "No sense calling out the troops. I mean, we'd feel like idiots if we were wrong, with all the press this thing's been getting. I'd hate to get the officers riled up for a false alarm. We'll do some surveillance. If we spot him there, we'll call for backup."

Captain Blanch considered Valerie's words with a hand on her chin, ever the thinker, and agreed.

"I know I don't have to tell you this, but don't approach him alone. You've seen what this man—if it is, in fact, one man—you've seen what he's capable of; I couldn't live with myself if that happened to either one of you. Much less both of you. I know I don't have to tell you this, but if you see him, stay put. No—better yet—hide. Hide your asses, far away, and call for backup. We'll use SWAT for this bad boy if we have to. And if I hear either one of you did differently, I'll have your ass for disobeying a direct order. Got it?"

They got it. They also planned to disobey it.

*   *   *

"Why did you do that?" Noah asked, holding the door open for Valerie without realizing it. For once, she didn't berate him for it. They paused on the stationhouse steps. Tiny drops of rain had begun to fall. One landed on Valerie's cheek and trickled down like a tear to her chin, where she brushed it off.

"Do what? And why didn't I grab my umbrella?"

"You told Blanch to leave the troops behind, that we'd

call for backup. Why did you do that?"

"What was I supposed to do? Let 'em tag along and interrupt you while you're getting your exorcist on? What kind of a partner would do that?"

"So, you believe me?" he asked.

Valerie sighed. "I know *you* believe it. And, so far, I hate to admit it, but it's the one thing in all of this mess that... well, I can't say makes sense, but all the clues add up. Ghosts, demonic contracts, crazy men with vendettas possessed by spirits—it's not my thing, I'll admit. But you seem so convinced." She tipped her head up at the gray-blue sky and blinked as another raindrop touched her forehead. She put her chin down. "Noah, I've never doubted anything you've ever told me until yesterday. It suddenly occurred to me that it wasn't time to start doubting. Not when so many lives are at stake. And not when such an incredible tale comes from such a credible source as you."

She had never looked so beautiful. His heart soared with her trust in him, then plummeted at the idea that he was about to bring her along in the most perilous case of their careers. He'd rather bring her along in a drug raid filled with PCP-fueled junkies with guns than against the thing he'd seen kill one hundred and thirty-six people. There was no telling what would happen once they confronted Ducharme.

Maybe they'd be lucky. Maybe Ashley was right, and Ducharme was dormant, recuperating from his recent gunshot wounds. He might be immobile enough for them to find and read his book. Then again, Ashley had said he wasn't easy to kill. Sleeping or not, he was as lethal now as he'd ever been. Perhaps waking him would be equivalent to rousing an immortal hibernating bear with samurai training.

He looked at his watch. As much as had happened

today, he was amazed to find that the time was barely coming on six. There were two hours until sunset—plenty of time before the hours of darkness when one felt most vulnerable, most at risk to the darker forces that hid in one's subconscious. Noah knew that they both carried with them the overwhelming sense that once they stepped into the cemetery, they may never leave. That this might be their last case, their last moments.

"What do you want to do?" Valerie asked.

"I was thinking steak and shrimp and a big, fat booth where we can pour over this book, learn what we need to know," he said. "I mean, it might be our last meal, no time to worry about living large or beyond our budgets."

She laughed. She had a beautiful laugh, even when it was tainted with nervous tension. "Great idea, Hal."

*   *   *

The bistro Valerie chose, a place called "Phillip's" hidden in a tiny corner of a half-closed shopping center in the heart of Gryphon, was one Noah had never visited before. He gave in the second she swore that its surf and turf was divine.

The decor was as humble as its name. Primarily red, the ambiance might be mistaken for an Italian restaurant; garlic cloves strung from the ceiling, red and white checked tablecloths, and candles in red hurricanes burning on the table gave the place subdued lighting. The maître d' knew Valerie and greeted her with a kiss on each cheek before he gave them a pleasant seat near a window.

Valerie placed the book Madame Ubora had given them on the table beside her to study. She'd paged through on the way to the restaurant and found what they were looking for—what the book called a unity spell. According to the book, the "possession" was only temporary. It had been written in Latin, a language of which Valerie understood a little of the workings; as it turned out, she did speak Italian.

"Valpolicella?" the maître d' asked. Valerie shook her head.

"Not this time, Howard. On duty."

"All the more reason!" Howard said with a smile. "Make them pick up the tab."

"Thank you, but I'll have a diet coke. Is Freddie here?"

"No, not tonight. He's at home with the wife and bambino," Howard said. "Been doing that a lot the last three months."

"Well, he *does* own the restaurant," Valerie said. Howard smiled, took Noah's order, and went to get their drinks.

"Why is it called Phillip's when the owner's name is Fred?" Noah asked.

"Freddie. Short for Frederico. He kept it the same so as not to throw off the loyal clientele. Didn't want to make any waves when he took over three years ago," Valerie replied.

Their drinks arrived, and they each ordered a surf and turf. When the waitress left with a flounce of her curly brown hair, Noah asked—trying not to sound too curious—how it was that Valerie knew the owner.

"Well, I ought to. We shared a playpen."

"Your brother?"

"No, my Siamese twin. Of course, my brother."

Noah stirred his drink with a straw—a ginger ale in no need of stirring. Bubbles clinging to the side of the glass flew to the top like divers starved for air.

"Do you want to visit him before we go? I understand if you do. We've got time. Sort of."

Valerie shook her head adamantly. "No. I don't. If I see them, or if I take one look at that precious little niece of mine, I'll never have the guts to leave their house." The last part of her sentence came out sounding on the verge of a sob. Noah didn't have to see her eyes to know they held tears.

They didn't speak again until they were halfway through their meal, which, as Valerie had promised, was prepared without a flaw.

"There's one thing about this that really bothers me," Valerie said, swallowing a lump of mashed potato.

"What's that?"

"What if we win? What happens?" She sawed another piece from her filet mignon but waited to spear it.

"Well, I believe Ducharme dies. The silver cord holds him and the ghost together. Ashley and I sever the cord, and he reverts to the way he was when he signed the contract, I imagine. According to Gardner, he was mostly dead when he signed the contract. So... I guess he'll die."

Valerie poked at her meat but made no move to eat it. "And if he dies, then what?"

"What do you mean?"

"Don't you see? This fight is going to be you and Ashley and him. The plan is to walk in on him while he's more or less sleeping and use this *Run with Spirits* book and that spell to kill him. If we can kill him, that is. If he didn't sign when he was more alive, which we won't know until one of us looks at the book. We have no evidence against this guy. He left no traces at the scenes; he's been like—pardon the god-awful pun—a ghost. Top that off, if he dies, we're culpable. It'll look like we used unnecessary force on a man we can't prove committed the crimes. What are we going to tell people? How will we explain his death?"

"Valerie, if it comes down to losing my job and going to jail versus the lives of God knows how many other people, there's no comparison. I'll take the hit. I'm going to be the one to do it, anyway."

Valerie put down her fork. She stared at her steak as if she'd discovered a band-aid under it. Noah reached across the table and took her hand in his for a brief squeeze, an action that had felt so natural before, but this time was wrong, too artificial. He let it go.

CHAPTER 47

A child. The hunter had been a child the last time he faced them, and though the first incident had terrorized him, now he tracked them with the same single-mindedness of a dog hunting a fox.

A clever fox, who will kill the dog.

He chuckled, and the sound resonated off the smooth stone of the mausoleum.

This confrontation had all the difficulty of having a pizza delivered to his door. The idea of having his next sacrifice willingly walking to his side tickled Delroy. A victim practically placing his hands around their neck. He laughed again.

The *Muerto Fuerte* had given him the boy's name—Noah—and had shown him what had happened the last time the hunter had seen Delroy's face: the boy's parents dead, sliced into neat halves while the boy and his sisters fled, panic-stricken and terrified, in the family vehicle.

Now, one of the sisters was dead, the other an alcoholic with a dependence on prescription drugs. Only Noah had managed to survive the attack without forming some chemical dependency in adulthood. His vice was an addiction to his work—a misplaced sense of justice, Delroy supposed.

That wasn't to say Noah had escaped unscathed. He carried with him the power to see and communicate with the gray people. He, too, had dreams and visions—had shared the prophetic dream he'd had last night. And still, he came.

His hunter was brave. He was handsome. He had an

unnatural power. They were so much alike. Too bad they hadn't met another way, another time, or in another life.

Then again, maybe they had. Perhaps this was some twist of fate, destined to play over and again with each incarnation until he and his hunter reached the necessary conclusion. Delroy, unlike some, did not carry with him the memory of his past lives. He wondered, sometimes, if he was a new soul. His parents hadn't said, and the gray man would not tell him. No spell he'd worked had revealed a definite answer, either.

Strange, the way events unfolded. If he'd tracked his hunter down as he'd originally planned, Noah's death wouldn't have given him the satisfaction that it would now. Noah didn't fear death, didn't have any trepidation about the afterlife. As someone who saw the grays, he knew there was life even after his body stopped functioning. His death would've brought no terror, no fuel to their immortality, no joy to his life.

The woman, his partner, was the human's newest and greatest weakness, and could be used to their advantage. Noah would do anything to protect her, even if it meant his own life.

Her death would make the hunter's sacrifice more valuable. His tears, shed in love and grief, would strengthen Delroy and the warrior within him more than his blood.

How ironic that a boy who escaped would grow into a man who died at their hands two decades later, trying to catch them. The irony of life was often humorous.

It disrupted his plan, and now his list was completely out of order, but there was still beauty in it. Noah was forgiven.

CHAPTER 48

John C. Wright Memorial Cemetery was hidden on the rural outskirts of the Gryphon town limits down a winding road sided with thick live woods and clumpy winding strands of kudzu. After what felt like a long drive in a blue-black, rainy haze interspersed with brilliant lightning flashes, Noah parked the unmarked SUV in the sand outside the gate and cut the engine.

Quiet pervaded as the air-conditioner stopped its desperate thrum and the wipers their hypnotic rhythm. As their ears adjusted to the loss of noise, they became aware of the falling rain whispering on the hood and windshield as the heat began creeping back into the car.

They said nothing but exited in sync, a plainclothes Fred and Ginger.

Noah was surprised to see the wrought iron gate unlocked at that hour. He lifted the heavy padlock and let it drop with a clang that somehow sounded rustier in the drizzle. The caretaker, whoever he was, had not performed his duty.

He's making it easier to find him. Noah's stomach turned. It looked like Valerie was right. Ducharme was only steps away.

They entered the graveyard. Nautical twilight reigned; they had lingered too long at the restaurant. But somehow, Noah sensed it was right to face the creature they had to kill now, when daylight ended and night began. Although he had no reason to believe that nighttime benefited his opponent, the mere act of entering a crypt for the final face-off gave the battle a vampiric quality. Facing him in the daylight felt too similar to taking a pot shot—unsportsmanlike, unfair, like shooting a fleeing suspect in the back or without warning. The balance of day and night felt more evenhanded.

Valerie had voiced no complaint as they drove to the graveyard. If the idea of facing Ducharme in the dark frightened her, she was putting up a marvelous front.

They made their way into the cemetery. Valerie, who'd had the foresight to grab her flashlight, now lit the beam and scanned headstones for names. Thomas, Swain, Mackinnon, Drake. She flicked the beam from stone top to stone top. No Ducharme. They headed toward the mausoleums in the rear.

Grass grew in variations of long to short as if the caretaker had too busy a schedule lately to trim the whole lawn at one go. Flowers in planters throughout the cemetery—some new, some half-dead—now drooped under the burden of the storm.

He found he wished he'd buried his parents in another part of town. John C. Memorial, although closer to his apartment, now felt contaminated, malign. He half expected a fog to roll in from the shrubs in the rear of the yard or to rise from the graves, though he knew the weather was exactly wrong.

"You're clear on what we do, right?" Valerie asked, brushing one stone with the light, then another.

Noah released a breath he hadn't known he'd been holding. "I stand there and let you read from the book. Once Ashley steps inside, I sneak into the mausoleum and see where Ducharme signed the contract. If he's more dead than alive, I sever the cord that holds him to his body somehow. How hard is that?"

From the corner of his eye, a motion caught his

attention. He started and then snorted back a frightened chortle as his sister's spirit emerged from a head-high azalea bush to his right.

"Ashley, you scared the life out of me," he signed, speaking the words for Valerie's benefit.

Ashley's hands flew, and he watched, too busy keeping up with her quick fingers to translate.

"Right place. Very funny. Yes, we're ready, I guess. Do you understand what to do?" He watched again. "Yes, I understand. I'm scared to death, but I understand." Nothing for a second. Then he signaled with a point.

"She says he's this way."

*   *   *

The mausoleum wasn't hard to find: it stood at least twelve feet high and was made of taupe granite with large black columns and a heavy-looking arched gold door. A well-kept patch of grass led to three broad matching granite steps. The Ducharme monument was a tribute to wealth, but without a word, it said more than that. In a cemetery of graves left more or less cared for, the Ducharme memorial was immaculate. The grass was green, surrounded by neglected brown Bermuda grass. It shone. It was perfect.

"He works here, just like he did at St. Anne's," Valerie breathed. "That's how he's been able to get in and out whenever he wants. He has a key." She took a tentative step into the square patch of grass before the monument as if she expected Ducharme to have placed alarms around the perimeter.

She clutched the leather book to her chest, like a shield, and tiptoed forward until she stood in the center of the manicured grass, admiring the monument that looked as new as the day it had been erected. "I hope someone takes this good care of me," she said.

"Valerie—"

"Don't!" she snapped, her voice a hushed whisper. "Don't tell me someone will care for my grave like this. Don't tell me that if you live and I die that you'll make sure I get a place just as pretty, 'cause it isn't true. My family's broke, and all I got is a tiny savings and a measly term insurance plan that'll barely cover my burial. So don't get all sentimental and mushy, 'cause I won't believe a word of it." She swiped a tear away with a finger, sniffed, and wiped the other eye.

"I was going to suggest we get started," Noah said gently.

Valerie released a pent-up sigh and pulled the book away from her chest. Noah heard the patter of heavy raindrops on the cover. The storm was picking up. He tried not to read too much into nature's unwillingness to cooperate.

"Oh. Well, yes, we should," she said, blushing and blinking in humiliation. She turned to the correct page, marked with a white napkin bearing the "Phillip's" logo in red. The ink had run, staining the top of the page with a bloodlike blur that reminded Noah of a tie-dyed shirt he once had.

Strange what one thinks in times of stress.

Valerie sat on the wet grass, the book propped open in her crossed legs.

When Noah gave her a curious look, she explained, "Wouldn't do to fall and lose my place. Ready?"

He took a deep breath, intending to slow his heart a little. It didn't work; the sound still pounded in his ears. He tried another. No luck.

"As I'm gonna be," he said.

CHAPTER 49

Voices trickled through the crack in the golden gate. Their pursuers had arrived.

They expected them to be asleep, he saw. They thought the man's sister... Aha. No, they would receive a surprise. He and the warrior would render Noah incapable of moving, they'd crush his windpipe until he could barely breathe. Then…

He considered his bag of weapons. The silver blade? No. The gun? No, too distant. He wanted to lay his hands on the woman with Noah, to defile her body with their touch.

The obsidian knife. Perfect.

He fished through the bag, grabbed the blade, and tucked it into the back of his pants. Wouldn't want to run the risk that their hunter might grab it while he was flailing about in their grip.

Delroy leaned back and envisioned his tactics. A surge of excitement raced along his spine, his arms, tingled his skull, pumped his heart like a marathon runner.

Not too much. Keep your calm. Keep your wits about you.

But it's so close! This will be the first time I will kill one who wants to fight back!

More reason to stay level in the head. Do not get overconfident.

But he can't kill us. You've said so. I've signed the Book of the Dead. We cannot die!

I tell you to take caution. He has had more

*thoughts about this matter than you. **He is not unprepared.***

Do you mean we can die?

Don't be ridiculous. We will not die as long as you keep your head and listen to me.

The gray man had never spoken with any uncertainty before. Delroy's hands and knees shook, but whether it was due to adrenaline or fear, he was not sure.

*   *   *

"Here lies vile body must be destroyed..." Ashley's hands flowed with Valerie's clumsy Latin, and Noah wondered if it was so he understood or if the motions were also part of the spell.

Raise your hands. Valerie said you're supposed to raise your hands. He lifted his arms to the sky. Warm rain spattered his palms and drizzled down to his elbows, his shoulders, down his shirt. He tipped his head back and closed his eyes, blocking out all superfluous sensory input and opening his mind up to the idea of relinquishing possession of his body. That way, his sister could enter him as Ducharme's deviant ghost had. They would be on an equal spiritual footing.

Or, at least that was the idea.

Without warning, the air around him grew icy. The rain no longer felt like a warm summer shower. Instead, the sensation was like large, fat, wet flakes of snow landing on warm, exposed skin. The air around him wafted, the frigid breezes encouraging his body to move back and forth like a charmed snake. He was sure if he opened his eyes, he'd see his breath coming out in clouds with each exhale, but he kept his eyes frozen shut.

Instead, through some mental portal to the outside

world, he saw Ashley approaching him, caution evident with every tentative step. She stepped right behind him, and although Noah knew it was a ridiculous thought—she was dead—he imagined he felt her cold breath on his neck.

Then she stepped inside, as easily as a foot into a well-loved slipper.

His body tensed, his nature resistant to this large foreign intruder. His skin felt stretched taut, a sausage casing filled to bursting.

Law of physics, Noah. Two things, one place, same time, not possible!

Though the logical part of him knew that one of those things was not, technically, solid in the same sense he was, it was difficult to convince his body of that fact. Noah's eyes bulged as his mind surged with the presence of Ashley's mind in his.

Ashley's mind, with all of the awareness of the collective unconscious. His thoughts became a muddled swarm of languages unknown before that moment. He tried to focus on one, but it was impossible.

Desperate for an anchor to the physical world, his eyes shot around for a focal point, a single item to process. As he scanned his surroundings, details from every nuance within that glance inundated his overtaxed human brain.

Too much. Too much! Noah became aware of the dampness on his knees and the feel of grass under his palms.

Stay with me, bro, Ashley's voice ordered, and it occurred to Noah that he heard her voice, though not with his ears.

He tried to stay alert. God, how he tried. But the knowledge and strength that flowed through him now were so overwhelming he found it impossible to hold on to a single coherent thought.

Incidental things came to his awareness, tiny minutiae

of detail that were of no consequence. Still, they were the first handholds graspable in an ocean of knowledge that threatened to drown him. In a high school in Michigan, a young woman named Nadine had slipped during cheerleading practice and had fallen on her knee in the grass, drawing blood. In Montana, a man fished in the dark, obsessed with the idea of catching a hopper that he had mentally dubbed—for reasons he kept to himself—Big Dick. Now his mind flew farther, across oceans and new time zones, and he caught the dreams of flying in the mind of a child in a village outside Sao Paulo. He experienced the overwhelming pain of a mother giving birth in a hospital in St. Petersburg.

He hadn't realized he was crying out or that he had collapsed on the ground in the wet, spongy grass. His voice bounced off the headstones around him. The sound waves echoed in his ears, on his skin, through his hair.

This is too much! This is too much. I can't do this!

But he was doing it. As he struggled with the flashes of knowledge, desperate for a foothold—*Too much knowledge, too much*—Ashley took control of his body. His dually manned carcass, with someone else at the wheel, eased up from the ground to his knees, then staggered to his feet and came face-to-face with Delroy Ducharme.

CHAPTER 50

Ducharme looked the same as he had in Noah's dream that night before his family left for Lightning Fork. Eighteen years had done no damage to his body. It was as if time had stood still for Ducharme: he had the firm build of a man in his twenties, the same dark, curly hair, the same youthful face. The same scar angled from cheek to chin. His dream of eternal youth had been achieved.

The only difference now was that with the help of Ashley's eyes, Noah saw a cord—a sleek silver line as thick as a rope that tied the ghost to Ducharme's body.

Now that he saw the ghost, he understood why Pamela and Richard had had a difficult time telling the difference between the human and the spirit. The face of the ghoul loomed over Ducharme's in a way it hadn't twenty years ago. At times Noah saw more of the man, then, with a shimmer like a drop into a pool of mercury, Ducharme looked more like a demon than anything he'd ever seen. He was a creature, ancient and malefic, a horrible soul that had found its way back into the human world by weaving itself into Ducharme's body. Its face was twisted into a permanent scowl, a frown with sharp teeth ready to tear into anyone who got in his way. The body that overlapped Ducharme's body was muscular and bare, the body of a warrior gone off-beam, who'd sought power in a darkened place.

They were two powerful killers in one youthful body.

I don't stand a chance!

Noah's heart, already overloaded with the shock of

harboring Ashley's spirit alongside his, threatened cardiac arrest. He wavered on his feet, but he wasn't sure if it was due to an action of his own or if Ashley's spirit was suffering shock, now that she'd come face to face with their parent's killer. He sensed it was both.

Ducharme, on the other hand, appeared unaffected by the presence of another man-plus-spirit entity. He licked his lips, blinked, a man awakened from a nap by the harmless gong of a doorbell. The ghost guise overlapped his human face, a sneer on his lips. Then it was gone.

"You," he said in a pleasant voice with a contemplative cock of his head. "You... were there. I should've killed you. But you got away. That doesn't matter. It's better this way. You didn't know that, did you? Of course not. If you had, you wouldn't have come."

Noah had found a buoy in this ocean of knowledge: Ducharme. He had to kill Ducharme. If he didn't, Ducharme would kill him; then he'd proceed to kill Valerie, and dozens, maybe hundreds more as if they were nothing more than cattle trapped in a slaughterhouse. He'd kill however many it took so that he lived, and he'd continue to live until someone else learned about the silver cord.

How in the fuck am I going to sever—?

They were screwed. Madame Ubora had given them a book that allowed Ashley to enter his body, but no supernatural weapon. He'd supposed that once Ashley had entered his body, he would have a way, a weapon would appear from the heavens, an answer would materialize before him, and he'd have some heavenly insight. The book, the spell, would give them what they needed to carry out this supernatural task.

He had nothing. All the knowledge on earth flowed through his mind—their minds—and he had nothing. Ducharme was protected by the *Libro de Los Muertos*.

The Book. I have to see the book. I need to know if I can kill him or if we need to get the fuck out of here.

In the corner of his mind, he heard Valerie continuing with her incantation. He prayed that she'd hit on a useful verse that would cause a spiritual sword to materialize in his hand.

Wait a second. I was mostly alive. Doesn't that mean I can't be killed? But I didn't sign anything. I didn't shed any blood. This isn't a Book of Life that counteracts his Libro de Los Muertos; this is a spell in a book with the charming title To Run with Spirits. *Oh, damn! What in the hell do I do now?*

The memory of his dream loomed over him. The distance between them was similar to the way it had been in his dream. How long until Ducharme had him dangling by his neck? Or—and this thought kept Noah sane—might he manage, for the first time, to avoid fate?

Valerie's voice sang the spell in Latin, and the answer came to him unexpectedly on the flood of knowledge in which his spirit buoyed. Ducharme's link had to be broken by another spirit. By Ashley's translucent hands.

Ducharme regarded him like a scholar studying a student who had espoused a ridiculous solution to an elaborate problem beyond his comprehension.

"You think you can kill me." No jest, no resentment. Ducharme stated the fact without pretense, without surprise, but, most disturbingly, without fear.

"I'm going to try," Noah replied. His voice sounded odd to him, like a voice dubbed over with a female voice.

He'd expected he'd have to stop Ducharme from ducking back into the mausoleum and grabbing his bag of tricks. He braced himself to leap forward, to try to get his hands on the cord as soon as Ducharme's back was turned, to see what it was made of. Maybe it'd be an easy task. Maybe, with some luck, the rope was made of ectoplasm and—

There was no time to think, to react, to even register what happened next. In a fraction of a second, Ducharme hurdled the distance with ease, and in one effortless move, took Noah by the throat with a colossal arm. Before Noah could respond, Ducharme lifted him several inches off the ground and cut the flow to his windpipe.

CHAPTER 51

His oxygen was getting low; his head grew light and felt strangely detached. The world spun at the edges of his fuzzy vision. Worse, he knew that Ashley shared the pain that racked his body.

Do something, Halabrin!

Stars danced before his eyes, and his body longed to relax and fall asleep. He fought the blackness that wanted to take over his exhausted body, wanted to hand control over to Ashley permanently. He knew if he gave in, chances were excellent he would not wake up—at least, not in his body.

From the blurry corner of one eye, he saw Ducharme reaching around his body for the cord that bound him and Ashley.

And a gray foot.

And another. And yet another.

Valerie's voice droned on, white noise to his muffled hearing, like tires on the pavement.

Ducharme's hold on Noah's neck wavered. For the first time, Ducharme looked frightened. Terrified. He eyed Valerie and seemed to be weighing the odds of being able to reach her without a battle.

The ghosts of Wanda Murphy and a man he knew from their similarities must be her father Brogan stood a few feet away. Beside them stood Walter and Naomi Pilgrim, and fanning out behind them were dozens more—the victims of the Lightning Fork killing.

With what little strength he had left, Noah gripped the

elbow of the arm that suspended him and yanked down, though the pain it set off in his neck caused stars to dance before his eyes and his vision to tunnel. Ducharme's grip faltered for an instant, but it was enough. Noah slipped from his grasp and collapsed to the grass, scrabbling toward the gray shapes and away from the killer.

"He was mostly dead, Noah," Stephen Harper signed, emerging from the mausoleum behind Ducharme. "The book is inside, in the bag where he keeps his weapons. I learned a little something while being an extremely bored ghost these last few days. Turns out I can turn pages of books after all."

The ghosts that encircled the grass of the Ducharme memorial shared a wordless moment of contemplation before stepping onto the grass. One by one, they advanced and entered Noah's body.

It was a euphoria that surpassed the wonderful strangeness of Ashley's joining him. At first, the air around him grew chilly, then frigid. Goosebumps raised on his body from his toes to the follicles on top of his head. His muscles stiffened, and his heart slowed, certain that he had taken a quantum leap into the Arctic Sea. Yet, at the same time, he felt bloated, huge. This time, however, he felt spiritually stuffed, not physically. Empowered

Invincible.

He rose and faced Ducharme, who stood frozen with fear.

Noah's mind, too, flowed with knowledge once more. The buoy to which he'd clung had floated away on a crashing new tsunami of knowledge. He was powerless in his own body and mind; the spirits in the Noah suit had complete control and worked together to move him in sync. Through his mind's eye—their eyes—he saw a multitude of gray arms stemming from his torso and reaching for his opponent. He was reminded of Shiva, the Hindu god of destruction and regeneration, multiplied.

Ducharme tried to charge toward Valerie. He only managed to turn before the spirits in Noah's body propelled him forward, capturing Ducharme within their spider-like embrace. While Noah's physical body restrained Ducharme with a rapturous strength he'd never known, the ghostly hands sought after and found the silver cord, easily beating back the Ducharme warrior-being that scrabbled to grip Noah's body with clawed hands.

The physical contact he shared with Ducharme, combined with the knowledge that flowed through him, made it possible for Noah to view the memories that Delroy had struggled so hard to repress. He knew that Delroy saw them, too.

Delroy. I've never thought of him as Delroy, he's always been…

*   *   *

Ducharme. No. What are you doing? Get out of my mind. You're trying to make me believe the lies again! It's not true! This isn't a memory. It's not! It's a lie! A goddamn, man-made, manufactured invention. I don't believe it!

*   *   *

It was so hot that day that Delroy didn't have to moisten his fingers to turn the pages of the book he held—the sweat on his body extended to his fingertips. From behind a leaf-strewn mound of dirt, he watched as his parents put the finishing touches on the picnic basket.

Funny. To look at them, you'd think they were so normal.

Delroy knew better. He knew where they went at night

now. He knew about the *Muertos Fuertes*, about the plan they'd had since the moment he was conceived to give him to their Sun King—the Holder of the sun.

The problem was, the Sun King hadn't wanted him, ironically because his parents hadn't told him why they'd brought him, why he'd been born. They'd thought in his ignorance, he would agree to be sacrificed in this life for a better life in the hereafter, and with his death, they would inherit his youth and vitality. However, the Sun King had seen through their plan and had denied their sacrifice. Because of his parents' greed, Delroy wasn't worthy.

His parents had not seen it that way. Over the last few months, the abuse had gotten much worse. He spent days at a time locked in his closet now with only the stinging of his bruises and the rumbling of his stomach to remind him that he was alive.

He'd been bred to be a sacrifice, and he had failed in the sole purpose for which he'd been born. Now, his parents searched their books for ways to improve him as a creature, to purify him, to make him better, more acceptable. Only for these rituals or for his education was he released.

And lately, ironically, his parents believed that to make him perfect, he needed fresh air and sunshine. He was brought to the campground to eat healthy amounts of food and to bask in the sun that they coveted so much... a sun he'd barely seen.

He'd learned a lot from books cultivated from their collection. One by one, he'd taken volumes from their library and hidden them away in his room and learned by the light of a pencil-sized flashlight he kept stowed in the sleeve of a jacket that hung above his head. He learned about demons, and hell realms, about sacrifices, and the names of gods and archangels. He taught himself spells, first simple, but growing more complex every time. One of his first spells had eliminated his need for the flashlight and stolen batteries; he'd taught himself to conjure a magical source of light. He taught himself how to unlock his closet door, so he could creep outside at night and replace a book he'd finished with a new spellbook.

Today, he planned to use his newest, most complicated spell. The book he held in his hands would conjure up a Foxfire demon. This demon would do his bidding during the spell, after which he would be cast back into whatever dimension he normally resided. It sounded simple enough: an incantation accompanied by the assembly of a few particular sticks, oils, and powders he found readily available in his parents' cupboards during one of his nightly clandestine jaunts through the house.

Delroy's forehead was drenched, and not just from the humidity. He spoke aloud softly, not wanting to arouse his parents' attention. He assembled the oiled branches in the necessary shape and sprinkled them with a yellow powder that smelled horribly. With one match, the spell was ignited.

The air around him changed; it practically sparked with energy. Though he saw nothing, the atmosphere surrounding him became occupied with an invisible being; his eyes searched for the entity he knew was there.

It had worked.

The urge to reach forward, to see if it was tangible, swelled in him, but he resisted. He didn't want to lose his chance to use the Foxfire demon to grant him the wish for which he'd been summoned.

Delroy asked it one favor: that the demon would do whatever it took to ensure his parents were happy.

The demon, without a word, consented. He felt the warm air currents around him shift as it dove away and drew near his mother and father.

His parents stood. A trail of leaves rustled, marking the path of the demon as he reached them like a wake of wind. His mother and father faced Delroy, then each other. In their hands, he saw the flash of sunlight on the blades of two long, thin knives.

"No!" he cried. He knew now what the demon planned to do. He watched in horror as his parents cocked their elbows back like the hammers of two pistols and stabbed each other in the ribs, the blades guided to the heart with deadly accuracy by the Foxfire's unseen hand.

Delroy looked at the symbol in the twigs at his feet. He kicked it, stomped out the guttering flames, screaming as he did, telling the creature its presence was not wanted, that it needed to return to whatever unholy realm from which it'd come.

His parents collapsed in each other's arms, then fell to the ground, their eyes unmoving and glossy in death.

Delroy fled into the wood.

CHAPTER 52

Transparent newcomers to Noah's body pulled and twisted the silver cord in Ducharme's back, yanked with all of their spiritual strength. At the same time, Ducharme and the *Muerto Fuerte* scrabbled for the cord attached to Noah, but they were beaten back by others defending Noah's connection. It looked like a spiritual tug-of-war.

Ducharme's silver cord ripped.

He heard it happen. It sounded like someone had torn a large book in two with their hands.

The spirit within Ducharme let out the most mind-splitting, desperate cry Noah had ever heard, the chilling cry of a dying ghost. Noah's soul recoiled in a strange, sympathetic fear.

He hadn't known a ghost could perish, and he watched in amazement as the deviant warrior ignited like a match head. His long, fierce face contorted in agony, his arms flailed as he died. Engulfed in a blue flame, the warrior turned into spiritual dust and wafted away.

Ducharme collapsed, but not before Noah noticed deep, jagged red gouges on both of his wrists and silver tears on his scarred cheek. As his lifeless body met the ground, the thirsty grass drank the summer squall and the blood of a serial mass murderer.

*　　*　　*

Valerie shut the book.

Noah approached the mausoleum with extreme trepidation. He pulled the golden gate open and stopped as if he caught a voice she didn't hear. He probably did.

One by one, they exited his body. She counted no less than twenty-seven souls exiting Noah's body. She'd been able to see them since somewhere around the second sentence of the incantation she chanted. The battle hadn't lasted seven minutes, but it was the most incredible seven minutes she'd ever lived.

As the last spirit left his body, Noah buckled and then tumbled to the ground. Valerie made to stand, but was stopped as a beautiful ghost with what must have been blond hair in life approached her, a physical match to Brittney, but slightly younger. Valerie tore her eyes from Ashley long enough to make sure Noah's chest rose and fell. She exhaled a pent-up breath of relief.

"Valerie?"

She'd never heard her name sound so beautiful. She faced Ashley.

"Yes?"

"What you need? Those things you worried about? They're in there," she said with a finger pointed at the crypt.

Valerie had no idea what she was talking about; the events of the past hour had erased any thought of evidence from her mind.

Wait a minute. It's all over, and I'm still seeing ghosts! How did I understand her?

"Ashley?" Valerie asked, "will he be all right?"

Ashley smiled. "Yes. And don't worry. He's just waiting for you."

"What—?"

Ashley turned. Where twenty-seven ghosts had exited now stood two spirits, ones that hadn't been present for Noah's battle with Ducharme. Valerie knew the instant she saw how similar their features were that they were the Halabrin parents. Ashley greeted them with a smile and a tear-filled embrace, and they vanished in a flash of light.

CHAPTER 53

"Valer—"

"Shh... sit back and be quiet. The doctor says you shouldn't talk for a while. You've got some pretty bad bruising on your throat."

The light in the hospital was blinding and unforgiving, but she managed to look like an angel. He glanced around him. Brittney was sitting in the single chair next to the window, relief in her eyes. Flowers decorated the handful of flat surfaces around him. At the foot of the bed, a half dozen helium balloons clung, stirring on the air-conditioner breeze.

"What—?"

"What did I just tell you? Just relax. Sit back and take a load off your brain."

He tried. He tried, but there was so much he didn't remember. Everything that happened from the moment Ashley had entered his body had been swallowed up in a vacuum of bright images and strange, terrifying half-memories, some of which he was positive weren't his. He had a vague memory of the battle, had a pretty good idea that Ducharme had died, but it was all impressions, like trying to remember drowning.

Valerie smiled, and he knew everything had turned out all right. "I'm guessing you want to know what happened after you blacked out."

He nodded, and as he did, he noticed that his throat felt as if his windpipe was partially crushed. He felt a little hesitant about sharing the story in front of his sister, but she knew what he could do.

"I wish you could tell me what you remember, but... Do you recall the fight? Opening the door to the crypt?"

He shook his head, cautious this time not to move more than necessary.

"Well, Hal, that's where I stepped in. You passed out, and I ran back and radioed for help. But as I waited, I had to investigate that place that our pal Ducharme had called home for the past couple of years. I walked into that creepy-ass tomb, and you know what I found?"

Noah shrugged. He guessed it would hurt less than a headshake.

"Trophies. He kept trophies! Body parts, things he pilfered from the homes—little stuff that wouldn't be missed but will help trace him to the scene of the crimes. Noah, we have nothing to worry about. He nailed his own balls to the wall. When the EMT's got there, I warned them not to disturb the evidence, of course, but I'd called for yellow tape and... Noah, it worked out okay! I can't believe it, but it worked out okay."

He asked her for water, and she poured him a short glass of icy fluid that both soothed and scorched his throat. After he swallowed, he asked, "Ducharme?"

"Dead. We had a good idea that he'd die, you remember? But I kind of led Blanch to the conclusion that he caught wind that we were on to him and committed suicide just before we got there. I mean, it was the only answer that makes sense to anyone who wasn't there. I guess he used the blood from slitting his wrists to sign that contract in the Book of the Dead. Once the spirit left, he was simply a man with his wrists bleeding out, on the verge of dying. Gardner was right. He was 'mostly dead.'"

He had no idea what Valerie had told the department about the bruising on his neck, and he imagined Brittney had about a million questions, but he'd worry about that later. He pointed at her Valerie.

"Me? Oh, I'm all right. I had a hell of a hangover from that spell, and some things lingered for a while. But things have calmed down a lot since you've been in here, and to help me fill in any blanks, I've got a few new friends to talk to from time to time."

Before he had a chance to ask her what she meant, the door to his room opened, and Madame Ubora burst in, all but hidden behind an enormous bouquet of sunflowers.

"Why couldn't you be a Sagittarius?" she demanded. "Then you could have done with a nice little bouquet of Shasta daisies."

"Madame Ubora, you shouldn't have!" Valerie laughed.

"Don't worry 'bout it. They're to help him heal." She glanced around and, with a little effort and some help from Valerie, cleared a space near the window. "There. Now look on those for at least ten minutes a day. You'll heal quicker and hopefully put a smile on that bruised face of yours. You looking awful mawga. Rest, man. Ease up."

It was then that Noah noticed that Valerie had waved at a ghostly figure standing behind Madame Ubora. Her son Peter had followed her into the hospital.

"How are you?" she signed. Noah blinked.

"Fine," Peter signed back. They smiled, having reached a conversational standstill until Valerie learned a little more.

Valerie sat on the edge of his bed and took his hand. "Funny thing, though. I can't hear them anymore, but I can still see your ghostly friends. You'd better hurry up and heal, partner. You've got a lot to teach me."

He grinned so hugely he thought his face would crack in half. Using both his hands and lips, he said, "I will. Don't worry. I will."

Support Indie Authors

BUY
READ
REVIEW